CW00762161

THE ROSE GODDESS

Also by this author

Sacrifices

The Black Princess

CHILDREN'S BOOKS

Sunita Makes Friends

Sunita Goes To The Zoo

Sunita's Special Day

Good Terms

Refugee

PLAYS

Norah's Story

Self-Willed Women

An Enchanted Brew

The Rose
Goddess

Maggie Voysey Paun

MOONLIGHT BOOKS

The Rose Goddess
FIRST EDITION : 2019
ISBN : 978-81-936839-9-6

Cover design by Rich Voysey at Forge Branding Ltd.

Published by
MOONLIGHT BOOKS
20 Ekjot Apartment, Pitampura, Delhi-110034, India
Email : moonlightbooks2016@gmail.com
Website : www.moonlightbooks.in

This book is based upon a true story, however, some of the characters and events have been fictionalized.

The views expressed in this work are solely those of the author and do not necessarily reflect the views of the publisher, and the publisher hereby disclaims any responsibility for them.

Printed by Avantika Printers Pvt. Ltd., India

With love and gratitude to
Rashmi
who has brought me so much happiness for so long

CONTENTS

CHARACTERS

PART I
THE JOURNEY

11
1824, Dover, October

12
Lyme Regis to Dorchester

13
1824, Dover to Calais, November

14
Dorchester

15
1824, Paris, November

16
Ringwood to Southampton

17
1824, London, November

18
Southampton

19
1824, London November

20
Portsmouth

21
1824, London, December

22
Portsmouth to Horsham

23
1824, London, December

CHARACTERS

Kitty Phillipps, 1802-87, born Noor-un-Nissa, baptised Catherine Aurora

Lieutenant-Colonel James Achilles Kirkpatrick, 1764-1805, her father

Khair-un-Nissa 1786-1813, her mother

Sharaf-un-Nissa, her grandmother

Captain James Winsloe Phillipps, 1802-59, her husband

Mary, James 'junior', Emily, Bertha, their children

Mir Ghulam Ali, later William George Kirkpatrick, 1800-1827, her brother

Catherine , 1802-1848, his wife

Isabella,1788-1849 Julia 1791-1847 and Maria, 1786-1861, Kitty's Kirkpatrick cousins, who were married to Charles Buller MP, 1774-1848, Edward Strachey, 1774-1832 and Admiral Sir John Louis 1785-1863 respectively

Thomas Carlyle, 1795-1881

Jane Baillie Welsh, his wife, 1801-1866

Edward Irving, preacher and Thomas' friend

Isabella, his wife

Helena Bennett, born NurBaksh, long-term resident of Lower Beeding, Sussex

Mary, her maid

Walpole Mohun-Harris, later Emily's husband

Norman Fitzgerald Uniacke, James' junior's friend, later Mary Phillipps's second husband

Daniel Byrne, Emily's first love (fictional)

Robert Elliot and Georgina, fellow travellers of Kitty and Emily (fictional)

Reverend Richard Astley, of St Mary's Parish Church, Horsham (fictional)

OTHERS MENTIONED

Charles Molyneaux-Seel, Mary's first husband

Lieutenant Colonel William Kirkpatrick, 1756-1812 Kitty's uncle

Colonel James Kirkpatrick, 1729-1818, Kitty's grandfather

Faiz Palmer, Nur's sister and Khair's friend

William Palmer, Faiz's son

Benoit de Boigne, later Comte de Boigne, Nur's ex-husband

Charles and Anne, Nur's son and daughter

Ernest her grandson the third Comte de Boigne

Adele d'Osmond, Benoit's second wife

Henry Russell, 1783-1851, Kitty's father's assistant, later British Resident in Hyderabad

Jane Casamajor, his wife

Charles Russell, his brother

Sir Henry Russell, 1751-1836, his father

Lady Russell, his kinswoman and author of '*The Rose Goddess and Other Sketches Of Mystery And Romance'*, London, Longman's Green & Co, 1910

Mountstewart Elphinstone, the young Edward Strachey's colleague in India

Colonel Arthur Wellesley, later Duke of Wellington

Richard Wellesley, his brother and Governor General of India

Harry, Kitty's gardener, (fictional)

Mrs Redford, Nur's friend and landlady

Mrs Potts and Millie, Maria's housekeeper and maid (both fictional)

PART I

The Journey

1

1853 Stitchill House, Torquay, September

Kitty's hand falls to her side holding the letter that has cast her mind into such turmoil. She leans on the balustrade of the belvedere which gives the house an uninterrupted view over the whole of Torbay. Uninterrupted, that is, until this summer, which, being by turns extraordinarily wet and extraordinarily hot, near tropical in effect, has seen an extraordinary growth in the shrubbery which lines the southern edge of the garden.

Ten years past, James had thought to give their fine new villa some privacy with a row of fast-growing evergreens newly imported from the Himalayas. There was then no knowing how much further the fine sweep of hillside encircling the bay would be parcelled into building lots to satisfy the stream of newcomers to this most pleasant and salubrious part of the British Isles. In the event she and James had been fortunate, their nearest neighbours on either side being out of earshot and hidden from sight by banks of surviving oaks and beech, and those in front too far below their line of view.

She can see James now, deep in conversation with Harry the gardener, pointing out redundant branches with his walking stick, which he does not need thank goodness, while Harry responds with some tool of his trade, it is hard to see at this distance. They move to the nearby rose garden, which still boasts a second bloom of many of its varieties if nowhere near as profuse as the first glorious crop of summer, and she sees their conversation become more animated. Stick and long-handled shears, she can identify them now, gesticulate ever more fiercely, in fact are almost locked in battle. She smiles, recognising the signs of an ancient conflict, folds the letter and feels again the strength of its appeal.

'*The pen is mightier than the sword.*'

'Edward Bulwer- Lytton, the famous novelist and playwright.' It is the voice of her middle daughter Emily, who has come out to find her.

'Did I speak aloud? It seems to happen more often of late. I am getting old.'

Emily rests her head a moment on her mother's shoulder. 'Don't say that, Mother. You are still beautiful.'

'I was never as lovely as you.' Kitty looks at Emily with, as ever, that brief shock of recognition.

Her daughter is the image of her so long-dead mother. Or rather, the image of the miniature that her grandmother sent her not so many years ago, for she cannot truthfully remember her mother's face, having been torn from her arms at so very young an age. Emily has the same thick dark-auburn hair that has never quite submitted to braids or ribbons, the same almond-shaped black eyes and porcelain complexion, no wonder her father had been captivated. Kitty sighs. At Emily's age, eighteen, her mother had already given birth to two children. Herself and William.

'You have received bad news?'

'Oh, sad news more like.' Kitty hesitates. 'News that recalls the past.'

'Hence the quotation from Mr Bulwer-Lytton?'

'In some degree.' She considers. 'He expresses a sentiment the strength of which I have just had occasion to experience.'

Emily frowns. 'You speak in riddles, Mother.'

'I meant only what is perhaps a commonplace observation,' she holds up the letter, 'that this piece of paper with its black ink markings by a stranger should have such unexpected power to affect. I may be required to go away for a while.'

Emily opens her mouth to speak, perhaps to protest, but Kitty turns towards the house. 'You shall know all,' she promises. 'But I must first speak to your father.'

They enter the drawing room through one of its three floor-length windows which overlook the garden and sea. A small low table and several easy chairs are ranged at each window. Emily's tapestry is strewn over the nearest table where she had been sitting, while at the furthest sit her two sisters, heads bent together, one light, one dark. It

3

would have made a pretty tableau, but for the sights and sounds of discord that become more apparent as Kitty crosses the room.

'Tidy yourselves and wash your hands,' she says, hoping to divert them. 'Lunch will be in a quarter of an hour. I am going into the garden to call your father.'

'Bertha refuses to complete this sum I have set her.' Mary's black curls are set dancing by her indignation and her pretty face is flushed with frustration, due also perhaps to the fine work on which she was been engaged all morning. She has given herself the task of making her own lace for her wedding veil, the date for which ceremony is fortunately some months hence.

Thirteen year old Bertha is also out of temper. 'I have been worrying at it half an hour, Mother, and still Mary won't help me.' Bertha looks up with her father's blue eyes. Had she been a boy, Kitty reflects, not for the first time, she would have been his image, only her hair is somewhat darker. She reaches down to close the copy book and drops a kiss on the frowning forehead.

'We have all been sitting still too long,' she says. 'After lunch we shall go for a walk.'

***

James is cross too, still deep in altercation with Harry. She can hear the substance of their disagreement as she crosses the lawn. Harry believes in brutal autumn pruning of roses, James wishes him to clip only the dead heads and straggling branches now, and to return in spring to reduce them further.

'You'm the master.' Harry abandons the argument without conceding the point and stomps off to his tool shed and thence no doubt to his lunch.

James remains still, gazing across the bay, the sloping of his shoulders betraying to a seasoned observer such as herself a degree of dejection surely unattributable to the recent disagreement. He lacks occupation, she thinks sadly, for one who was a man of action before all things. He hears her approach and straightens as he turns, a smile lighting up the still handsome face as it had that first time she saw him in the splendid, braided, dark blue uniform of the 7th Hussars, across Maria's London drawing room.

'Lunchtime?'

'Very near.' She takes his arm. 'I see you have had your annual argument with Harry.'

He laughs, she can always make him laugh. 'Regular as the seasons. But I've given him his head with the rest of the shrubs. To restore your view.' She smiles, but briefly which surprises him. 'You are not pleased?'

'Read this.' She takes the letter from her pocket and gives it to him. 'I have just this half hour past received it. Read it aloud if you would for I should like to hear it again.'

James reads at speed, his raised eyebrows several times reflecting doubt, if not disapproval at its contents.

*"Chateau de Buisson Rond, Chambery, Savoie, 3rd September 1853
My dear Madame Phillips,*

I am the grandson of General, later Comte de Boigne, who for many years was in the service of an Indian prince, and of his first and Indian wife Nur Baksh, later known as Helena Bennett, who has lived in England for more than fifty years. She is the sister of Faiz, who was the wife of General William Palmer of the East India Company, and, as you will surely know, your own mother's dear friend who was with her at her early sad demise.

I had never met my grandmother, but a few short weeks ago we were eagerly awaiting her arrival at our home in Savoy, my father Charles having visited her in July and discovered her in good enough health to make such a journey despite her advanced age. But cruel fate intervened. Shortly after my father's return from England, he sickened and died, it seems of some undiscovered condition of the heart. We are bereft at our sudden and unexpected loss. I wrote immediately to my grandmother and have maintained communication with her through her local executors, by which means I know how sorely afflicted she was. She removed almost immediately from her country house to lodgings in the nearby town, where I believe she has a few friends and the attendance of a maid of whom she is fond. I should say that her only other child, Anne, died at the age of fifteen.

I should like to think that there was someone in whose company she might unburden her soul and find solace, recognising the true

5

sympathy born of some degree of common background and long-standing connection. Madame, you must now have guessed my intent. I believe that, having such similarities of history and coincidences of connection, that person may be you. 'Why do you not first go to her yourself?' you may protest. Please be assured that I have considered the matter and have indeed not entirely abandoned the project but fear that my most well-meant advances may appear to her more as the unwelcome intrusion of a stranger than as the loving sympathy of a close relation, and thus serve to increase rather than alleviate her distress. Herewith please find some necessary information of names and addresses should you feel able to attempt what may sadly be a hopeless task, but knowledge of the performance of which will be of the greatest comfort to myself and my family.

I am dear Madame your humble supplicant who begs you to be assured of my continuing regard should you for whatever reason be unable to undertake this commission.

Ernest Comte de Boigne

'Do you wish to go?' James returns the letter to Kitty before taking her arm in his as they walk slowly towards the house.

She looks up at him. 'I think I ought, do you not?'

He shakes his head. 'Dear Kitty, I do not. I think it only the *duty* of this Comte. But I am not surprised *you* feel it so. You with the kindest of hearts.'

She brushes this aside. 'It is not hard to imagine this lady's grief.'

'No indeed, it is quite tragic to have lost her son, just as she was to visit her family at last.'

They have reached the open front door under the high two storey porch where he guides her over the step ahead of him and into the hall beyond.

'When she had already lost her daughter,' Kitty adds. 'And surely more besides. I wonder...'

She raises her eyes as she always does to the great painting that for the past year has hung above the staircase, arresting the attention of all who enter. It portrays in life-size two small children dressed in resplendent Mughal gowns of red and blue edged with gold, with golden pointed slippers on their feet, caps like crowns upon their heads and long strings of pearls hanging to their waists. She meets the serious gaze of her five year old brother, who entirely understood the fate that was soon to befall them, while she, with eyes cast down and swollen-faced from weeping, at three knew only what she had lost. How long ago, how far away and yet she could recall exactly... she fingers the locket at her throat.

'I wonder how came this – Mrs Bennett - to be so alone, so far from...' She stops abruptly with what one might think a guilty flush upon her cheeks.

'Home?' He puts his arm around her waist, draws her to his side and looks up at the painting. 'It is that, isn't it? Your common heritage and history. Go, my darling, help this lady as well you may. Only...' It is his turn to hesitate.

'Only?'

'Well, there are two matters in truth, though they are related. I am concerned for its effect on yourself, that you may not be sufficiently recovered from recent griefs to bear those of another, which will in any case recall the saddest parts of your own life. And besides, you must not travel alone. The journey is long and not at all direct, I believe. Horsham is surely on no principal coach route to London. There will be changes, more than one, I shall make enquiries.'

'Thank you my dear,' she raises her face to kiss him and on impulse asks, 'Shall you come with me? We could go on to London, visit little James, before he is posted who knows where.'

He laughs. 'Not so little, he o'ertopped me before he left, Lord knows how army life has enlarged him further. And the Kaffir war is over though tis true there may be another very soon with this trouble between Turkey and Russia ...but no, in answer to your question, I think not, dear. There would be no place for me. I know there is a corner of your heart where I do not quite belong.'

'Oh James!' She wants to deny this truth but is too honest, as they both know. 'Then join me later, in London. Perhaps you might bring the girls and we shall make a family excursion before the bad weather sets in.'

He nods but is still not quite persuaded. 'But I think you should take Emily with you. And I shall accompany you both by train to Exeter to see you onto the coach.'

It takes Kitty a moment to see what good advice this may be. 'What an excellent idea. The more I think of it the more I see it.'

She regards her husband with renewed admiration and not a little wonder at his perspicacity and foresight, under which scrutiny he looks a little abashed but, she thinks, happier than he has been for some time. She might have kissed him again, but for the sudden descent of their daughters, newly washed and tidied and in considerably better spirits than she had left them. They are in truth quite boisterous, and so wrapped in some recent remark or event that has caused their mirth, that they do not notice their parents until they are almost upon them.

'Oh, Mama, Papa, forgive us.' As ever, it is Emily who first registers their more sombre mood. She casts a quick glance of enquiry at the painting as if it might hold a clue. Then she notices the letter in her father's hand and turns to her mother. 'You had received news?'

'I shall tell you about it over lunch,' Kitty replies. 'How would you all like a visit to London to see James? We may stay at Maria's in Eaton Place. They are going up early this year.'

'Mother,' Mary turns an animated face to Kitty. 'May we go shopping in Regent Street for materials for my trousseau? I am sure there will be far greater choice than in Exeter.'

'I am sure you are right,' affirms Kitty. 'And perhaps we may ask Maria to recommend a London dressmaker who will stitch them in the latest fashions.'

'I should like to see the Green Jackets on parade,' says Emily. 'It is hard to imagine my brother as a soldier.'

'We shall find out where best to see them,' James promises her. 'I am eager to see James myself, though I do wish he had joined the 7th.'

'I think James will be guarding the Queen at Buckingham Palace,' says Bertha confidently.

'Oh Bertha!' her sisters turn on her. 'That is another regiment entirely.'

'But we shall be very near Buckingham Palace,' her mother quickly intervenes. 'And who knows, we may see the Queen out riding in one of the great Parks. But first I must leave you for a while. Come now to eat and I shall explain.'

As she leads the way, her arm in that of her husband, her three daughters following, the very picture of a happy family, Kitty cannot help but think of someone else she will be near, someone with whom her life might have been equally closely entwined and taken a very different course.

2

1824 Goodenough House, Shooter's Hill, June

I was in the rose garden at cousin Julia's country residence in Kent choosing a few blooms for the hall table when I saw him striding up the driveway with Edward Irving. I had been curious to meet him since he had tutored cousin Isabella's two oldest sons and been spoken of with great admiration. The boys had loved him. He had come recently from Edinburgh to London to pursue his career as a writer and I had seen him briefly once, the day of his arrival, at the Irvings' in Pentonville. We had not then spoken. In fact, Julia and I had been on the point of leaving and only passed him in the narrow hallway where lay his baggage much labelled with the name of the ship upon which he had travelled. On a whim, and quite unseen, as I thought, I tore off one of these tags as I passed.

This afternoon, my hair was in disarray as usual and it tumbled further about my shoulders as I slid into the house by a side door, unnoticed, or so I hoped. When I entered the drawing room a few minutes later he was gazing out of the window. He turned to greet me.

'Dear Kitty? Is this she of whom the world speaks so well?'

Julia was seated in earnest discussion with Mr Irving in whom, at that time, she had great faith and to whom she was most generous in support of his congregation. But she came hastily to introduce us with Mr Irving a pace behind.

'Mr Thomas Carlyle,' she informed me. 'Mr Carlyle, my young cousin Katherine Kirkpatrick, Kitty to all who know her well, and very often 'dear Kitty' as you have rightly remarked.'

I extended my hand which he took in his and bowed.

'And your partner, I believe, in the magical furbishing of Edward's living room in his absence?'

'Indeed,' Julia smiled at me. 'The project was almost entirely Kitty's. The generosity entirely.'

'Unimaginable generosity,' Mr Irving put in. 'Evidence of the purest Christian heart.'

'Oh, pray!' Such praise made me uncomfortable. 'I thought only that it seemed a shame to have such a pleasant room and not be able to enjoy it.'

'Whatever your thoughts may have been,' insisted Mr Carlyle, 'to act upon them in such a fashion is rare and remarkable.' He bowed again and released my hand. I think my heart already beat faster.

He was good-looking, dark-haired, slim, light of step and, to all appearances, of heart also. His present expression was merry, his eyes somewhat narrowed, his lips curved in ready good humour. I liked him, though he had already made me blush. We went to stand together by the windows and admired the view.

'Such beautiful green and clean country around here,' he remarked, 'Yet so near London.'

'It is only a mile south of the river,' I confirmed. 'Indeed Edward, Julia's husband—'

'Mr Strachey?'

'Yes. Edward sometimes walks to his work, at India House, you know, in the City.'

We both gazed out across the fields to the Thames where could be seen a continuous procession of ships of all sizes sailing up and downstream against a smoky backdrop of spires and domes and other densely packed edifices.

'There is a ferry,' I added.

He nodded. 'Edward and I took it. And then we walked, not finding other conveyance.'

'Oh,' I blushed again. 'Then you know exactly of what I speak. I should have thought. I have been tedious.'

He regarded me a moment in silence. 'It is not a word I would use,' he said softly. 'Magnificent perhaps. Fascinating certainly. A person with an unaccountable interest in luggage labels.'

I must have blushed yet again but, before I could speak, he turned his gaze to the garden and then appeared struck by some observation.

'Oh, the creature has gone. When I arrived,' he hastened to explain, 'There was some apparition amongst the roses, almost buried in them in fact so that I almost doubted my eyes. But now it is gone, so perhaps it *was* a fairy as I then imagined. For she had about her the most unearthly air, with a blaze of red bronze hair the like of which I had never – oh!' He breaks off and clasps his hand to his mouth as he feigns to notice mine.

It was so transparent a stratagem that I laughed aloud. 'Mr Carlyle, you are teasing me. It was, of course, I, and it is true that some of the rose bushes are much taller than I am and currently in the fullest of bloom.'

'Aha!' He bowed low. 'So part of the mystery is explained.' He straightened and eyed me closely. 'But not all. Whence came your wondrous colouring, your hair, your deep dark eyes - '

'And dark complexion?' I interrupted. 'You do not know? You are not teasing me again?'

He put his hand to his heart. 'Though I would not say 'dark'. Dusky perhaps.'

'A little foreign shall we agree? Well, it is all from my mother and perhaps before her from the Persian Royal family, or so my grandmother told me. And they were direct descendants of the Prophet Mohammed. While my father was an Englishman, representative of the East India Company at the Court of the Nizam of Hyderabad.'

'Well! No wonder you trail an aura of such mystery and romance, with a heritage one could scarcely imagine and certainly not invent. There must be a tale to tell that I should like to hear. Well!' he repeated. 'For once I am speechless!'

His directness made me daring. 'All appearances to the contrary!'

We both laughed and became aware that the other two were observing us and, by unspoken accord, moved to join them.

'Edward!' Thomas, as I soon came to call him, accosted his friend. 'You did not prepare me for such entirely captivating company. Mrs Strachey! I am indebted to you for allowing me into your house.'

'My door will always be open to you, Mr Carlyle,' responded Julia and my heart leapt a little for I knew her to be ever sincere. She liked him too, we could meet again with her approval. And so we did, all that summer.

3

1853 Torquay to Exeter, October

Emily shrugs herself into a corner of a front facing seat in a first class carriage of the South Devon Railway Company train, where the morning sun lends her face a golden glow. Her parents, seated opposite, catch each other admiring their daughter's beauty and exchange a complicit smile. After more than twenty years of marriage they can often guess the other's thoughts. Emily smiles back at them.

'I wish we could travel all the way by train,' she says. 'How much quicker and more comfortable it would be.'

'But we shall be able to travel all the way home from London by train,' James points out. 'In fact, we shall have a choice of route via Bristol or Salisbury.'

'And you do not know how comfortable travel by coach has become compared to thirty or forty years ago,' adds Kitty. 'Why, I marvel we so often visited Uncle William in Exeter when the journey from my grandfather's in Bromley took so many days.'

'You will be travelling at twelve miles an hour!' James affirms. 'And with such improved suspension that any unevenness of the road will be scarce noticeable. Such wonders I have lived to see! Such ingenuity of the human mind! Though I hear Mr Brunel has now quite given up on his atmospheric system of propulsion, I was speaking with the station master while you were checking your baggage. He told me—'

'Oh Papa!' Emily interrupts. 'You are making yourself appear a hundred years old. Engineers invent things. That is what they do. Just as you were a brave soldier and commander of men.' She smiles at him.

James does not respond. He looks out of the window and one might think him offended by his daughter's interruption, however fondly meant. Kitty knows different. In truth he did not see much action and bitterly regrets not having had the opportunity to show his worth. She seeks to divert the conversation and takes two folded sheets of paper from the bag at her feet.

'Emily, you have not read this second letter which I received yesterday from the Comte de Boigne.' She opens out the pages and hands them to her daughter. 'He thought we should know more of Mrs Bennett's history since she may tell us little herself. Do read it aloud. I have scanned it only in haste.'

Emily sits up straight the better to deliver her reading.

'"My dear Madame Phillips,

The knowledge that my grandmother will soon be the beneficiary of your company gives our family great comfort. My mother suggested that I should tell you more about Helena's life since she may be unable to do so herself.

So, in my previous letter, I intimated that my grandmother's life had been earlier struck by tragedy when her daughter, my aunt Anne, died at the young age of fifteen years. I know my grandfather was much affected for the death occurred on his daughter's visit to France to see him for the first time after many years. She died in his arms of a fever in his new chateau near Paris a few days after her arrival. He always blamed himself for calling her to visit him when travel between England and the Continent was still difficult owing to the ongoing hostilities with France.

I understand that it had been my grandfather's intention that Helena accompany their daughter, but difficulties in securing travel documents had already delayed the trip for around two years and were still unforthcoming for Helena, probably because the British authorities did not regard her as Benoit's legal wife. (Although my father did tell me that he had found evidence of some malpractice amongst my grandfather's agents who were paid to look after the interests of Helena and her two children). How so? you may ask. Did a marriage contracted according to Indian customs count for less? The answer is yes, in the eyes of some, including, sad to say, Benoit. For, within a matter of months after their arrival in England from

India, during which time Helena and the children were baptised in the Catholic church and given the names by which I have always known them, he had met and married a seventeen year old French aristocratic emigree, Adele d'Osmond.

I daresay one can construct some sort of excuse for his behaviour – he had been living in India for well over twenty years, having left home when a teenager to become a soldier. On his return to enjoy the cultured delights of Europe for the very first time, he would, with his fame and fortune, have found himself able to mix in high society. To have a wife who was part of that world, indeed moved in the very highest circles (she had been brought up in the household of the doomed Queen Marie Antoinette) must have appeared very desirable. It was clearly a temptation he could not resist.

However, I doubt not that your sympathies will be entirely with Helena. Benoit did ultimately ensure that she was well-provided for with the country house and estate from which she has only recently moved, but for some years her circumstances were most constrained. Despite this, my father told me that he never heard Helena speak in anger against her husband and ensured that he and his sister maintained a loving and respectful correspondence with their long absent father, to which assiduity he attributes his eventual recognition by Benoit as his rightful son and heir.

My dear Madame Phillips, I trust that this brief history will help you understand my grandmother's character and state of mind and hope that your meeting will distress neither of you and be of benefit to her. I am, and shall remain forever, in the debt of you both, whatever the outcome of the next few weeks.

Ernest Comte de Boigne. "

'What a tale!' Emily passes the letter back into her mother's hands. 'We certainly should not have guessed how very much Mrs Bennett has suffered before this most recent loss. Indeed, did I not know it to be true, I should accuse the author of over-burdening his story, any one or two circumstances having been sufficient to gain the reader's sympathy and explain this lady's extreme grief. First to lose her husband, then her daughter and now her son. Surely there is nothing more cruel than for one's children to pre-decease one—' she breaks off suddenly. 'What, Father? You wish me to appreciate some more of our railwaymen's ingenuity?'

James is indeed trying to distract his daughter, has changed his seat to sit beside her and is pointing ahead up the track. 'We are coming to the first of the many tunnels that have made this line possible. If you do not look now it will be too late.'

Emily looks but is not entirely diverted. 'I only wished to remark that, whilst common, it is surely yet unnatural, not in the natural order of—'

At this moment the train whistle blows loud and long, the carriage is plunged into a minute's noisy and sooty obscurity and she does not finish her sentence nor can she notice the pain in her mother's face and sadness in her eyes.

'You see?' insists her father. 'And there will soon be others. Until we reach Dawlish station the line follows the very edge of the land, whether at the foot of, or inside, the precipitous cliffs. Is it not a wonderful sight and, yes, feat of engineering? Could you have imagined such a journey to be possible a few short years ago before its construction?'

'Dear Father,' Emily puts her arm through his and lays her head briefly on his shoulder.' It is not the first time we have made this journey, although I know that I am fortunate to be able to say so. And yes, it is thrilling to be carried in safety along the very edge of the sea and I admit I cannot begin to understand the calculations and inventions that have made it possible.' She plants a kiss on his cheek. 'Only—'

'Only you care more about this strange old lady than humouring your old father.'

'Oh Papa!' Emily strikes him gently on the hand as Kitty laughs at them both.

'Who will soon bid you farewell and return alone to his humble abode while you—'

'Your father is right,' Kitty intervenes at last. 'Let us enjoy this last hour together as well as the delightful scenery through which we are passing.'

And for the next half hour all three keep their gazes fixed on the extraordinarily picturesque view from their carriage windows of red sand cliffs and beaches, blue green sea, and the wide estuary of the

River Exe. But Kitty's thoughts are elsewhere, for she cannot but be struck by the parallel between Mrs Bennett's situation and that of her parents. The legality of their marriage had been doubted for many years, her father's word not having been found sufficiently convincing. To Uncle William at first, who, by then in Calcutta, must have been informed by letter from her father, and hence to the rest of the family. It was one of the matters about which, once she was old enough to understand its importance, she had tried to secure more knowledge over the years, until her grandmother sent her the eyewitness account for which she had yearned. And what a miracle it had seemed to establish contact with her after so very many years! Kitty is jolted from her reflections as, with much releasing of steam and grinding of brakes, the train pulls into Exeter St David's station.

They are a half hour early for the coach. The driver has not yet opened the doors, being somewhere taking refreshment, the four horses are still enjoying the contents of their nosebags and no other passengers have yet arrived. A porter finds them a bench to sit on.

'We could have taken the later train,' explains James, taking a seat between his wife and daughter. 'But I thought it better to take no chance, you having so long a journey ahead of you.'

'I am very content to sit awhile in the sunshine,' Kitty assures him, tipping her face to better feel its warmth. 'Surely when we return home the chill of autumn will be in the air.'

'And we shall have first choice of seats,' adds Emily. 'I could not bear to be obliged to sit between strangers and unable to see where we are passing.'

'It will be a scenic route,' her father promises. 'If not quite the shortest. I have besides arranged that you will not traverse it as quickly as you might, for on no day will you travel above fifty miles. Which will mean that, with stops for luncheon, no part of your journey will last more than two or three hours. Which I think you will find quite bearable, Emily. And moreover, you will have leisure to explore a little of Lyme and Portsmouth when you stop for the night.'

Kitty smiles at her husband. 'I think you have cleverly contrived to give us a holiday before we commence our mission and am very much looking forward to seeing these towns again. It is many years since we travelled there, is it not?'

'I think it more of an adventure!' Emily exclaims before James can respond. 'Never having seen either.'

James looks from one to the other with a small smile of pleasure and seems about to say more but the driver makes his appearance, closely followed by the porter, so he hands Kitty and Emily up the steps into the empty coach. They settle into window seats opposite each other on the right hand and sunny side.

'Just in time,' Emily whispers to her mother as an elderly clergyman hoists himself with some difficulty up the carriage steps and, on seeing them, removes his tall hat. He acknowledges them with a faint frown and nod of the head before taking the third corner along from Kitty, where he closes his eyes and appears to sink into a deep sleep.

'I had better go and see that your bags are safely stowed,' says James through the open window.' Take care of each other.'

Kitty reaches for his hands and holds them briefly to her lips before letting them go. 'I shall write,' she promises.

'I am going to keep a journal with a full account of my experiences,' claims Emily. 'Illustrated with sketches of memorable places and events.'

'I shall look forward to reading it,' her father replies. 'If it is for public perusal. Goodbye my dears.' He disappears from their sight.

4

Exeter to Sidmouth

'All aboard!'

The driver's command is answered by a female voice calling on him to 'wait up', the owner of which, a middle-aged woman of countrified appearance, shortly clambers up and into the fourth seat. She is red-faced from exertion and rather portly and she carries several bundles which she stuffs beneath the seats and a large basket which fills the space between herself and Emily.

'Wheel came off the trap,' she explains with a deep sigh as the driver cracks his whip, the horses pick up their hooves and the coach clatters over the cobbles towards the highway southwards out of the city.

Kitty and Emily express polite sympathy but are then engaged in waving farewell to James who has reappeared on the far side of the road. By the time that they can no longer see him, their companion has other concerns and, having uncovered her basket, begun to eat her way through its contents. Kitty points out a last sight of the squat towers of Exeter Cathedral rising out of the surrounding trees and houses.

'How huge it seemed to me when I was a child,' she muses. 'And how loud its bells! For Uncle William's house was very near. We used to play in the cathedral square, with bats and balls and chasing each other, my brother and I with our cousins...'

Kitty can see her brother's handsome laughing face so clearly as he ducks away from her reaching arms and darts nimbly aside, and Julia also, ten years older but always happy to amuse them. Very likely she had escorted them on more than one visit from Grandfather Kirkpatrick's where they had all spent much of their childhood. Although, quite soon after Uncle William had returned from India to Devon, Julia had gone to India to join her older recently married sister Isabella in Calcutta, and within the year had met and married Edward Strachey. While Maria at five years older must have already been expecting her first child...

'Great Uncle William's children?' prompts Emily.

'Some of them,' Kitty affirms. 'I cannot exactly recall who might have been there on which occasion.' My brother would have remembered, she thinks, dearest William, always her touchstone and protector. 'As you know,' she reminds Emily. 'We also all lived together at some time with our grandfather, either in Kent or London, before Uncle William came home. It was a large and somewhat disorderly household. Although quite happy I think. It included also Cecilia whom you scarcely met and Robert whom you never knew, for he soon went back to India...'

Emily frowns and then remembers. 'The children of Uncle William's Indian wife? Whom he left behind?'

Kitty nods and sighs. 'All dead now, save Maria. There is no-one else with whom I can vouchsafe my memories. How the years go by.'

Emily reaches across to touch her mother's hand. 'Yet you still are so youthful,' she says.

But Kitty pursues her own train of thought. 'Do you know, Maria was born in the same year as was my mother. Which does not seem possible, so long has she been gone.'

Kitty is being unusually revealing on the subject of her past life and Emily takes her opportunity. 'Mother, you have always said that when I am older—'

'I will tell you my whole history,' Kitty nods. 'And so I shall but not just now. Let us rest a little and enjoy the journey for we shall have views of the Exe for most of the way to Exmouth.'

***

'Quarter of an hour!' shouts the driver as the carriage comes to a halt on the Exmouth quayside and the clergyman stands and gets down from the coach in such rapid response that it is as if he had never been asleep.

Emily's neighbour elects to stay inside. 'Nip in the air,' she sniffs the sea breeze entering through the open carriage door. 'Don't mind me, if you can just climb over me legs.'

There were no more passengers waiting to embark, only several crates of freshly caught mackerel to be transported to places further along their route. While she and Emily walk to the end of the quay, Kitty observes their driver's heated negotiations with a small group of fishermen. 'I think it is some private business of his own,' she smiles. 'And yet I am glad of this unexpected stop, the chance to see again where once we lived and all you children were born.' She loosens her bonnet and allows the wind to lift her hair from her face. 'I always liked this view across the Exe, perhaps more than in the opposite direction. I used to come here often and watch the boats sail west and dream that they were bound for the Americas and I a traveller with them.' She laughs and then turns quickly to her daughter. 'Not that I was not happy, you must know, only that Exmouth was, is, a little quiet, a little dull after London and the other places I had known.'

Emily seems satisfied. 'So that was why you moved to Torquay?'

Kitty does not reply.

'Mother?'

'Perhaps. But no,' she amends her response immediately. 'For there were most unhappy associations with this place. Do you remember your Aunt Catherine?'

'Your brother's wife? Did she not die some years back?'

'Five years ago,' Kitty nods. 'But before that and for many years she was – most disturbed, some said mad. She never recovered from my brother's death which was when all their three girls were still small. Soon after I was married your father suggested she move to Exmouth, to be near us, so that we could assist her. But it was more a burden than we imagined especially when we began to have our own children. We found her a housekeeper who understood her moods and of course we continued to visit on occasion, but I fear her last years were most unhappy, with her daughters married and living far away. Especially Christine, in Florence.' She sighs deeply.

Emily looks pensive. 'I guess,' she says after a moment, 'it is well that she was not alive to hear of Christine's death this year nor those of the two little ones. And all three within a year of each other? So very tragic. I think it would unhinge the strongest parent.'

'Yes indeed,' says Kitty with an emphasis that gains Emily's instant attention. 'As you know, we lost three little ones,' she says. 'It was another reason for our move to Torquay. Your father said we needed a change of scene, more neighbours and activities to distract us. And Maria was there some of the year.'

Emily is distraught. 'Oh Mother, I do forget, they were so very little, the two born after me, I scarcely remember. I am sorry, it is hard to think I might have had two more brothers and a sister. I should have remembered earlier too, instead of thinking only of Mrs Bennett.'

Kitty secures her bonnet, takes her daughter's arm and steers her round to walk back towards the coach. 'But then I still have the four of you while she has none. And Papa so cleverly discovered our splendid house in yet unfinished state, we moved at quite the best time before Torquay became so very fashionable and, indeed, expensive and it is certainly a more pleasant place for its climate which some find almost tropical—'

Emily is not presently so interested in such practical matters and they have almost reached the coach. She returns to her earlier preoccupation. 'Mother, is it worse, do you think, to lose your children to death or to their forcible removal?'

Kitty stops and stares at her daughter before allowing her gaze to drift beyond her and out across the blue-grey sea to where it becomes a sheet of dazzling silver in the path of the midday sun. It is a question she has often asked herself.

'I don't know,' she shakes her head. 'I must think about it. I *will* think about it while we journey on to Sidmouth.'

The road follows the coast quite closely but, for much of the time, is in deep narrow lanes with high hedges on either side. These are full of autumn fruits: scarlet rosehips, crimson haws, black sloes, blackberries and pretty, if inedible, pink and orange spindle-berries, growing so near one could reach out if one so wished and pick them. But they obscure the longer view, there is less to distract, and progress is slower, especially when they must pull into a gateway to allow other vehicles or animals to pass. Kitty's fellow passengers are very soon slumbering, allowing her to ponder in peace the problem her daughter has set her.

The difficulty is, she knows very well, that her memories are so mixed with what other people have told her, people who had visited Hyderabad like Edward Strachey as a very young man, others who had known either or both of her parents as had Isabella, and Uncle William, who had maintained a frequent correspondence with his brother after himself leaving Hyderabad. Above all, there was her brother William, who certainly remembered more than she did and from whom she never tired of hearing the story of their life before they left India. And there were pictures, engravings, of the splendid house in which they had lived.

5

1818 London, Fitzroy Square

'Come and see, Kitty.'

William called me to the table where, with his one good arm, he had spread some etchings recently acquired by Edward and Julia to comfort us in our sorrow. Our dear Grandfather had passed away some weeks before at the great age of eighty seven years.

'This was our home,' continued William. 'The British Residency, built by our father.'

'It is very grand,' I peered over his shoulder. 'Like a palace, fit for a King or Queen.'

Edward joined us. 'Or a Nawab or Rajah,' he observed. 'It is very much a mixture of styles of architecture. One might say part Islington, part Hindustan! And a great improvement on the previous construction. When I visited your Uncle William, when he was the Resident, the accommodation was a ramshackle hotchpotch of bungalows around a rundown *baradari* pavilion. William's own bungalow leaked, letting in the monsoon rains. It was not at all a fit setting for the representative of the King of England at the Nizam's court. It did not command respect and Lord knows the British had need of it. William was never on such good terms with the local dignitaries as your father. Although your father was the recipient of some criticism for his extravagance in this building. From his compatriots.'

'Arising from jealousy no doubt.' Julia's voice was full of scorn. 'Frustrated ambition. I daresay there were older men who thought your father unfairly preferred for the position. Calcutta was full of such meanness and spite. It is one reason I was so glad to leave.'

'I do not think this is a fair representation of the house,' my brother said suddenly. 'The front was similar, I remember columns like this, which I might now call Greek, and a great flight of steps to the entrance. But the length of the building, these great extensions on both sides...why Kitty, even you may remember how we would run the length of this verandah in no time at all?' He fixed me with his dark eyes, demanding corroboration.

'I can picture a line of what seemed to me to be tall stone vases which towered over me and which I think must have been the balustrade of the verandah,' I offer. 'Though in relation to myself it did seem rather long. And Mama's house had pretty arches covered with flowers, roses I think. And I remember the gardens,' I said, eager to please him. 'Where was the model house which was a very small replica of our own, commissioned by our dear father for us to play with.'

'For you, Kitty. Do you think I played with dolls?' William smiled at me fondly. 'I wonder if it is still there.' But then his face darkened and he turned to Edward. 'I think this drawing was intended to distort the extent of my father's supposed self-aggrandizement. A deliberate ploy to cast aspersion where there should only have been praise, which must have made his task still harder, the performance of which undermined his health and brought about his early death.'

His shoulders shook with anger but I could see also that his eyes were full of tears, which made the greater impression, for my brother did not cry except on that terrible occasion when, aged eleven, he somehow fell into that copper of boiling water. I regarded his deformations sadly, the empty coat sleeve, the stiff and shrunken left leg, results of that accident which, it sometimes seemed to me, had also twisted his perceptions of the world. It was during his convalescence that he had applied himself to studying our history.

'Perhaps it was less a personal attack,' Edward clapped his hand on William's shoulder. 'And intended more as an abstract aggrandizement of British power.'

'Which was certainly a common phenomenon,' added Julia and then she smiled and took my hand and led me to the window. 'What else do you remember, Kitty?'

I looked out into Fitzroy Square, a pleasant enough space of trees and flowers to find in the heart of London, and tried to imagine the sweeping meadow beside my Indian home, where my father had tried to create something like an English deerpark.

'I remember the blackbuck, the way their horns rose in unison above the long grass when we approached, like a line of staves or a picket fence. There were sheep too, though not like English sheep …and I remember William telling me there were snakes, though I never saw any so I think he may have been teasing.'

William laughed as he hobbled to join us. 'I expect I was, dear sister. Although there could have been snakes.' He threw his arm around my shoulders and kissed me on the cheek, his bitterness forgotten.

6

Sidmouth

'I'm hungry.' Emily's complaint recalls Kitty to the present day. 'I think Papa's estimates of our speed a trifle optimistic.'

'Well, look,' Kitty points through the carriage window.' We are arriving in a town, which must be Sidmouth, I recognise that church and, if I am not mistaken, we are near our destination. There it is: The Old Ship Inn.' She points across the road to a low two storey thatched building, on the front of which hangs a board bearing a rough painting of a galleon.

'It is certainly old,' says Emily as they alight and make their way across the cobbles.

'Five hunnerd year,' confirms their fellow passenger, the country woman.

The clergyman nods. 'Once part of a monastery. But later the haunt of smugglers and ne'er do wells.' His sudden eloquence surprises them, but his mournful air discourages further conversation.

'Mind yer 'eads,' warns the woman, leading the way through the front doorway. 'Seems to me folks must've been smaller in them thar days. Smaller than me at any rate!' She laughs good-naturedly.

'See how thick are the walls,' observes Kitty. 'A good yard.'

'And how low the ceiling and how dark.' Emily clutches her shawl closer as she peers into the room beyond.

A fire burns in a wide hearth with seats in inglenooks on either side where one old man nods over his pipe. There are low wooden trestles and benches, most occupied by fishermen in oiled woollens and long boots whose conversation dies as the strangers enter.

'Shall we all sit together?' Kitty leads the way to a table in a corner out of the general view.

When they have eaten a passable mutton stew and potatoes Emily leans to whisper in Kitty's ear. 'Can we find the privy?'

The countrywoman, who they have discovered is a farmer's wife, bound on a visit to her sister in Portsmouth, overhears and directs them to a curtain beside the bar.

'Behind thar,' she tells them. 'Take the passage to the end and you'll find what you require in an outhouse in the stableyard beyond. I'll be going there myself afore we leave.'

'I fear it will be quite frightful,' Emily whispers as she follows her mother down the dark corridor to the yard beyond.

But her face clears when Kitty pushes open the privy door and they discover a clean enough facility and a waterbutt besides with a tap under which they wash their hands. Kitty looks around her, she is getting her bearings and remembering her previous visit, with James, just after their marriage.

'See the gateway opposite?' she points across the yard. 'It leads directly to the church whence, I recall being told, there is an underground passage to the manor beyond, I forget its name.'

'For smugglers?' Emily is shocked. 'Then parson and squire were in collusion with the lawbreakers and facilitated their escape?'

Kitty laughs. 'Your father was also shocked, I remember,' she says. 'And a little critical that I was not. But he readily appreciated my reasons.'

'Which were?' Emily is still sceptical.

'Come, let us make our own escape and walk to the sea front and I will tell you. But you must be a little patient while I unfold my story.'

There is a brisk wind blowing from the west when they reach the path along the top of the beach but it is in this direction that they turn for Kitty has remembered something else.

'I recall that there are rockpools along this way,' she says, 'To which I promised myself I should bring my children when I had any, thinking how they would enjoy finding crabs and other small creatures. Only we never did. And I did not at the time tell your father out of modesty for we were newly wed.'

Emily glances at her mother whose cheeks are flushed by the wind and smiles. It is not difficult to imagine her much younger face.

'So you will take me now?' she asks. 'It is perhaps a little chill for fishing.'

'Indeed. Nor is it pleasant walking into this wind. Let us walk the other way and then find our way back through the town where there is more shelter.'

The eastern end of the beach is marked by sheer redstone cliffs, on top of which newly ploughed fields rise to a line of woodland along the crest of the highest hill. Further stretches of cliff are visible beyond where the coastline curves back a little on itself before turning away and out of sight.

'Our road to Lyme must somehow traverse those hills,' observes Emily. 'T'will take some time.'

Kitty takes her daughter's arm and walks more closely beside her. 'All the longer for me to enjoy your company,' she says. 'You asked me if it is worse to have one's children taken from you as my dear mother had to bear, which you already know. Or to lose them to death. Perhaps you may help me decide for there is something in my history I have never quite been able to understand.' She takes a deep breath.

'Our parting from our mother was terrible. I can recall precisely her cries when we left her and see the very place in which she sat when we parted, under a rose arbour in front of the Rang Mahal – the small house where she mostly lived with us and our grandmother, a little apart from the official residence. She was tearing at her beautiful hair in her extreme grief and I am sure I was screaming and fighting whoever it was that carried me off.' She clasps her locket in one hand.

Emily observes the gesture and nods. 'I remember how happy you were to receive from your grandmother the lock of your mother's hair,' she says. 'May I look at it again?'

She leans close as Kitty opens her locket. The single curl is a little faded but the unmistakeable ancestor of both Kitty 's and Emily's own hair.

Emily looks from one to the other in wonder. 'It makes me feel so close to her,' she whispers.

Kitty closes the locket carefully. 'Since I have been a mother myself I have so often thought about the anguish she must have undergone, until I fancy I can feel it for myself. she continues. 'And what would have been worse was that, until the very last, she thought that she would be travelling the first part of our journey with us, and we would spend some weeks together in Madras before we embarked. Only my father's health suddenly declined and she chose instead to remain with him. My brother's and my departure could not be delayed on account of the season, the imminent rains always made roads impassable for travel by cart, bullock carts they would have been. Some of this I have discovered later you will understand.'

Emily nods. 'So then it was too late for them to join you?'

'And there was another circumstance. There had developed an extreme famine in the region, due to the previous failure of the rains I daresay, and my dear father further delayed his departure until he could not even ride to Madras in time to see us embark, though he tried and I daresay in the process worsened his state of health still further. Our ship having sailed, he travelled on to Calcutta by sea on some official business, and died in the house of cousin Isabella. She was but lately married, my parents were in fact to have attended her wedding.' Kitty sighs deeply. 'But it was all too late, too late. And my poor mother never saw him again.'

'Which compounded her grief beyond measure,' Emily says slowly. 'And beyond my comprehension.'

'Indeed. I have wept many times at her loss besides my own. But mark one lesson I have tried always to remember – for we must make haste back to the inn - my father put his duty to the people of his region before us, before his children and his wife.'

'Hence your sympathy for the smugglers? Your understanding of the collusion?'

'Well deduced, my darling.' Kitty hugs her daughter. 'They were, and I daresay are, mostly but poor fisherfolk supplementing an unreliable income and enabling their customers to avoid paying very high taxes on their whiskey and tobacco. I believe there are worse crimes.'

'I shall try to remember it,' says Emily gravely.

They walk on in silence until they are within sight of the inn when Emily is struck by a further consequence of what she has learned.

'And the painting, Mother, when was it executed? Surely after your parting from your parents, else why should you both appear so sad?'

'My father had commissioned it, knowing that Mr Chinnery was to be in Madras. But I think he had intended that it would be a family group.'

'Oh Mother. How much comfort would that have given your mother. And you. A portrayal of the happy life you shared for surely it was happy, was it not? Your parents having married out of love for each other and doubtless overcome opposition and difficulties in order to do so?'

'Oh *I* was entirely happy I am sure,' Kitty says instantly but then reflects. 'Or, perhaps I should say, I have only happy memories.'

'Tell me.' Emily hangs a little more heavily on Kitty's arm, forcing her to slow her pace. Kitty can see that she has not understood or does not care about this careful distinction.

'My mother was for ever making things, or commissioning others to make them according to her design. There was a tailor's shop just outside the gates to our home, I recall going there with her and my grandmother to try on a blue satin gown, she had shown me a picture she had drawn, and told me to colour it as I chose, and here it was miraculously transformed into a real dress I could wear. I remember the tailor crouching beside me, his mouth full of pins as he adjusted the length and then sitting back on his heels and all three smiling at me as I twirled in front of them. And then being allowed to choose a border. So many different designs there were, you cannot imagine, reels and reels of them thrown out along the carpet in front of me. I can still feel the one I selected, the scrolls and flourishes picked out so intricately in gold thread and tiny beads...'Kitty raises her free hand and allows her fingers to describe their memories in the air, thereby, it seems, bringing to mind something else.

'And in my mother's rooms there were always bowls and trays full of beads and jewels, semi-precious stones I daresay, opals, pearls, perhaps garnet and jasper, all shining and sparkling in the light, which she magicked into necklaces and bracelets and earrings and with which she let me play.' Kitty cups her hand and then slowly opens it as if to allow its contents to fall through her fingers. 'Just as you used to play with my jewellery.'

Emily smiles as she in turn remembers. 'I can exactly recall the sound and rhythm as I let a string of beads cascade back into its container.' But then she stops abruptly. 'Mother,' she drops Kitty's arm and steps back a little to survey her, her head on one side, her hands at her own throat. 'Do you not possess one of your mother's necklaces? Made of opals with bracelets to match? I am sure you once showed me, held it round my neck for me to admire, but I have not seen it since.'

'I am glad you remember,' Kitty smiles. 'And one day you or one of your sisters may have it. But it is too fragile to wear and too precious. She made it as a wedding gift for cousin Isabella, who gave it to me on my own marriage. Come now, the driver is calling us.'

7

Sidmouth to Lyme Regis

Reinstalled in the coach, Kitty and Emily find the churchman replaced by a young woman who, the farmer's wife informs them, is travelling to Portsmouth to help in her brother's household where there is a new baby. The two women are soon so engrossed in their own intimacies that Emily can continue her questioning.

'So were your parents also happy? Even though your father, I know, was ill.'

'Of which I have no memory. And yet of his state of mind I have reliable proof for, by very strange coincidence, I have read a letter he wrote about this time in which he said,' Kitty frowns in the effort to recall, 'that he is *"as happy and comfortable with his wife and his dear little children as he could ever imagine himself being, and wants nothing to complete his happiness but"* – oh, absent family and friends, something to that effect. He wrote that to Sir John Kennaway, who was his friend but also your father's uncle which is how I heard of the letter. You see how fragmented are my sources of information.'

'And your mother?'

'She would have known for some time that her children would be sent home.' Kitty speaks slowly, thoughtfully.' There would have been preparations, only I was not aware. I think my brother knew that one day he would be sent to have a proper English education. And I suppose they thought it best to send us together.'

'But so very young! Was it the common practice?'

'I think not. I do not really know, though I have asked.'

Emily frowns as she considers. 'Is that what you have never understood?

Kitty hesitates before her careful reply. 'Part of it, or, I should say, in some ways, yes.'

Emily is satisfied. 'No wonder your poor mother died so young. Of grief no doubt.'

'When I was but eleven or twelve. Do you know,' Kitty decides on impulse that there is no harm in proffering this particular confidence, 'I used to wonder why she gave up hope of seeing us again, for there was no known reason for her death, only her loss of the desire to live. I think for a while I was even a little angry at her for not living on, for depriving us of the comfort of knowing she was still there loving us and that we might one day be reunited.'

'Truly your story becomes more and more sad,' Emily sighs. 'I am so very lucky in comparison.'

'Yet see how my fortunes changed!' Kitty leans to squeeze her daughter's hand in gentle remonstrance. 'Come now, let us leave these sad reflections and look forward instead. We shall soon be at Lyme at the end of our day's journey and I believe you will find much there of interest.'

But while they complete this stage of their journey, Kitty's thoughts return to the past. Her mother died the year after her brother's accident and she is not ready to tell Emily of another circumstance. She and William were never allowed to write to their mother, not even to reply to their grandmother's letter of condolence on William's injuries, though it was read to them. Surely there must have been other letters, perhaps many others, which were not read to them, about which they never knew? And that is what she has never been able to understand, what even her kindest cousin Julia could never explain, not even when Thomas had so closely quizzed her during their stay at Dover later that year.

8

1824 Shooter's Hill, September

We were at Julia's house in Kent and I remember it being a warm and sultry afternoon, it must have been in early September, when Julia proposed the trip. There had been no rain to speak of for weeks and we were all glad of the patchy shade afforded by the apple orchard. The apples were not quite ready to pick though some had fallen and the two older boys, Edward and Richard, had been encouraged by their mother to gather them to make a chutney, tasking five year old William to collect any they dropped. Baby John was having an extended nap in his carriage. Finding so useful an occupation tedious however, Edward and Richard had turned instead to climbing the larger of the trees, which of course dislodged more of the ripest apples which were fast becoming a danger to their younger brother below.

Julia and I were seated by a low table on which we had placed a workbasket of small items requiring repair but we felt equally indisposed to constructive activity, while Edward made no such pretence and lay on his back conversing with us in a desultory way, occasionally reproving his sons when the deluge of apples grew too intense. There was, in short, an end-of-summer feeling engulfing us all. School was to begin the following week and we should therefore in a few days have turned our backs on the countryside and returned to London.

We had not seen Thomas for several weeks for, in the hope of improving his state of health, he had accepted an invitation to stay with a doctor friend in the vicinity of Birmingham. I missed his lively company in which I felt myself enlivened, but matters between us were not then so advanced that he would presume to write to me. I knew he thought that Mr Irving had been compromised by some similar indiscretion and would have rather married a young lady he met subsequent to the now Mrs Irving. I did not then know that Thomas himself was in a similar position as regards a young woman who did in fact become his wife. Howsoever, fortunately, or perhaps by design, for she had remarked several times on my listlessness and regretted my lack of young company, Julia had maintained some degree of correspondence with Thomas. I believe it was one of his letters, perhaps received that very morning, which promoted her sudden change of plan.

'Thomas is still not well,' she announced. 'Despite spending large amounts of time riding around in the open air visiting castles and coal mines and suchlike, his dyspepsia continues unabated. I propose a sea-party and he must join us. I do believe there is no ailment that does not quail before a dose of clean salt air. Which is what he was promised by Isabella some weeks back.'

'Why did they not go to Cornwall as intended? Did Charles' constituents not after all desire his visit?' Edward enquired, and I thought I detected a note of irony in his voice. It certainly seemed to me that Charles Buller travelled to East Looe but rarely.

Julia shook her head. 'All I know is that there was a great deal of indecision and very little consideration for Thomas' own potential plans. In my opinion they do not value him as they ought. But,' she waved away the topic, 'I shall invite the Irvings and you, dear Kitty, may travel ahead with them while Edward and I see the boys off to school. Let us go to Dover which is not too far. We should rent two properties since the Irvings now have a baby.'

9

1824, Dover, October

And so it transpired. The house that Julia, or her agents, I do not know exactly how matters were arranged, found for the Irvings, was closer to the shore but smallish and a little dark. Hers was brighter, in a new row higher in the town... Liverpool Terrace! I had quite forgot the name. We were all to stay at Liverpool Terrace until the Stracheys' own arrival, which made me the hostess, albeit temporary. We, or I rather think it must have been I, since Mrs Irving was much taken up with her infant, had not long established the two households, when Thomas arrived.

I opened the door to Thomas myself and caught him unawares, his hat held in both hands and leaning slightly forward almost in an attitude of supplication. But the moment he saw me he adopted an altogether more casual demeanour, his mouth curling in the way I well-remembered as a prelude to some teasing or otherwise outrageous statement. What I had not quite remembered was his eyes, their extraordinary violet hue and their fiery depths which seemed to flare up when he was excited by something. As now. His eyes betrayed him, of that I was sure. He was very happy to see me.

'Well well, by what strange coincidence or quirk of fate do we meet?' he prevaricated. 'I am arrived to stay with my good friends the Irvings and, upon meeting me in town, they informed me that you also were in Dover and, moreover, awaiting the arrival of your cousin Mrs Strachey and her husband. Of course I hastened here to discover if it could be true.'

'As you see.' I smiled. 'I do believe Dover is become quite fashionable following the re-opening of passages to France so perhaps it is not so great a coincidence. And besides, as you surely know, the Irvings in fact are also resident here with me, until the Stracheys are come.' And then I laughed and so did he. 'What is strange,' I continued, 'is to find myself suddenly become mistress of a household but even the servant is at present out and I am therefore alone and unable to offer you hospitality. I don't think I should invite you in,' I clarified. 'Do you?'

'Perhaps not,' he affirmed. 'Particularly since we are in the provinces and might offend such sensibilities. But then what is to be done if we are to continue our conversation?' He frowned and, finger to his lips, appeared to give the matter serious thought.

'If you cannot come in, then perhaps I could come out?' I ventured. 'Perhaps to walk a little together in the open air would not be too offensive? And meanwhile you may leave your baggage in the hallway.'

Of course my diffidence was affected in the extreme and Thomas knew it. He had nodded his agreement but, eyes narrowed, was still contemplating some appropriately arch rejoinder when I returned from fetching my bonnet and joined him on the step. I made a further suggestion, this time unsure myself of its sincerity. 'Perhaps we may find the Irvings and invite them to accompany us?'

Thomas gave a shudder which appeared to be quite involuntary. 'I believe them to be currently entirely taken up with infant affairs and apparatuses,' he observed. 'And my good friend Edward is quite brought down by it. He is a Goliath in chains, Gulliver in Lilliput—' he broke off then, perhaps ashamed at having so far revealed his feelings. 'Or perhaps it is of myself I speak, thus displaying my own small tolerance and ignorance of marital bliss. No, today let us, you and I, walk alone. I have great need of fresh air.' He placed such an emphasis on these last two words that I glanced up in surprise to find his eyes locked upon me with a burning intensity that I felt might consume me altogether.

I swallowed hard and moistened my lips before managing some response. 'Then perhaps tomorrow we may make a larger party.' In truth, I think that if someone had told me at this moment there would be no tomorrow, that I had just this one evening left on earth, I would have thought myself blessed if it were to be spent it in Thomas' company.

'You know,' he continued, as we climbed westwards to view the rapidly sinking sun. 'I do truly love Edward as a brother.' I think he was still troubled at his outburst.' On many occasions he has made it his business far beyond the call of friendship to assist me, to smooth my path through life, introduce me, including of course,' he looked sideways at me with a glimmer of his habitual mischief-making, 'effecting my employment with the Bullens and hence eventually my meeting with the Stracheys and of course your charming self. It is just that of late I find him overly solemn, preoccupied with his great mission, while I of course, having turned my back on the Church, am still adrift. I daresay he finds me equally annoying, though he is far too charitable to say so.'

But Mr Irving was delighted to walk with us the next day and other days, in fact every new scene seemed to awaken some happy comparison with past outings and escapades, of which there had been many, when both he and Thomas were beginning to make their way in the world. They became so animated on occasion that I might have insisted they walk alone had I not understood that I served as an audience for their show of camaraderie and love that might not otherwise have found expression. They would not, for example, have found cause to tell of the strange bond that linked them long before they met, which was that Mr Irving's uncle and Thomas' father both had such large heads that they had to send to a hatmaker in Dumfries, no hats large enough being available in their village. I laughed of course, but not nearly as much as they.

'There was a third Bighead,' Mr Irving chortled when at last he could speak. 'Don't you remember, some Doctor?'

But Thomas shook his head. He was, after all, several years the younger.

And then on another walk, the following day perhaps, I remember we were somewhere high, the air bracing, when they recalled with admiration an influential schoolmaster who had taught them both at different times.

'I only wish dear Jane had found my teaching as inspirational,' Mr Irving sighed.

Thomas frowned and made no direct reply and I guessed 'dear Jane' was a person he had rather not discuss in my presence. What he did say was that this teacher had favoured a Socratic way of teaching which was 'a praise and a glory' for well-doing boys who learned the skills of clear-headed argumentation which never left them.

'Except in some cases, very much to be regretted,' he confided in a low voice, slowing his pace while Mr Irving strode on, his longish curly hair streaming behind him. He was always an imposing sight. I glanced at Thomas in enquiry and he continued.

'When somehow, overhanging the primeval logic and clear articulation, there develop strange draperies and huge superstructures foreign to the matter in hand, which thereby becomes entirely obscured. He,' Thomas nodded at the figure ahead, 'is being misled I fear, by the uncritical approbation of those less well-schooled than he.' Thomas stopped and looked closely at me to see if I understood what was clearly of great import to him, but when I remained silent hastily clarified. 'I do not mean your cousin, Mrs Strachey, who is a *schöneseele*, a singular pearl of a woman, incapable of inveracity, pure as dew and full of love. I mean others in his flock and even closer to him—'

'Hush,' I said. 'He has made his choice. And perhaps you misjudge.'

The next day I did remain behind to give Mrs Irving company, out of duty rather than sisterly affection. I always found her bloodless complexion alienating,, in fact her manner generally lacked warmth. I daresay she did not like me either. But I have sometimes wondered since whether, had I cultivated her friendship, she might have saved me later grief. I might have challenged Thomas earlier and required him to resolve matters sooner, whether in my favour or not. In the event, the baby requiring both her attentions and those of the nursemaid, I found myself redundant. On the whole I was relieved when Julia and Edward arrived.

'So Thomas, tell us of your travels,' Julia invited him as we took our first meal together. 'We have been very quiet and unadventurous all summer in our rural retreat.'

Thomas held up his hands in a great display of self-deprecation. 'But you have already seen half the world and returned to tell the tale,' he protested. 'Even Irving has a brother in India who is an army surgeon. One can scarcely compare these experiences with my poor Midlands roaming. You must know I regard you Anglo-Indian people as an entirely new species and quite exotic.' He laughed again, glancing briefly at me, and I saw his humility then as genuine, and a contrast to his spirited discourses with Mr Irving.

'However, do ask him about his journey down here,' I urged. 'For he found it truly epic. Worthy of Odysseus, Marco Polo even.'

'You fabricate,' he protested, a small flame flickering briefly in his eyes, but I took no pity on his discomfort.

Julia looked from one of us to the other and smiled. I think it was then that she recognised how our affections had developed. 'I think you must tell, Thomas,' she decreed.' And let us judge if Kitty lies.'

But I felt bold that night, secure in the knowledge that we were drawing ever closer, and heedless whether I made it apparent to others present. 'I shall tell and he may counter as he will,' I proclaimed. 'For the facts are few enough. He was forced to ride alone on the roof of the coach all the way from Canterbury and, forgetting the driver of the carriage, not to mention those snug inside, imagined himself the last person alive in the world after some great disaster and headed who knows where, perhaps across the very Styx itself, and in any case, chilled to the bone, he wondered if he should ever again arrive at a place of human habitation, if by now such existed. For all he could see on either side was darkness and shadows in which one might imagine any number of evil monsters to lurk, the odd flicker of light being as likely from their preying eyes as from a humble cottager's rushlamp...'

The whole company was by now laughing, including Thomas, for it was very clear that I was elaborating and extemporising upon what had been a very small complaint about the discomfort of one part of his journey from Birmingham. He only shook his head at me in mock reproof and returned to his earlier preoccupation.

'So,' he continued, 'now that you have so rashly invited me into your company for an extended period it is my firm resolve to satisfy my curiosity and make of you a closer study. Mr Strachey?'

'My experience of India has been from behind a desk in Leadenhall Street these many years past,' protested Edward. 'But it is true that having seen such far and different places does permanently influence one's perceptions of those close to home.' He loosened his cravat and sat further back in his chair, warming to his theme, his fine mellow voice an invitation to his audience also to relax. 'Many of whom appear, I must confess, quite small and mean, their preoccupations trivial, their prejudices insupportable. Naturally I speak of the English, the Scots being in general a great deal more entertaining. Hence your invitation,' he waved a hand in Thomas' direction. 'And yours, Mr Irving.'

He added this last quickly but it was clearly an afterthought. Edward was never as enamoured of the evangelists, including Mr Irving, as were Julia and Isabella. In truth, if one were to judge from his conversation alone, he found more inspiration in the works of Chaucer than in the Holy Bible itself - and I daresay Thomas would have seconded him.

Thomas picked up his glass and toasted his host. 'Howsoever,' he insisted, 'it is your turn to be spied upon. Think yourself, yourselves,' his gesture included myself and Julia, 'specimens in a glass case, butterflies pinned to the wall, while I subject you to scrutiny. I say,' he turned to Julia. 'Might I smoke? I find it improves my digestion and therefore, it ought to follow, makes me more agreeable.'

Julia gave her permission while shaking her head in remonstrance. 'I am sure your doctor does not follow your analysis, Thomas.'

'In fact, he counselled quite the opposite,' Mr Irving affirmed. 'I should be happy if you could exert your good influence, dear Mrs Strachey.' He spoke with the solemnity of his sermons.

I thought quickly to preserve the prevailing mood of geniality.' Perhaps it is another peculiarity of the Scots,' I suggested. 'Pertaining to their digestion or to their medical science. Which we all know to be quite advanced.'

Thomas wagged a finger at me in reproof. He had indeed on previous occasions discoursed at length on the intellectual accomplishments of his countrymen. But he was not now to be diverted and returned to his inquiry.

'I want to know what it is like to be an Englishman in India,' he said. 'So that I can see it with my own eyes. Or rather, my eyes as they would be if I were an Englishman abroad.' He closed his eyes the better to imagine.

'Of course,' Mr Irving intervened again, 'there are many Scotsmen in India. Seeking their fortune, opportunities being less favourable at home.'

Thomas opened one eye, looking a little irritated at this latest pedantry, but then he nodded, conceding that perhaps his friend had a point. 'Although I fancy that most who go there of any nationality have the same intention and, I daresay, also make some common ground of their shared European heritage. When they are not fighting each other for domination of the sub-continent.' He closed his eye again and spoke to the assembly. 'So who will first take up the challenge?'

'Well, I was certainly there first,' said Edward. 'At the age of about twenty-five I went out to India to work for the Company and first travelled with another new arrival, Mountstewart Elphinstone, who was even younger than I. Twenty-one as I recall. We managed to delay the onset of our labours for a year, criss-crossing India in a great cavalcade of elephants, camels, horses and bullocks with a guard of sixty and near two hundred servants. Perhaps our contribution was not as much valued as we thought such pomp suggested. Why, we had one elephant simply to carry our books!'

There had been several gasps of astonishment from the Irvings up to this point, but Thomas still looked sceptical.

Edward nodded. 'I know, it seems fantastical now to me also, while then it seemed only our due. Like many young men, and I do not include those present, we did have a very high opinion of ourselves. In any case, we travelled far and wide, including, as Kitty already knows, to Hyderabad. It was in 1801 before young Kitty was born.' He turned to me.' And I do not recall seeing your brother William, Kitty, perhaps because he was a babe in arms and therefore secluded in the women's quarters. '

'I should rather like to hear what Kitty herself remembers,' Mr Irving put in, 'before I, or indeed she, is influenced by more adult perspectives.' He looked to Thomas whose fleeting displeasure at the interruption swiftly dispelled as he saw the logic of his friend's position.

He nodded. 'Kitty? You are in the dock.'

I nodded. 'But you must understand that my memories are already heavily over-laden by what others have told me, present company included.' I indicated Julia and Edward. 'For example, I have a clear picture of Hyderabad but I am almost certain it is informed mostly by Uncle William's descriptions for a small child would not be capable of such an overview. I can see immense black crenellated castle walls sweeping across hills and down valleys, an endless expanse of towers, walls and gateways, while inside their shelter I see well-watered fields, gardens full of fountains and peacocks, groves of palm trees and orchards of many kinds of fruit. Then the living quarters, narrow crowded streets of merchants houses and workshops, above which rose shining domes and minarets, their walls bearing glorious tilework of the brightest hues, and somewhere, I guess, our Residence in its own garden—' I hesitated as Edward cleared his throat in a way I recognised.

'Dear Kitty,' he said gently. 'I think you describe Golconda, the great fort which is outside the city of Hyderabad or perhaps,' he nodded correcting himself, 'Bidar, which is further still and where I am certain you would not have been taken. It was indeed an awe-inspiring sight, so massive and in such contrast to the desolated landscape all around. Or most likely, some combination of description of all three locations.'

'And I,' added Julia. 'Have the very same picture in my head and I never went to the Deccan at all. It is certainly a tale told by my father and perhaps even somewhat embroidered in his oft-befuddled state. He smoked opium,' she paused and looked pointedly at Thomas. 'It was his medicine for illness often sustained in the sub-continent, which eventually required his return to England. Many, I believe, similarly dosed themselves for a variety of ailments. But I would not advise it for he became less and less attentive to the world of others, which of course included his children, and moreover less and less… content in his own mind.'

She sighed and looked sad and I wondered if I should intervene and break the ensuing silence, for I knew she must be thinking of how Uncle William had died, some said from an intentional overdose of opium. But then she straightened and turned to Edward with a bright smile. 'Tell them about the Nizam,' she commanded. 'For I believe your reception was much as that described by my father some years earlier when he became Resident.'

At this point the servant girl came in to clear the dishes and replace them with a selection of desserts. Edward had had time to consider his account. 'We were invited to attend the Nizam's *durbar*, his public audience,' he began, 'to which we were conveyed in great state in a palanquin escorted by elephants, horses, soldiers etc. We passed through several courtyards before dismounting and were then led by the chief minister to an open-sided pavilion where sat the Nizam to whom we presented gifts and made our *salaams*. He was very old by then but still a fine handsome figure dressed in brocade, many splendid jewels and a high cone-shaped headdress. The surrounding nobles also were all swathed in pearls and other precious stones and he gave us some to wear in our turbans, which you may not be surprised to hear I hardly wore. In fact, I gave my jewels to Julia on our marriage to make into necklaces or some such.'

'A ruby pendant and a pearl necklet,' Julia clarified.

'But your father, Kitty,' Edward continued, 'as you know, often dressed like a native and certainly in that situation behaved like one. I daresay our less-practised demeanour gave some offence, although we intended only courtesy in deference to our host and his position as the Company's representative. Despite having been somewhat prejudiced against him by Arthur Wellesley when we stayed at his garrison on the way to Hyderabad.'

'Which is another story entirely,' Julia interrupted firmly. 'Come Kitty, Mrs Irving, shall we retire and let these men discuss the important matters of the world with which we never bother our heads.' Which we did, amidst much merriment and protestations on all sides for there existed no such arbitrary distinctions in that blessed household.

But it was not the end of Thomas' enquiries which he pursued on several subsequent occasions, with fateful consequences.

10

1853 Lyme Regis

'We've arrived, Mother. At our hotel.'

Emily's voice recalls Kitty to the present. She follows her daughter out of the coach. 'Let us leave our bags here,' she suggests, 'and go out immediately to view the town before evening draws in.'

Ten minutes later they are walking along Bridge Street in the centre of town.

'Oh mother, you were right, Lyme is quite delightful.' Emily takes a deep breath as she turns a corner and peers down the steep street ahead that descends to the sea. 'I cannot wait to see the famous Cobb, where took place the famous and indeed fateful scene in Miss Austen's last novel.'

Kitty is looking about her and considering. 'If I am not mistaken,' she says at last, 'we have only to walk but a little further along this way before turning down to the harbour and we shall find the other feature of the town which has given it world-wide fame.' She hastens ahead in the direction she has indicated.

'It must be something connected with the discovery of fossils?' Emily quickens her pace to follow her mother along the sloping street that follows the contour of the hill. She comes to a halt beside her at the foot of a flight of four steps which climb to the entrance of a shop that boasts a large curved glass window on either side.

'Anning's Fossil Depot,' she reads. 'The house of the famous Mary Anning?'

'Just as I remember it more than twenty years ago,' Kitty nods, 'When Miss Anning was still to be seen collecting her fossils on the seashore. Shall we go up?'

They find both windows full of small rocks and fossils, grouped with their names and prices indicated on neatly lettered signs. Emily peers into one window, Kitty the other.

'Ammonites known as 'snakestones',' Emily reads. 'Belemnites or "Devil's fingers", 'Vertebrates—'

She breaks off as the door between them opens and a young gentleman emerges holding a rolled up sheet of paper. He is of average height, of pleasant if unremarkable appearance and in the midst of donning his hat when he spies them, again doffs it and bows. 'Ladies.' He begins to descend the steps.

'Local people had collected these stones for years,' Kitty explains to Emily. 'Not knowing that they were the relics of ancient animals.'

'It is interesting,' Emily says slowly.

'Yet you are disappointed?'

'I expected something altogether larger,' admits Emily. 'Having seen some drawings thereof. I guess that I mistook the scale.'

'Perhaps there are larger specimens inside,' Kitty suggests. 'Although the very largest would I am sure be sold for, as I recall, the Annings were always poor.'

A low cough makes Kitty turn. The young man has stopped at the foot of the steps and clearly wishes to speak.

'Sir?'

'Forgive me for interrupting,' he is twisting his hat a little nervously with both hands and his face is a little flushed. 'I thought perhaps I might be of assistance, having been resident in Lyme some weeks and made something of a study of these phenomena, whereas you, I fancy, are recent visitors to the town?'

'Mrs Phillips, from Torquay,' Kitty extends her hand. 'And this is my daughter Emily.'

Emily bobs a small curtsey at which the young man is emboldened to spring up the steps and join them. 'Walpole Mohun-Harris at your service.' He sweeps another bow. 'The Reverend Mohun-Harris, I should say, but keep forgetting being but recently ordained and still without a position.' He laughs in self-deprecation.

Kitty warms to him. 'We have indeed only this last half hour arrived although for myself it is a second visit but after many years.' She smiles. 'In fact, I was recalling seeing Miss Anning herself strolling on the seashore looking for the fossils that have rightly made her celebrated.'

'I envy you,' the Reverend Mohun-Harris replies.' And yet perhaps there are more curiosities on display now than on that visit. You must go inside and, if you will permit, I will accompany you.'

He moves swiftly to open the door and follows them inside and perhaps does not notice the slight frown on Emily's face as she catches her mother's eye. But Kitty shrugs and, besides, her attention is instantly attracted by a portrait hanging on a wall.

'Miss Anning, just as I remember her,' she points. 'Wearing a strange high hat which we discovered was for protection from rock falls.'

The Reverend Mohun-Harris nods gravely. 'Indeed she was almost killed in one such in 1833. And her faithful little dog did not escape.'

Emily has noticed something else on the opposite wall, a print of a landscape entirely populated by a variety of strange creatures large and small. She reads the title beneath.

' *"Duria Antiquor."* That is more as I imagined I should see.'

'Dorset in times gone by,' supplies the Reverend Mohun-Harris and indicates his roll of paper. 'Of which I have just purchased a copy.'

'Mother do come and see! Is it not amazing?' Emily leans in to look more closely. 'Those are surely much larger ammonites, that creature there looks like a tortoise and that a crocodile, the others are quite fantastical.'

'All are creatures of which Miss Anning found the fossils,' says their new acquaintance. 'Drawn by a patron of Miss Anning with the intent of providing her with funds through sales of copies. The 'crocodile', which is indeed what it was called at first, was her first great find, then named an *ichthyosaurus* or "fish lizard", now a resident of a museum in London.'

'What is that odd bird?' Emily points.

'It is a *dimorphodon* or *pterosaur*. Not a bird but a reptile, a flying lizard if you will, and that very large creature eating an unfortunate smaller specimen is a *plesiosaur* or sea dragon. Another reptile, it has been called the Age of Reptiles.'

47

'We must acquire a copy of this engraving, Mother, would not Papa find it fascinating? May I take your purse?' Emily walks to a table at the back of the shop and rings a small bell which summons the immediate attention of an elderly man.

'Is it not near impossible to imagine that this was our world? 'Kitty steps closer to the drawing. 'So very different to what one was brought up to—'she breaks off as Emily re-joins them, her face a picture of dejection. 'What is it my dear?'

'There are no more copies available although some are awaited,' Emily sighs.

'I daresay we may find it in London,' Kitty consoles her.

'But you must have mine,' says the Reverend Mohun-Harris quickly, holding the package out for Emily to take. 'I am sure the owner will post another copy on to me. I have placed an order for a number of other items besides. Please, do take it.'

Emily looks quickly at her mother, her desire to accept so clearly apparent that Kitty agrees without further demur. 'It is extraordinarily kind of you,' she smiles. 'But now, Emily, we must make haste if we are to see the Cobb before dark.'

***

Emily walks carefully along the top of the oddly inward-sloping high harbour wall that protects the town and its fishing fleet from the wild western storms. She stops at a particularly treacherous flight of steps and calls down to her less adventurous mother on the quayside below.

'I do believe this must be the very spot described by Miss Austen where Louisa Musgrove falls down and her whole life changes, with quite unforeseeable consequences for those connected with her and the happiest of outcomes for Anne the heroine. Or perhaps it was the steps further back up which I climbed, though they seemed less challenging.'

Kitty gazes up at her daughter and attempts to bring her mind to bear on this question. She has been thinking of entirely different matters, connected with the rolled up print that she is carrying while Emily explores. James will of course be pleased that his daughter thought of him and wished to give him a gift, but he will show nothing like his interest in steam propulsion and other mechanical matters. They rarely discuss their religious beliefs, Kitty's own indeed being something of a mystery to herself, but she knows he prefers not to think of the great challenge to the Christian story of creation posed by the discoveries in this unlikely place.

Emily has become impatient. 'In *Persuasion,* Mother, wherein Anne has been persuaded to break off her engagement to one of lower birth, remember? A sea captain? I am sure you have read it.'

'So I did. But eight years later he returns from his voyages a rich man and they are reunited and, one is led to assume, live happily ever after. I thought it contrived.'

'Miss Austen was far too clever a writer for such cavalier dismissal,' Emily protests. 'In quite a different class to those of the more popular romances. Why should not there be a happy outcome?'

'Indeed it is always to be preferred,' Kitty acknowledges. 'Only – well, I cannot believe that after eight years she would not have been *persuaded* to marry someone else. Eight years is a long time in a young girl's life.'

Emily laughs and flings her arms heavenwards. 'It was because she loved him, Mother. Is that not easy to understand? If anything I thought it a little contrived that she would allow herself to be dissuaded from marrying the man she loved. *I* most certainly should not prefer another's counsels to those of my own heart. Not even yours, dear Mother.' Emily executes a pirouette, her long curls lifting in the freshening wind, and then she stops, peers into the sun and finally waves. 'Oh mother, look, it is that young man again. And now he is coming our way...'

'Do come down before you fall,' Kitty urges, holding up a hand to assist. 'We should walk to meet him since you have acknowledged his presence.'

The Reverend is a little out of breath, 'I say, I hope you won't think me presumptuous seeking you out, only I was on my way to search for fossils, there being perhaps a half hour left before the sun quite deserts us, when I saw you on the Cobb and the thought occurred that you might care to join me and profit by what little expertise I have acquired?'

'Oh!' Kitty sees the doubt in Emily's face, no doubt she is expecting her mother to think it too little time to extend their expedition, but Kitty is feeling indulgent.

'How kind, Reverend!' she smiles. 'I believe Emily would very much like to accompany you since we shall have no time before the coach departs in the morning. But you two young people will be able to walk much more quickly without me and I am in any case a little fatigued. I shall sit here,' she indicates a bench, 'and await your return.'

'We shall stay well within your sight,' the Reverend Mohun-Harris says hastily. 'There have been recent rock falls a short distance in that direction, where new fossils may therefore have been exposed.' He points westwards. 'And I beg you, both of you, do call me Walpole.'

Kitty sits where she indicated and waves to the departing pair. Better by far, she believes, to allow some freedom to young people so that they may form their own opinions and select their own spouses, with guidance as necessary. Dear Julia had thought the same. But Isabella had not and she, Kitty, had allowed herself to be dissuaded, if under circumstances which would surely have urged caution on anyone. Emily still sees such matters in black and white. Right and wrong. Perhaps her own mother had been the same. So young, yet surely so strong-minded in securing the husband of her choice. Kitty's gaze turns eastwards and lights on a distant group of perhaps half a dozen people walking along the shoreline away from the town. Thirty years ago, she thinks, that could have been us, at Dover.

11

1824 Dover

We had walked to the beach, the six of us in various groupings that shifted in shape and composition according to individual fancy and circumstance. There we parted company with the nursemaid, who professed herself capable of propelling both babies in the three-wheeled baby carriage that Julia had, thoughtfully, brought with her and promised to give to Mrs Irving upon our return to London. In truth, little John who was now able to walk a little, was too large for his chariot although as yet reluctant to give it up entirely. But he was also too heavy to carry over any distance or uncertain surfaces.

Mrs Irving and I were squired down the shingle bank to the foreshore where the receding tide had exposed flat sand on which it was easier to stroll. I took my arm out of Thomas' and we lingered to allow Edward and Julia, who together were now helping five year old William clamber over the shifting stones, to join us. There he shook off his attendants and ran ahead of us towards the sea. As the rest of us followed him, the Irvings dropped behind a little way, while Thomas moved to Edward's side.

'What troubles of Kitty's father were you referring to yesterday, Mr Strachey?' he asked. 'And why did the Duke of Wellington so dislike him?' Thomas looked from Edward to me and back again to Edward. 'And were the two matters connected with each other?'

Julia instantly looked unhappy and I believe would have spoken, but Mr Irving engaged her attention and she was forced to fall back and walk with them.

Edward held up his hands in mild protest. 'You are too scientific, Thomas, too rational. Or I have given you cause to think such matters can be easily defined and ordered. And it was Richard not

Arthur Wellesley whose opinion was the more important at this stage, being India's Governor General at the time. However,' he pursed his lips as he considered. 'I think 'the connection' may be the easiest place to start, for the heart of the matter is the circumstance with which you are already familiar. Kitty's father James was an admirer, in fact a lover, of Indian culture, particularly I should say Indian Muslim culture, that being primarily what he had encountered. And this in some ways both led him to his marriage to the renowned beauty Khair-un-Nissa and to being distrusted by the English authorities. And his marriage only increased that disapproval which made many difficulties for him.'

It was Thomas' turn to protest. 'I fear you are not scientific enough!' he exclaimed. 'I am bemused.'

'Hmm. People do say I can be too succinct,' Edward paused and bent to pick up some multi-coloured pebble. 'Very pretty. And no doubt with an intriguing history if one could but read the signs. How and of what it was formed, how came it here to this particular beach…You should make me a drawing, Kitty, and I will perhaps find some geologist who can explain it.' Edward turned back to Thomas. 'Very well, Thomas, I shall eschew generalities and tell you what I have myself observed.' Again he stopped and pointed down. 'Another such stone, Kitty, but smaller. Surely we might carry it home?'

Thomas bent quickly to pick up and present the stone to me before turning the full force of his attention onto Edward, who nodded and coughed before continuing his account. I hung as avidly on his words for, even if they proved not new to me, it was joy to hear my parents remembered.

'Before our visit,' said Edward. 'Elphinstone and I had been told that James often wore Mussleman's dress, hennaed his hands and kept his mustaches Indian style and we found it to be so, though not on all occasions. He took us hunting deer with cheetahs, which I may say was great sport. But we also shot grouse and played cards and backgammon and billiards as if we had been at home in a London club. I would say his somewhat hybrid life well reflected his role in mediating between the British and the local ruler, the Nizam. It certainly facilitated it and it also made it more – understandable -that he should be allowed to marry so high-born a woman.'

'A descendant of the Prophet Mohammed,' Thomas observed, casting a sideways glance at me for confirmation.

Edward nodded. 'But it also led to rumours, allegations even, that James had entirely 'gone over' to the other side, changed his religion, become, in effect, a traitor. Some even thought that Khair's family had deliberately courted him for that purpose. It is almost certain that they sought him rather than the reverse but it was because Khair wished it rather than marry a cousin of her grandfather's choice. James apparently resisted for a while , or so he told his brother William, Julia's father, who attempted to prevent the alliance.'

'There were official enquiries,' I added. 'Requested by the Governor-General. I daresay you may still read the reports though I have not, their subject matter being thought too intimate. What I do know is that my father had served the company loyally and well, for the same Lord Wellesley had not long before recommended him for a baronetcy!'

We had reached the water's edge where William was, none too expertly, dodging the incoming waves.

'Extraordinary!' Thomas stopped pacing and, turning seawards, looked far out to the horizon as if the answers to these mysteries might there be visible. But then he shook his head as if to clear it and addressed me directly. 'I wish I could invent such a tale.'

'The truth can be strange indeed,' Edward nodded and bent to pick up a whole handful of pebbles which he scrutinised not at all but, calling William to his side to assist, began to throw at the incoming waves as if to emphasise each remark. 'James' diplomatic skills had secured the expulsion of the French from southern India , without a drop of blood being shed, and a Treaty of alliance with the Nizam, which more or less secured British ascendancy in India. I have to say I only understood some of this later.'

'More extraordinary yet!' Thomas turned to me with fire in his eyes. 'Imagine that one man could have such an effect upon the course of history. And that he was your father!'

'While Julia's father—' continued Edward.

'My Uncle William—'

'Was Wellesley's trusted aide in Calcutta, with therefore very divided loyalties.' Edward threw his last stone.

Thomas was still shaking his head in disbelief at the Gothic twists and turns of my history when Julia re-joined us.

She took Edward's arm. 'Of what are you speaking with such animation?'

'Oh, some trivia!' Edward waved a hand dismissively. 'James' Kirkpatrick's single-handed defeat of the French and your father's equally important role in formulating British policy in India.'

Julia smiled at him fondly. 'I suppose you did not mention Admiral Nelson's sinking of almost the entire French fleet at the Battle of the Nile? I believe historians might make something of this coincidental occurrence.'

We all laughed then and made some remarks about our old enemy being just across the sea and it being as well we were no longer at war or we could not have enjoyed this walk in such serenity. Thomas stopped and stared out to sea for quite a while before observing that he had never been in such close proximity to France before and how strange it was to think one could now visit that country with such ease and entirely for pleasure.

'Assuming that the new King observes the Charter as well as did his predecessor,' Edward agreed. 'Meanwhile it is true that one hears that there is so much pleasure to be had in Paris that it is fairly over-run with English and at any one time one may find in residence a third of the House of Lords! Although proportionately more of the Scottish and Irish peers, who find it not only a more congenial but cheaper place to live than London.'

I daresay there was more laughter at this point, and perhaps some scepticism, although Edward was not commonly given to exaggeration. In any case we then, by common accord, began to stroll along the beach to rejoin the nursemaid whom we could see some distance along the beach with John toddling around her. I think we might have abandoned the whole subject at this point had not Thomas again become thoughtful.

'Indeed, Nelson was a very great man and further proof that without men of judgment acting upon events, the outcome, the consequences will be, must be different, if not readily foreseen. Or perhaps intended.' He seemed almost to be speaking to himself, for he looked neither to left nor right, his brows drawn close in concentration. 'And even if the individual is not properly recognised by history, as sadly seems to have been the case with James Kirkpatrick, perhaps partly due to his early and most tragic demise.' At this point Thomas woke from his reverie and spoke in quite a different tone as he returned his attentions to this particular case. 'When Kitty and her brother were already en-route for England, which left his wife, their mother, unexpectedly and entirely alone, in what may have been a most compromised condition in regard to her own people, as well as the British.'

'She was not quite alone,' I corrected him. 'She did have her mother, and her grandmother. I think they lived almost always together. And there were servants of course.'

'And she was received by the family in Calcutta,' added Edward. 'After she had completed a period of mourning, she came to see her husband's grave and stayed for some months. She became great friends with Isabella by all accounts.'

'She brought her some opal jewellery as a belated wedding gift,' Julia nodded. 'Of course I was still in England.'

'And had not met me.' Edward held her closer. 'Little did I know I too would be marrying into this illustrious family!'

'A most just and enlightened family,' Thomas smiled at us all in what seemed to be the conclusion of his investigation. 'She was not abandoned. Respect and understanding can triumph over differences of language and race.'

Thomas appeared satisfied but I was not. This happy picture did not at all accord with my experience. If I had ever been told that Isabella and my mother had been on good terms, I had forgotten for it seemed to make little sense of what I knew with utter certainty.

'Then why, Julia, if my mother was so well-received by our family, by Isabella, why were not my brother and I allowed any correspondence with her? Why were we never given news or allowed to write? Even when dear William suffered his accident? Why? Why?' My voice rose as my distress increased. 'Why did you break her heart and ours?'

'Hush, hush,' Julia attempted to comfort me but I daresay I shrugged her off.

'You must ask Isabella not Julia,' Edward advised. 'Julia was not there.'

'But *you* were in Calcutta at the time,' my voice had already begun to falter. 'And you were both there when William and I were growing up in England.' I sighed and became silent. I knew I had lost the argument as I had long ago when my only weapons were tears and tantrums. I was now grown but Edward and Julia were still my elders, still acting in what they felt to be my best interests. And even I did not wish to voice at this moment what had become my own conclusion: that if my parents were not married my brother and I were therefore illegitimate, and that if the connection with my mother were severed then our reputations might better be protected. But then Thomas spoke and I think the fire must have been in his eyes for both Edward and Julia recoiled a little.

'Kitty never wrote to her mother? Nor received letters from her? Was not that excessively cruel? And what possible reason can there have been? Other than prejudice and racial pride born I guess from Britain's growing power in that place. It seems to me a sad betrayal of James, not to care for those he loved when he was no longer there to do so and not at all what I should have expected of your family.'

Edward looked very uncomfortable though surely not the main target of Thomas' critique. 'As I said, Thomas, you would need to ask Isabella.'

To my renewed distress, Julia was almost in tears. 'We are neglecting our other guests.' She straightened her shoulders and I suppose would have turned aside to wait for the Irvings who had trailed somewhat behind. But dear Thomas' response was immediate. He hastened to join the Irvings, who did indeed appear in rather silent and sombre mood, and clapped his friend on the back. I remained with Edward and Julia but overheard the beginning of the ensuing conversation for Thomas' voice was unusually loud and hearty.

'Edward, does this not recall to you our time at Kirkcaldy, that fine mile-long beach of the smoothest sand, where we walked so often by moonlight as much as by day? Do you remember watching the waves coming in, steadily, gently and then the break of them, rushing like a mane of foam from south to north the whole mile's distance? What happy days! And you gave me *'will and waygate'* – that finest Annandale expression! -of your library, being already

56

well-established when I arrived, which invitation I was pleased to make full use of.'

Mr Irving responded with the genial laugh which he always seemed to have ready, at least in Thomas' company, and Mrs Irving said something more quietly, I guessed to do with how she had there met both Thomas and her future husband for I knew she was a Kirkaldy girl, a local clergyman's daughter. Both men then laughed and I was happy to observe the three of them walking together in apparent harmony until we turned homewards. However, I recall with shame how later that evening, after supper, I aided Thomas in again betraying his old friend and benefactor, which doubtless did little to endear me to Mrs Irving. And besides, we again upset my dearest, kindest cousin, Julia, whose own mother had died in childbirth when she was very young and whose childhood had been almost as unusual as mine.

We had acquired the habit of reading aloud to each other in the evenings and, on this particular occasion, Mr Irving was reading from Phineas Fletcher's *Purple Island*, reading with much solemnity despite Thomas' and my jocular interruptions and teasing. We two made some sport, as I recall, of trying to guess to which parts of the body Mr Fletcher's cumbrous allegory referred. The others soon became silent although I did not much notice this at the time.

'River' was easy, being of course the vessels that carry the blood and we also guessed the 'cave' to be the mouth, though not that the teeth were 'porters, receivers of the rent', nor the tongue 'a groom who delivers all unto near officers'. Upon mountain we disagreed. Thomas argued for the protuberances like shoulders and knees, I wanted to include the head. (The more general 'bones' was the correct answer).'Goodly cities' had us entirely foxed until Mr Irving told us that the 'arch city' was the liver, from which it was easy to deduce that the other principal organs were lesser cities.

Edward then again took part, and being more familiar with the work, recalled that the island's prince is the intellect, who wages war on disease and vice with the aid of his counsellors, the five senses, and his allies the virtues. Thomas wondered, with thinly feigned seriousness, if this would prove a model for the analysis of recent European conflicts in which new game Edward and I soon joined, throwing out wilder and wilder suggestions as to why some battles had been lost, how secure were present victories and so forth. Our wit eventually enlivened to such an extent that Mr Irving at last admitted defeat, snapped shut the volume and, rising to his feet, announced to his wife that they should return to their lodgings. She stood up instantly, clearly unamused by our antics and eager to leave but as immediately, Edward recalled his duties as host.

'Do stay,' he urged. 'I would hear of your experiences in Glasgow which I believe to be a much up- and-coming city, if still secondary to Edinburgh.'

'Oh indeed, sir.' The Irvings resumed their seats and Mr Irving leaned eagerly forward to satisfy his audience. 'I was most fortunate to be taken on by the great Dr Chalmers whose preaching was such an inspiration to me.'

But Edward's interest was of a more secular bent. 'Were you not there at the time of the radical uprising?' he enquired. 'Amongst the weavers? Against whom was called out the yeomanry?'

His tone was impartial, though I knew him likely to take the part of the workers who had found themselves so cruelly displaced by the new mechanical looms, and was glad soon to hear both Mr Irving and Thomas profess a similar opinion.

Some half an hour later when the Irvings did at last depart, Mrs Irving having begged the need of sleep, Julia sternly addressed the three of us.

'*The Purple Island* is not so absurd a book,' she insisted. 'I believe it displays a rare knowledge of anatomy.'

'But in twelve cantos?' protested Edward. 'In such *purple* verse? Are there not better ways to learn of such things and to pass one's time?'

'I see you are in need of diversion,' Julia frowned and, calling me to join her, bade the two men goodnight.

The very next day she came up with her proposal to send us on a trip to Paris and leave her in peace to enjoy the Irvings' company. Strange punishment of our misbehaviour indeed! I never did discover how sincere were her stated motives, whether she truly wished more time to discuss matters of the spirit with Mr Irving, for she surely did not reckon to be undisturbed having also her two infants to consider. At the very least they were mixed, for how could Thomas and I not have grown closer in such circumstances, and how could she not have foreseen, if not intended this to be the case?

12

Lyme Regis to Dorchester

Emily turns to her mother, a small frown clouding her habitually frank expression. 'The coachman is getting up on his box,' she says. 'And Walpole is not come.'

They are alone in the coach for, as they discovered at breakfast, the young girl was sick in the night and the farmer's wife has kindly stayed to nurse her. They plan to take the next day's coach.

'Oh my dear, and are you very disappointed?' Kitty is not sure how far her daughter's affections have yet been engaged.

'Well, he *promised* he would be here to bid us farewell,' Emily's voice rises and her lower lip trembles. She twists a pocket handkerchief in her hands as she leans from the coach window and peers anxiously up and down the street.

Kitty does not quite find in this the answer to her question but wishes to console her daughter nonetheless. 'Then there must be some very good explanation for his delay,' she asserts, with more confidence than she feels. Young men can be unreliable, this she knows from bitter experience without having ever suffered herself in quite this fashion. She suspects that young James in London is already discovering how easy it is for a good-looking young man in uniform to encourage a girl's expectations and she is hoping that any such dalliances will not prove too compromising for anyone concerned.

'There he is!' Emily's whole demeanour is transformed in an instant. She sits up, a flush in her cheeks, her eyes bright, and leans out further. 'Walpole!' she calls, waving her handkerchief. 'Oh do hurry! Look Mother, he is running, he has even removed his hat. Oh, can we ask the coachman to delay? Oh, he has seen.' And with this she opens the door and would jump down were the steps not removed and Walpole already arrived and saluting the driver for his delay.

'I have brought you this.' Kitty sees him hand Emily what looks like a stone. 'I went early this morning acting on the best information, only it took longer than I expected and I am come directly from the beach.' He is out of breath, perspiring but radiant with his success. 'It is the best specimen I have ever found.'

'Oh Walpole, it is wonderful!'

Emily's response is clearly gratifying enough for, as Kitty watches, any lingering uncertainty in Walpole's upturned countenance disappears to be replaced by a wide smile. What more would have been said it is impossible to know for the coachman can wait no longer.

'Close the door!' he shouts and Walpole bows briefly to Kitty, slams shut the carriage door and steps back.

He waves to Emily and Emily to him until the coach has turned out of Bridge Street and begun the long climb out of town and onto the east-bound road. Emily sinks into her corner seat and inspects her gift, which Kitty can now see is an ammonite four inches across and in perfect condition. The previous evening, Emily and Walpole had returned in some dejection, having found only the smallest ammonite imprints and a broken belemnite.

'Is it not wonderful,' Emily says slowly, 'to think that this was a living creature in the sea near here, but millions and millions of years ago when the earth was a very different place and we humans did not exist and would not appear for – well, millions and millions of years? I must say it makes the story in Genesis seem like a children's story.' Her hand flies to her mouth. 'Or is that a terrible thing to say?'

'It is what many people are thinking, I believe,' her mother carefully replies. 'And I suppose it is better to face one's doubts and overcome them than let them fester and destroy all faith. What does Walpole think?'

'Oh, he believes we must take account of whatever science uncovers. We had quite a discussion about it.'

Kitty is surprised both at her daughter's new interest and at Walpole's attitude. 'But does this position not pose problems for his chosen career?'

'No.' Emily slowly shakes her head and pauses, remembering. 'He says that everyone sooner or later will experience such doubts and that he, like a good shepherd, can help his flock to face them and lead them to a new understanding which will strengthen their faith. Something like that anyway. Very much as you just said in fact. Oh, do look!' She points with excitement from the window in the direction from which they have travelled. Kitty is then obliged to turn in her seat, which she does with the aid of a leather strap suspended beside her for the coach is now on a steep incline. 'Do you see the Cobb?' Then her tone changes and she sighs. 'I wonder if I shall ever see it again.'

Kitty leans back in her corner and smiles at her daughter. 'I am sure you will,' she says. 'In fact, I think we should all make the trip again next year in our own carriage,' she reaches for the strap again as the coach jolts over some irregularity in the surface of the road. 'Which might be a deal more comfortable. I do hope we shall not have to get out and walk.' Emily does not respond to this, which makes Kitty think she is still thinking of her experiences in Lyme. 'Walpole's ambition is an admirable one,' she suggests.

'Yes, isn't it.' But Emily's voice has lost all enthusiasm.

'A worthy aim to which to dedicate one's life?'

'It is.' Emily sighs again and Kitty decides to risk rebuff.

'So why the sighs and sadness?'

'I am not ready to be the wife of a country vicar, Mother, however much I may admire him.'

'Walpole has asked you to marry him? With so little encouragement? After so short an acquaintance?'

'Oh no!' Emily is shocked. 'I am sure he would do no such thing without asking your and Papa's approval.'

'Then?'

'Oh Mother, one knows these things does one not? From glances, smiles, the drift of conversation? It is what one learns as one grows older.'

One does, Kitty agrees silently, and knows that she should not be surprised that, at eighteen, Emily has learned already.

'One can be misled,' she cautions. 'Some seek to mislead, to charm.'

'I should hardly call Walpole a charmer,' observes Emily a little testily, reaching for the strap on her side. The coach has reached the top of the hill and, with a jolt, begins an equally steep descent the other side. 'Anyway, he asked for our address in Horsham and said he might visit. He has a friend recently become curate of a church there. I could not easily say no.' She lets go the strap, wraps the fossil in her handkerchief, reaches under the seat for her travelling bag, opens it, puts the fossil inside and firmly snaps it shut again. 'And now, *please* let us find a new topic?' She kicks the bag back underneath her seat.

Kitty looks from the window whence it is not difficult to find inspiration. She points ahead to the sweeping seascapes visible between a succession of high redstone promontories. 'Similar but so much grander than ours at home,' she marvels. 'And how green the grass at this season.'

Emily looks with some reluctance but then laughs. 'All those small white dots! Are they not sheep?' she says. 'I wonder they do not fall off the hillside it is so steep.'

'And look inland also,' Kitty directs. 'Where the view is surely of equal magnificence.'

Emily turns her attention to the opposite window and silently observes the panorama to the north where line after line of tree-clad hills recede into the furthest distance, while Kitty wonders at the ballooning clouds that drift slowly across from the south-west and on across the land. How careless they are of we mortals here beneath, she thinks and is about to share this impression when Emily speaks.

'Tell me how your parents met, for theirs was surely the true romance that I crave,' she says, 'which did not let religious questions stand in its way. How I wish I could have known them.'

Kitty swallows hard. She could almost say the same. 'My dear! How very much *they* would have loved *you*.' She takes a handkerchief from her pocket and blows her nose. 'So. I will tell you what I have been told and you must judge if it meets your criteria. Do you remember that not so many years ago, and quite by chance, my grandmother and I were at last enabled to write to each other?' Emily shakes her head. 'You were a child at the time. I will show you her letters, or rather their translations, when we return home. She wrote that, having heard of my mother's beauty from an English lady who had visited the ladies of their household, my father then sought her out and they immediately fell deeply in love.'

'Ah!' Emily claps her hands. 'Just as I thought.' Her eyes are shining.

Kitty holds up a hand. 'Wait! There is another story. I have also learnt, from what others have told me, that, because of their religious differences, and also because my mother had been promised in marriage by her grandfather to a cousin, some of her family were much opposed to the match and this threatened relations between the British and Hyderabadi governments. My grandmother however did not like her father's choice for her daughter, no more did my mother, so it seems they encouraged my father's suit. In fact, I have been told that my grandmother contrived for them to meet on several occasions and that he, my father, at first resisted.' Kitty pauses. 'So what is your opinion? Was it truly true love or —'

Emily takes both her mother's hands in her own. 'I cannot pretend to understand the ways of a country and a time of which I know so little,' she says. 'But Mother, whether your parents fell in love of their own accord or were encouraged to do so by your grandmother is of little matter. They fell in love and remained so in the face of every opposition, including, I daresay, threats to my father's position. I can think of no better example of true love, can you? And is it not what every woman, nay, every person, would desire? And strive to achieve? I most certainly would.'

Kitty regards her daughter with mixed emotions. 'I believe you are even more like my mother than I had thought,' she says. 'And surely more than I.' She feels a little envy, of Emily's youth and certainty, and fears that actuality will not match expectation, as Thomas might have said and as in their own sad experience. But, she thinks, that could not be said of our trip to Paris, when we were as children escaped from the nursery. I remember the three of us, Edward, Thomas and I, leaning on the rail at the back of the boat watching the white cliffs of England slowly recede in the long wake of our vessel. With what excitement we pointed out landmarks to each other whilst they were still distinct, until they appeared so small that it was hard to credit it the home of all the places and people we knew and held dear.

13

1824 Dover to Calais, November

'How small an island it is!' I exclaimed. 'So insignificant one would think, compared to the great continent to which we are bound. How strange that it should wield so much influence in the world.'

'This narrow strait is like a great moat,' Thomas suggested. 'A constant defence against the frequent wars and invasions suffered by our nearest neighbours who lack such a natural boundary.'

'The cost being a certain insularity in our thought also?' Edward wondered, but Thomas seemed in no mood for philosophical speculation. 'Besides,' Edward added. 'Do not forget the importance of a strong navy to defend our very long coastline. And indeed our dominion around the world.'

'Do you know,' Thomas turned to me. 'The longest trip I have made by sea was that from Edinburgh to London, whereas you, and Edward, both have sailed half around the world. Such sights you have seen.'

'Except that I remember nothing, save being much afraid when there was a storm and being comforted by Mrs Ure who was accompanying us and because she was very fat almost suffocating in her embrace.'

Edward laughed. 'Poor little girl. I remember she was certainly an impressive figure.'

Still Thomas pursued his own course. 'Just think, when we have landed in France were we to continue on foot or carriage we would ultimately reach the far shores of China and the Pacific Ocean. How very different it is to have first-hand experience rather than discover another's in a book or painting. Oh, do I become tedious? Perhaps to you,' he addressed Edward, 'these are commonplace observations.'

Edward shook his head. 'Not at all. And I admire your constant sense of enquiry, may I say, of wonder.' He smiled. 'Most people are, I think, too sunk in the everyday, the immediate, to have such a perspective.'

Certainly our fellow passengers displayed no such inspiration. When it became too chill for comfort on deck, we found seats in the large refreshment saloon where there were a number of French, mainly men returning, I supposed, from some business venture, but rather more English, men and women, some children too. It soon became apparent from their conversation that many of them were acquainted, or at least enjoyed a great deal of shared experiences which they were keen to display.

'My dear, I can scarcely wait to walk again in the *Sham Elizas*,' loudly declared a lady at the next table to another sitting nearby.

Edward saw my incomprehension and leaned closer to whisper. 'Champs Elysees,' he translated. 'A large and fashionable thoroughfare in Paris.'

'Nor I to *do a little Tuileries*!' the other lady replied and both of them laughed immoderately at what was clearly a familiar phrase and pastime.

I looked to Thomas to share my own amusement but found him frowning. I might have commented but the first lady had thought of a further riposte.

'Nor I to receive the *galanteries* of the Frenchmen who know how to treat a lady,' she said with a sideways glance at our table. 'Our own dear men being so very glum.'

At this Thomas flushed, Edward pulled a very long face and we all three broke into loud and, I fear, somewhat superior laughter, which was quite unfounded, since none of us had any greater knowledge of France nor proficiency in its language. Edward's was perhaps the best but he made little effort and his accent was atrocious.

'Mon French est abominable,' he asserted after ordering us supper from one of the few French stewards and we did not disagree. Thomas' excellent knowledge of German was of course of no use, though he made some sport of speaking for a while in what he claimed was 'Frallemande', supposedly the language of a disputed border area between the two countries. We were in very light-hearted mood, still somewhat astonished to find ourselves on this unexpected adventure when it seemed anything might happen.

'This excursion will be quite unimaginable to my parents,' said Thomas. 'I have written to them and can picture their consternation, that we dare to go so deep into enemy territory.'

Yet his own amazement was almost as naïve. From Calais we travelled by private coach and much of the time I sat close beside him on the back-facing seat, while Edward claimed to prefer to remain with Jean, the girl I had engaged in Dover to be my maid. The countryside was flat and unremarkable, particularly at this time of year when most of the fields were brown and bare, but Thomas' interest did not flag.

'These names,' he said as we drove south, pointing to some sign or other, and sometimes contriving to touch my arm the better to engage my attention. 'Montreuil, Noailles, Abbeville. Of a sudden they are transformed from interesting words into actual places!'

14

Dorchester

'Mother? Of what are you dreaming? We are arriving in Dorchester. I have just seen the sign.'

Kitty is recalled to the present which, though precious since it has given her unaccustomed time in Emily's company, is not at this moment as engaging as that one journey with Edward and Thomas which had seemed set to change her future. Their coach has entered a wide paved street and soon comes to a halt at the entrance to what appears to be a large coaching inn.

'One hour's refreshment stop,' their driver informs them as he opens the door and assists them to climb down.

Led by a stable boy, the coach rumbles away through a high arched opening no doubt to the stableyard behind the inn where the horses will also be fed and watered.

'Oh do look!' Emily indicates a row of fine new buildings on the other side of the street. 'One would think oneself in a much larger city. What is that?' She addresses the driver and points to a long grey stone construction of elegant proportions with arched covered walkway along its front side and a clocktower its only adornment.

'That there's the Town Hall,' the driver replies. 'Built these five or six years past. Dorchester's a fast growing place. I seen it happen week by week, before my very eyes.'

'The one on the end is a church of course,' observes Emily. 'But the one between them also looks like a church does it not, with its fine large window and tall spire at the corner. Can there be need of two churches in such proximity?'

Her informant strokes his chin as he considers. 'Maybe there could, miss, depending on the demand, but that there's the Corn

Exchange, where the sort of business transacted is a fair bit different to what goes on in a church.' He chuckles, his eyes disappearing in the creases of his weather-beaten face.' And I should say it touches every bit as much if not more on the people's lives hereabouts. Dorchester's an important market town.'

'Hence the similarity of the buildings?' Clearly Emily is still puzzled and might easily, Kitty thinks, importune the driver further. She takes her arm to draw her away at which the driver doffs his hat and bows to indicate that they should precede him into the inn.

'Why, happen you're right, now you mention it.' He laughs aloud. 'Happen you're right. I'll be seeing you later, miss, ma'am. I'm off to the snug for a bite to eat. You'll find the dining room to the right there.' He is still chuckling as they enter the inn.

'Can the worship of God be so readily equated with the conduct of trade, Mother?' Emily shakes her head as they take their seats. 'Or rather, should it be?'

Kitty smiles fondly at her daughter, for whom this journey is unexpectedly providing such food for reflection. 'I think not, my darling, but I also think the coachman to be correct in his assessment. For most people material matters do prevail most of the time.'

And she is reminded of her own surprise at Thomas' entire lack of interest in visiting the ancient cathedral of Beauvais, of which they had a fine and uninterrupted view as they approached that city, where they intended making a night's stop. While she and Emily await the arrival of their dinner, she tries to recall more exactly what he said.

***

'Perhaps we can find time to visit it in the morning,' I suggested. 'I have heard it has the most wonderful stained glass and tapestries, besides being at one time the tallest building in Europe, nay perhaps the world.'

'For which over-reaching ambition the architects were rewarded with not one but two collapses in subsequent years,' Thomas retorted. 'Oh but look there,' he indicated in the opposite direction a café, within which could be seen a tall officer in some uniform or other striding to and fro in clearly dejected mood. 'Is he not the very image of human *ennui?*'

'He certainly does not look content,' I said. 'But surely you are wrong to dismiss the attempts of those long ago artisans. Perhaps it was not vainglorious aggrandizement which inspired them but the desire to please, nay even reach nearer to God.'

Thomas sighed deeply and then raised my hand to his lips. 'Sweet Kitty,' he said. 'Yes, it is possible. But in fact I have read that there was some race, some competition involved. In any case, I fear I cannot share your predominantly benevolent view of humanity and its religious practices.'

Of course by then I knew of his disaffection from the Church as a career but had not appreciated its depth or true nature. I daresay he had not yet formulated it as clearly as he did a few years later in that novel where he so bitterly attacked the materialism of our age. I returned to the subject when we were eating together later that evening and Edward, perhaps sensing my disturbance, put him on the spot, although not quite in the fashion I had imagined. In fact, Edward seemed less concerned with Thomas' spiritual condition than his material prospects and most particularly, it soon occurred to me, as a prospective suitor.

'So, Thomas,' he put down his knife and fork. 'If it is not to be the Church nor the schoolroom, how then shall you make your way?'

'Well,' said Thomas, pushing aside his plate, he never did eat much at a sitting. 'A literary life would do very well, and I am encouraged to believe it not to be entirely impracticable. A few small essays and other trifles were published in Edinburgh. And then there are my Schiller translations, you know? I have recently received an offer, they may be published together in one volume if I can edit them appropriately. And there is also my translation of *Wilhelm Meister*, by the great Goethe...I believe I have discovered a small niche in which I am regarded as something of an expert, though whether it will furnish a living I cannot as yet say.'

He began to toy with a piece of bread while Edward regarded him thoughtfully, as if appraising the accuracy of his self-estimation, or perhaps the degree of his determination in pursuing his stated ambition.

'And besides,' it appeared that Thomas felt the need to justify further his choice of career, 'I intend to have another try at writing a novel, having been inspired by Herr Goethe. The form you know, of

Wilhelm Meister, is far from those popular romances that fill every bookshop. Not only a matter of simple story telling.'

He fell silent and Edward not responding, I felt embarrassed on his behalf.

'Perhaps this journey may afford you material for some new writing?' I surmised. 'It is surely a moment of great interest to European readers, for a new King will bring change?'

Thomas held my gaze awhile and I thought I caught the glimmer of fresh inspiration stir in the depths of those extraordinary violet eyes. 'Perhaps,' he acknowledged. 'Though there are hacks enough to report the news, better placed than I to understand the import.' Then he frowned. 'But perhaps for once I shall not attempt to make comparison and analysis and reference , but to appreciate the present, which is wondrous enough.' Still he looked into my eyes as if wishing to say more but then he sat back, threw out his arms and exclaimed. 'Tomorrow we shall be in Paris!'

***

'Our food is served, Mother,' Emily rouses Kitty from her reverie. 'Are you well? You seem fatigued sitting so long with your eyes shut.'

'Oh, I was remembering another journey I once made, to a very great city. Paris.'

'With Papa?'

'No it was before I had met your papa. I travelled with cousin Julia's husband Edward and - a friend of his. We were very fortunate to be able to travel when we did, after the great revolution and before the later uprisings. We were there during the restoration. In fact, we saw the King when we were visiting the Louvre. Charles the Ninth I think he was. A most unimpressive figure I thought and indeed his reign was not a success.'

'Is there not peace again now?'

'Now that a Bonaparte is again in power? It seems so.' Kitty sighs. 'One has to feel sorry for the French people, suffering so many reversals of government in so short a time.'

'We are fortunate then, do you think, to enjoy such peace and continuity?'

'Oh yes, *we* are very fortunate.' Kitty makes this careful emphasis, but it passes unremarked for Emily's thoughts are taking a different path.

She is quiet for a moment. 'Mama, could we go to Paris? I should so like to see more of the world, like you.'

'I should like you to,' Kitty replies carefully. 'But you must ask your father. And perhaps when Mary is married for, who knows, she and Mr Molyneaux-Scel may take up residence there.'

But I shall not be the one to decide, she thinks, for she does not wish to go, knowing that the memories would be too painful, the comparisons nothing but unfavourable with those wonderful days.

An hour passed, the coachman comes as promised to call them.

'I was thinking, ma'am,' he says as together they approach the coach, 'the young lady taking such an interest in her surroundings, mebbe she would care to ride on the box with me awhile, the weather being fine and all? There's room for three if you would care to—'

'No, no I should not,' Kitty hastens to assure him. 'But Emily is welcome to if she would like. One certainly obtains a finer view when sitting outside but I fear one's comfort becomes more important as one grows older. I may in fact take a nap.'

Emily happily installed and well wrapped in a travelling rug on the box, Kitty rests her feet on the seat beside her but her dreams are of the waking variety for most of the remainder of the journey to Ringwood.

15

1824 November, Paris

I was so very happy at my part in enabling Thomas to so expand his horizons and experience such enthusiasm, for the costs of the trip were certainly beyond his present purse. And Paris did not disappoint us.

We approached the city along a fine wide highway with great old trees on either side, all brilliant in the October sun. It led through a tollgate onto the hill of Montmartre whence lay all Paris at our feet. I think no other city ever looked so fair, the whole utterly clear and sparkling with scarce a breath of smoke, thus quite unlike our own dirty capital. We arrived at our hotel in a mood of high anticipation, our rooms full of mirrors in which only my own reflection seemed faulty. I had already had glimpses of that *chic* style for which the French were famous as we drove along the boulevards surveying the passers-by, and I did not intend to be the object of mirth and scorn as English ladies so often were. I had seen their unkind caricatures in the press.

'Oh do look at those hats,' I exclaimed to Jean, she being the only member of our party likely to appreciate their style. 'Do not ours appear quite ridiculously small and fussy?'

Thomas looked quizzical. 'Those curiously speckled straw hats?' he enquired. 'You admire them?'

'I shall acquire one,' I assured him promptly. 'And some gowns besides if there is time to find a dressmaker. Why else does one come to Paris?'

For a moment he frowned and narrowed his eyes but then he saw that I was again teasing him and retaliated in kind.

'Quite so. One certainly is not interested in the art, the architecture, the history or the gastronomy, all of which are far superior at home. I speak of Scotland, of course.'

In fact, we were equally entranced by all we saw and heard in those too few and frantic days when we roamed the boulevards and gardens, visited the palaces and churches, sat in cafes and restaurants, and by happy coincidence of timing watched the famous actor Talma perform some tragedy. We were dazzled by the fabulous display of paintings in the Louvre which far surpassed any in London, and agreed that Paris deserved its claim to be the heart of Europe if not the world.

Notwithstanding his avowed intent to *carpe diem*, Thomas found historical significance at every turn. Along this street drove the tumbrils carrying the doomed aristocrats to the guillotine, he informed us, guidebook open in his hand; here the royal heads had rolled and here were they erected on sticks for the rude world to see. There the populace had stormed the supposedly impregnable Bastille, there erected barricades to frustrate the soldiers and guards' attempts to regain power. Yet twenty years on, now lay in state the body of the first king of the Restoration, Louis Dixhuit, and the same people and their children flocked past him in their thousands to show their respect. I found it hard to understand and said so.

'Twas the Allies' plan, those who had together defeated Napoleon,' said Edward. 'And had no intention of allowing his return or that of any other Republican. I remember hearing that the Tsar was particularly welcomed here, being so polite and quite unlike Napoleon.'

'I have read it was the women in particular who welcomed the return of the monarchy,' observed Thomas slyly. 'There are pictures of them crowding the streets around the new King.' He paused, perhaps thinking I would protest, but seeing I wanted further explanation, added: 'They had lost too many fathers, husbands and sons.'

'Which of course,' I remarked, 'makes perfect sense of their behaviour.'

'Indeed,' he agreed quickly, but then seemed to wish to say more. 'Perhaps I *could* write about this history,' he said. 'Taking the perspectives of those who were active in the events. So that one might feel one were there…'His eyes were glowing, his gaze elsewhere as he imagined the task.

'Then you will certainly have to visit here again,' said Edward. 'For there are surely still many people alive you could meet and talk to who will recall those days.'

I said no more at the time but intended to offer finance for such visits and hoped that I might one day accompany him. There was but one occasion which cast a passing blight on this imagined rosy future. On the afternoon before our departure Edward and I declared a wish to revisit the Louvre, there being so very many artistic works to appreciate, but Thomas cried off, saying he had to write some letter concerning the Schiller translations. Upon our return I saw that he had indeed written a letter, a very long letter which he made haste to put in his pocket.

'Is all well with your work?' I enquired.

'Yes, yes,' he quickly responded but flushed and did not meet my eye, which made me sure something was amiss, though not whether it should concern me.

He looked up then and I saw such a range of shifting and conflicting emotions in his gaze that I was afraid, it was almost as if he did not see me and in his mind was somewhere else entirely. But then he seemed to recollect his senses and smiled at me with what was surely tenderness and true affection. He proposed we take a last walk amidst the fallen leaves of the Luxembourg gardens and we both affirmed a wish to pay a more extended visit in the future, these few days having but whetted the appetite.

But, as far as I know, he never did return to Paris. He wrote his great work on the French Revolution from his study in London, drawing on his memory, his wondrous imagination and an extraordinary number of documents and other books. He had surely learnt French in the meantime for many of these titles were in that language. Or maybe She read them for him, for she was as clever as he, some say even more so. I found his book difficult, being quite unschooled otherwise in the relevant history and think it might have been improved by less surmise and more interaction where possible with the characters portrayed. We should have stayed longer in Paris!

I think Edward would have approved of the less fanciful sections but he did not live to see its publication. James pronounced it quite simply 'beyond him'.

16

Ringwood to Southampton

The previous evening, Emily having been somewhat chilled by her travel on the outside of the coach, Kitty had insisted they take supper in their room at the White Hart and go early to bed. Next morning Emily is entirely recovered and, as they breakfast, eagerly anticipating the next stage of the journey through the New Forest.

'Does not it sound exciting Mother? I have never been in a real forest. I wonder if there will be places with such strange names as yesterday! Let me see if I can recall some of them.' She takes a breath and then recites: 'Piddlehinton, Piddletrentide, Puddletown...'

Kitty becomes aware that they have an eavesdropper at a table close to their own, a prosperous well-fed looking young man on whose red lips plays an amused smile and whose eyes are fixed on Emily. Kitty is put on her guard, sees how much she may now have to protect Emily from unwanted attentions, how attractive Emily has become, one day to a young clergyman and now this farmer's son, Squire's son perhaps.

'Tolpuddle, Affpuddle, Briant's Puddle,' Emily continues. 'And a whole host of Tarrant somethings, only some of which we passed through.'

'We passed through Tolpuddle?' Kitty interrupts. 'I did not notice. That was whence were deported the so-called—'

'Martyrs,' nods Emily. 'The driver, Mr Standfield, told me about it. He is related to one of them. You know their real concern was the poor conditions of agricultural labourers? They were not revolutionaries like those in France as many people were led to believe. But I was glad to hear that a new law now prohibit deportation.'

The young man is shaking his head, though still smiling. Kitty is feeling she might challenge him, for his conduct surely borders on the impertinent, when Mr Standfield makes his entrance to summon them to the coach. But the young man stands also and follows them outside and Kitty is very relieved to overhear him ask to travel by the driver since he wishes to smoke. As they are about to set off, another young man of much poorer appearance leaps up onto the box next to him.

Emily has remarked none of this and her attention appears focussed on the journey. The coach traverses the wide open space of the market square and, once out of town, for a mile or so they pass close-shaved fields of some cereal crop, pale sheaves leaning against each other in neat stooks waiting to be garnered in before the arrival of winter. The road is edged with the last of summer's flowers, all faded, spindly or gone to seed. Thistle heads and wild clematis have burst into extravagant fluffy bundles of down ready to float off on the next wind and carry their seeds to further planting grounds. The day is bright, the sun burnishing the yellow and red leaves of the hedgerows that are full of small busy birds scavenging what berries remain. A lone crow perching on a gatepost caws mournfully, as if in warning of harder times to come.

'Oh look, Mother,' Emily has evidently had the same thought. 'He looks like a particularly serious clergyman. Do you think all crows are as pessimistic? Or has this one alone made it his mission to preach to the rest of us?'

Kitty smiles, glad to see that her daughter has not lost the delight in natural things that she showed as a small child. Quite abruptly the fields give way to bare heathland clad only in dry gorse and bracken and then it is not long before the light dims as the road enters the forest and on either side rise tall trees, oaks, birch and beech, ash, chestnut and elm interspersed with fir and other evergreens, making between them a dense canopy that at this season allows very little light to reach the forest floor. There are paths leading into the dark undergrowth and occasional cleared spaces for grazing or cultivation. In many of these there are ponies as well as cows besides the occasional goat and small groups of deer.

'It is every bit as wild and exciting as I imagined,' she says. 'And look, where there is that wisp of blue smoke curling up, could not that be a gypsy encampment? Mr Standfield told me yesterday that likely as not we should see some, squatters besides, for there is room enough and often no one to make them move on. Oh, I wonder why we are stopping.'

The coach comes to a halt and the two young men, hugging themselves for warmth, appear at the window.

'Pray excuse us,' the well-dressed one addresses Kitty as they climb up and settle themselves in the opposite corners of the carriage. 'I fear I am ill-prepared for the changing season, having brought no greatcoat. Had I been riding, I should have been better clad. Robert Elliott, at your service. And this is my man, Frederick Parker. Doff your cap, Fred,' he urges, for Fred is clearly discomfited at finding himself in such company and has not yet observed the usual proprieties.

'It is a public coach,' responds Kitty but graciously, acknowledging Robert Elliott's courtesy. 'Do you travel far?'

'To Lyndhurst only, for the pony sales,' he says. 'And I am hoping to purchase a new hunter also, or I should be mounted today. You have seen the wild ponies ma'am, miss? Or is it your first trip to the Forest?'

He contrives to address the final question entirely to Emily, the broad planes of his face a little at odds with the gentility of his manner.

Kitty replies before her daughter can speak, she is determined not to allow him such access as she had Walpole two days before. There is something a little too brash, too self-assured about this young man's manner, whatever his station in life.

'My daughter has never been here, although she has certainly remarked upon the ponies. I was here a very long time ago but am glad to say I have not as yet noticed any great changes.'

'Changes there be however, thanks to the railway. Oh yes!' He registers Kitty's surprise and perhaps imagines more interest in Emily's expression than she is likely to feel for he addresses her also with great enthusiasm. 'London to Southampton these five years past and not long since extended to Dorchester. City folks are finding it to be a fine place for their holidays.'

'Quite understandably,' nods Kitty. 'And no doubt on the whole a benefit to the area, though one might regret its loss of wildness.' She glances at Emily whose attention has however been taken by something outside and which, a moment later, she turns quickly to share with her mother.

'Oh do look, Mother, before we have passed.' All the occupants of the carriage follow her pointing finger and are in time to see a large herd of red deer cropping the grass in a small clearing near the road. 'What a wonderful stag! Such great antlers as I have never seen.' Emily's face is glowing with excitement, a picture of beauty which is surely not lost on Robert Elliott.

'We have even greater on our walls at home,' he says proudly. 'Though none as yet I can claim to have taken myself. But I hope for better luck this season, with my new horse.'

Emily looks at him directly for the first time and it is not with admiration. 'You kill them?' She is incredulous. 'For sport?'

Robert Elliott sees his mistake and hastens to make amends. 'Oh, but it is also in the necessary cause of deer culling,' he earnestly explains. 'There are too many deer, they destroy the timber, the trees. There was a new law passed, two years ago, wasn't it Fred? The Deer Removal Act? My uncle, who is the local Member of Parliament was most instrumental in having it passed.' He nods, confident that he has regained his ground.

So he is of some status, thinks Kitty, but not, I think, in my daughter's estimation. Emily's face has become a chill mask of barely concealed dislike and Kitty can pity young Robert now, might even assist him if Emily should prove too cruel. Meanwhile Fred, unwittingly or not, is providing a final nail in the young man's chances.

'It weren't only about killing, culling, the law,' he says informatively. 'It were about giving the right to enclose the Forest, large parts of it, to drive and keep the deer out so as to protect the timber.'

'That's right,' Robert says eagerly. 'My father's got ten thousand acres.'

Oh dear, thinks Kitty. Ten thousand acres where not only deer but gypsies and squatters will no longer be allowed to roam. Whatever the rights and wrongs of the matter, she knows where Emily's sympathies will lie and that there is no need to protect Emily from any more advances from this particular quarter. She realises this with great relief for she does not know how far she would or could go to prevent any of her daughters making what she regarded as an inappropriate match. She experiences a moment's understanding of cousin Isabella, who faced the same situation with regard to her own desire to marry Thomas. But Isabella displayed no such doubts as she herself harbours nor pity for her distress. Kitty never wants to cause her daughters the pain that Isabella caused her.

Robert Elliott alights at the Lamb Inn, Lyndhurst with very apparent relief, never again having exchanged a glance with Emily. She had steadfastly looked out of the window, making the occasional remark to her mother, while Kitty maintained a desultory conversation with the young man that just satisfied the bounds of courtesy.

'Thank goodness he is gone!' Emily exclaims. 'I think I shall remain in the coach rather than risk seeing him again.'

'Poor Mr Elliott! He was not entirely without merit. I learnt a considerable amount about the growth of the town of Bourne which is not far south from Ringwood. It is becoming a highly desirable seaside resort, very like Torquay we agreed, though he has never been to Torquay nor I to Bourne. He and his father are planning to invest in building along what will soon be a greatly sought after stretch of coast.'

'I know, Mother, I heard every word. You are an angel, for enduring such boredom and indulging such self-satisfied pomposity.'

'He will be rich,' observes Kitty. 'And no doubt has already attracted the interest of many young ladies or their mothers. But,' she smiles, 'I do not think *I* should like him as a son-in-law.'

'I only hope we have the carriage to ourselves again.'

'Ladies.' Mr Standfield appears at the window. 'Shall you not descend? There is a half hour before the coach continues.'

Emily exchanges a look with her mother.

'We thought the Lamb might be very congested, it being the venue for the pony sales,' Kitty extemporises.

'I will show you another inn close by if you care to accompany me.' Mr Standfield helps them descend. 'And along the way you may see some pens full of the ponies that are on sale which may interest the young lady in particular.'

No further passengers join the coach on its way to Southampton, during which hour mother and daughter exchange observations on how their family is faring without them, and on the passing scenery besides enjoying each other's silent company.

'Is it usual for mothers to like their sons-in-law?' Emily asks after a few minutes of just such peaceful contemplation.

'Oh!' Kitty is a little startled, her own thoughts having been quite similarly engaged. 'Well, it is clear that my grandmother liked my father, and – yes, I do think my mother would have liked your father. Who is perhaps not so very unlike my father, being kind and thoughtful of others and handsome besides. Oh yes, I can quite imagine how he would have charmed her.'

Whereas Thomas, what would my mother have made of Thomas with his boundless curiosity and his questions, she wonders? To him she would certainly have been an object of great scrutiny. But she never could have been, since she had died long before I met him. She sighs.

'But it is hard to imagine when I have so little real knowledge of her character,' she concludes. 'Such questions were not in my three-year-old mind when I observed her!'

'No indeed!' Emily smiles briefly. 'And then she died so very soon. How old was she?'

'Twenty-seven. I was eleven.'

'And why did she die?'

'Of a broken heart, if that is possible. My grandmother wrote that she simply turned her face to the wall. I think perhaps she had given up hope of seeing us ever again and so had nothing left to live for. And do you know,' she adds, 'my brother died also at the age of twenty-seven, which I used to think perhaps no coincidence. And now my brother's daughter also. Christina was also twenty-seven. Do you not find that strange? I do wonder if there might be some connection.'

But Emily is not so easily distracted.' But you were still alive, you and my uncle,' she insists. 'She could still have had some communication with you, which would have been of some comfort to all concerned.'

Kitty thinks quickly. She is not going to tell Emily that she and William were not allowed to write to their mother, she does not want to spoil her daughter's opinions of her cousins, Isabella in particular, especially now that they can no longer defend themselves. She again attempts to deflect Emily's enquiries. 'At least I do remember her a little, I did know her for a while and know that she loved me. And cousin Julia and her sisters also lost their mother when they were quite young. Julia was only seven.'

Emily frowns. 'Didn't you once tell me that her mother died in childbirth?'

Kitty nods. 'I did.' And so I believed for many years she thinks, as perhaps did Julia also, until Thomas undertook his inquisition of Isabella, on one of our visits to her house some time after our return from France.

17

1824 London, November

Thomas lodged with the Irvings and I mostly lived at Julia's London house after a brief stay at Shooter's Hill. But we also visited the Buller household in Kew more than once that autumn, for it was near enough to my brother's home in Isleworth where I had determined to see my two baby nieces as frequently as I might. Little Catherine was but a year and a half, her sister Emily six months old and my sister-in-law, also Catherine, had not yet recovered her strength. In truth, she had always been a little frail and there were those in the family who thought her more a burden on than helpmeet to William, quite besides the matter of her inferior origins.

Thomas' own relations with Isabella and Charles seemed enough reason for him to accompany me. Besides, I had some plan, I remember, to enable William, who fancied himself a poet, to meet his great idol Mr Coleridge with whom Thomas was on calling terms despite holding him in no great esteem.

'I have written a poem just now on the subject of *isht,* which is the Persian concept of romantic love,' William declared on one such visit, his handsome face alight with a strange mixture of pride in his achievement and deference to Thomas' greater standing as a writer. 'Do you think I might read it to Mr Coleridge?'

'I am sure you might,' Thomas advised. 'Though whether he would listen I cannot say. He is very old and, I fear, not very - susceptible to the interests of others around him. Bring it along anyway, just as soon as I have word of a suitable day.'

Isabella did not approve my scheme. She drew herself up erect on the couch where she was sitting and put her finework aside, the better to make her argument. 'Thomas, I distinctly remember you claiming that much as you wished you could venerate so renowned a sage as Coleridge, you could not elicit from him any comment of interest during any of your several conversations. Kitty, why do you thus raise poor William's expectations?' She regarded me with the pained expression that I had so often aroused in my childhood, but which had never marred her stately beauty, in fact perhaps it contributed to it.

'It is not as if recognition as a poet is a worthy aspiration under the best of circumstances.' Charles Buller turned from the window where he had been gazing out over the Green, taking the occasional imaginary pop at the ducks on the pond. He spoke in his habitual sonorous tone that was no doubt appropriate to Parliamentary debates and perhaps served well the interests of his distant constituents. 'Nor to belong to the scribbling profession in general. No offence, Thomas, and I might exempt the trade of historian from that judgment. But all these essayists and the daily expressions of opinion in the newspapers, frequently quite unfounded as I am in a very good position to know, why they simply create confusion, stir up the common people, and distract we who are trying to govern the country from doing what we know to be best.'

I think he might have continued in this vein but for Isabella's practised intervention.

'Speaking of which, my dear,' she rose gracefully to scrutinise the shoulders of his dark tailcoat for offending hairs or pieces of fluff, 'is it not time you took yourself off to the House? Albert has had the carriage ready this half hour past.'

Charles extracted his watch from a pocket in his waistcoat and consulted it before raising her hand to his lips. 'Quite right, my dear, as ever. Knew you were the one to keep me in order, the minute I spotted you when you'd arrived in Calcutta. Fought off a lot of other fellows to get you too. *"Titania of the Hoogly"*, remember Isabella? That's what people called you, the men anyway. Queen of us all.'

At this point Isabella turned her startling blue eyes to her husband and gave him a somewhat frosty smile, but Charles continued, unperturbed. 'Mark this well, Thomas, when you come to choose a wife, which won't be yet awhile since you are so far from established in any career.' He wagged a forefinger in emphasis. 'Every man needs a woman that can do that, keep you in line, up to scratch, so don't go making the mistake young Will—'

'Charles dear! Didn't you tell me you cannot be late for Questions today?' Isabella clapped her hands together as if she had just remembered this important fact, 'In fact, you need to be there in time for Prayers in order to reserve your seat for the Debate?'

'Indeed, indeed!' Charles beamed at us all. 'You see my point, Thomas? Choose wisely young man. When the time comes.' And he was gone, leaving a number of unanswered Questions in his wake.

Did he not suspect Thomas' and my feelings for each other? It seemed not. But Isabella almost certainly did. Perhaps we even betrayed ourselves during Charles' disquisition, by some unconscious exchange of glance or self-conscious flushing of the countenance? She was certainly astute enough to read such indications and draw the correct conclusions. Perhaps we had confirmed suspicions already generated? But on this occasion she said nothing.

On the way back to London that day, Thomas was unusually silent and I was afraid that my cousin and her husband had offended him.

'I think Isabella and Charles still consider you their employee,' I said, lightly touching his hand, thinking this might give him the opportunity to vent his annoyance, but the expression of puzzlement that swiftly crossed his face told me that his thoughts were entirely elsewhere. He shook his head.

'I am glad I am not, though it suited me well enough at the time to tutor the boys,' he said. 'Kitty,' he turned to face me, took both my hands in his own, fixed me with his eyes and spoke with much greater urgency. 'I have to tell you something which perhaps I should have told you before. I have a slight – entanglement - with a young lady I knew in Scotland. A misunderstanding in truth, though it is perhaps my fault for giving her some encouragement. I met her through Edward Irving, who himself was a little in love with her at the time. And she with him but nobly she insisted he hold to his prior commitment and marry the now Mrs Irving.'

I was confused. 'So your - young lady - is the same young lady that Mr Irving would have wanted to marry?'

'The very same. But in my case she has always led me to believe that she sees me as her teacher or at most brother, that she loves me but is not in love with me. Our talk, or rather our letters, for in truth we have seldom met, are almost entirely of abstract intellectual matters. She has a very serious mind. In fact,' his expression was rueful, if not guilty, 'I believe she thought me weak-willed and self-indulgent for making the trip to Paris when I could have been working.'

My heart was pounding. It seemed to me as likely that the young lady was jealous of the trip, if not of me. 'And this young lady, she has a name?'

'Of course, though I had not expected to need to utter it in your presence.' He smiled thinly. 'It is Jane. Jane Welsh.'

'Was it she you were writing to that day in Paris?'

'Yes, dear sweet Kitty, I am not surprised you have guessed, only that you are not more angry, more upset with me for, as you may think, playing with your affections whilst somewhat involved with another.'

'Surely I should be unreasonable to be jealous of any friend you may have had before we met,' I said. 'Even more if you and she are as brother and sister. And, dear Thomas, I do not think I could ever be angry with you.' I squeezed his hands and then attempted to free mine from his grasp, but he raised them to his lips and held them there for a precious moment.

'I do not think you could ever be angry with anyone.' He let my hands go. 'As in fact I once wrote to Jane.'

'*You wrote to her of me?*' I thought, wondering at the import of this revelation, but before I could speak he gave a deep sigh. 'Besides other very complimentary observations,' he continued. 'I am afraid I made her angry.'

I think he would have kissed my hands again at this point, perhaps even made some further declaration of his feelings, but it seemed to me wise to restore a little distance between us. Miss Welsh did not sound to me as dispassionate as Thomas had portrayed her. I remember even moving a little further from him on the seat of the carriage.

'Thomas, I thank you for your frank confession and pray to God Miss Welsh's feelings for you are as you believe they should be. But

I think you should, and would be very grateful if you would, speak also to Edward and Julia. Tell them what you have told me. For it is possible – do not distress yourself on this point too prematurely – but it may be that Julia would not have suggested our trip to Paris had she known of Miss Welsh and her - relations with you.'

Thomas recoiled in apparent horror. 'You think so? I had never thought, never sought to mislead any in your family, least of all so utterly good and kind a lady as Mrs Strachey.' He squared his shoulders. 'When we arrive at Fitzroy Square I shall come in with you and speak to them at once.'

18

Southampton

The coach comes to an abrupt halt and Kitty opens her eyes to a view of the distant masts of tall ships and nearby scurrying smaller boats and nearest of all, as her nose has already suggested, the stalls of fishermen selling the day's catch.

'Southampton! One hour's stop!' calls Mr Standfield, opening the coach door and helping them down. 'Gateway to the Empire!'

'Is that what it is called?' Emily asks her mother.

Kitty shrugs. 'I never heard of it. And we docked somewhere near Portsmouth when we arrived from India.'

Mr Standfield is listening with interest. 'Likely Southampton's been called that since the railway came here,' he suggested. 'Don't take long now to reach London. And the docks here'll be expanding again soon I'll be bound.' He helps them down and points along the quay. 'That way's the so-called Eastern docks, all new these last ten years. Just this side of them is the older one, the Ocean Dock, where all the ships of Empire used to come and go. But you ladies,' he half turns to point behind them, 'likely you'll want to walk up thataway. Where all the shops and fine buildings are. Why, I've heard it said there's not many towns can show so grand a main street and always kept exceeding clean. You'll find plenty of places to have a bite to eat besides.'

'I should like also to find a bookshop,' Emily says eagerly. 'For I think in so large a town there may be a wide choice and most particularly for ocean-going travellers to purchase. I may have need of more material with which to occupy myself, Mother, while you are speaking with Mrs Bennett.'

When they rejoin the coach Emily is the owner of half a dozen new titles and, despite her avowed expectation of needing occupation in Horsham, she is eager to begin reading them now. But then a girl a little older than herself, pretty and fair-haired with eyes the shifting blue-green of the sea gets in and the two girls swap literary opinions and more personal confidences for the remainder of the journey to Portsmouth. Kitty therefore finds herself alone again with her thoughts.

It is apparent to me now, she realises, that many events must have happened in close succession that wonderful month or two before Christmas 1824 during which I allowed my fondness for Thomas to grow, if still not have much expression. At the time, the days and weeks seemed long and full of the promise of many more to come, but in my memory all are compressed into what seems a fatal chain of causes and consequences. I daresay, for instance, that I went to hear Mr Irving preach and subsequently called on Mrs Irving on more than one occasion but I remember only one such, when Julia had accompanied Thomas and I. It was at the end of a service or meeting and the three of us were waiting outside the chapel in Hatton Garden, where Mr Irving was still besieged by a crowd of enthusiastic followers.

19

1824 London, November

'He is as popular as ever, perhaps more so,' observed Thomas.

Julia sighed deeply. 'But, I fear, less inspired,' she replied. 'He is not happy.'

'Oh, do you see it too?' Thomas turned to her eagerly. 'I thought perhaps it was my mis-reading of circumstances, which I am apt to do.'

There was a moment's silence as Julia acknowledged the truth of this before she elucidated. 'His speaking has lost its spontaneity, its simplicity,' she said slowly. 'It is strained, too intentional. I find it is no longer ... uplifting ... and I am not sure why.' Her furrowed forehead showed her distress.

Thomas was nodding throughout Julia's description. 'I was afraid it was my jealousy that, having myself lost my way as a churchman, I resented his very apparent success. I think,' he paused, 'I am only just coming to this opinion, you understand, that Irving also feels himself a failure. I do know that he had great expectations of the return of the Christian Religion in all its truth and glory, that it would rule the world at last, with him its chosen instrument. Not that he is overly full of self-love, as you, Mrs Strachey, know as well as I, only that he is too easily swayed by others' good opinion of him. And this leads him again and again to perceive evidence of the coming of the rule of God on Earth, hopes of which are again and again dashed.'

Julia smiled sadly. 'You love the man as I do,' she said. 'And after all, perhaps these jostling crowds gain something of lasting import from him.'

'Even while they turn his life into an uncomfortable huggermugger,' Thomas concluded.

I think it was on this same occasion that Thomas and I accompanied Mr Irving back to his home, while Julia returned alone to Fitzroy Square. What I certainly remember is the transformation in Mr Irving's countenance as soon as his front door was closed on the world and all his attention taken up with his baby son who appeared so very small in his father's giant arms. He took seemingly infinite delight in dandling the child, making him laugh, teaching him to imitate his clicking and lip-smacking and kissing him repeatedly as if he could almost devour him.

'Oh Carlyle,' he looked across at where Thomas was sitting on the other side of the hearth, where a somewhat paltry fire glowed fitfully. 'This little creature has been sent me to soften my hard heart which did need it.'

'He is very sweet and charming,' I said, glancing sideways to include Mrs Irving in my praise.

She had apparently not been in the best of health since returning to London, and reclined in front of the fire, her red hair hanging untidily around her thin white face, while I perched a little uncomfortably on a stool at the foot of her couch. There was no space in the room for more furniture. Thomas said nothing but smiled affably enough, though it was clear to me that he still had little understanding of the joy of parenthood. Perhaps he never would have, some men do not, some women also. But then I dared to hope that one day I should see him hold his own child with such delight, and that it would be *my* child also. My brief daydream was rudely interrupted.

'Edward dear, did you tell Mr Carlyle that we received a letter from dear Jane?'

I was sure I did not imagine the glitter in Mrs Irving's green eyes and thought briefly that perhaps I should have made more effort to befriend her when in Dover.

'Jane Welsh, you don't know her, Miss Kirkpatrick. She was *such* a friend of Edward and Mr Carlyle in Scotland. A very clever young woman, able to join in their every debate, far cleverer than most of we silly women.' She paused, eyebrows raised, but no one of us made comment. 'It *seems* she is hoping she may come south and stay with us awhile, did you know, Thomas? I am sure you must, for I know you are in frequent communication. I believe Edward had issued some such general invitation, but really dear little Edward seems to require so much space that I doubt we have room. Do you not agree, Thomas? Though I regret to deny you both the pleasure of her company.'

Thomas flushed and shrugged. 'I believe there is also some cousin she hopes to visit, near Brighton,' he muttered, while Mr Irving stuttered that he would write to Miss Welsh and explain that perhaps she might be able to come 'soon'. Then he allowed himself to be distracted again by his son.

I stood up abruptly. 'It is almost dark, I should return home. Perhaps, Thomas, you would be so good as to help me find a hansom?'

We made our farewells and Thomas left the room but before I could follow him Mrs Irving beckoned me to her and indicated that I should lean closer.

'Beware that girl!' she hissed in my ear. 'She sent Edward a lock of her hair when he was already promised to me! What sort of woman does that?'

My face must have betrayed as much shocked surprise as Mrs Irving had hoped to arouse, for she nodded with very apparent satisfaction and tapped the side of her nose. 'And I doubt that Thomas knows it.'

I joined Thomas in the hall and by common accord we walked a way together before we parted. I attempted to settle the disquiet that Mrs Irving had aroused.

'Shall you be sad not to be able to welcome Miss Welsh to London?' I enquired in as disinterested a tone as I could contrive. 'Since she is so clever, I daresay she would find much to interest her.'

'Oh undoubtedly,' Thomas replied. 'She is very jealous of my situation here.'

He spoke casually but in fact it was his apparent easy acceptance of what sounded to me a quite proprietorial attitude on her part that made me uneasy.

'*Jealous?* For what reason?'

'Oh that I am having such a fine time "*in the south*" where there are "*so many fine people to meet*".' He laughed briefly. 'Which is true, though I do not attempt to encourage such feelings I assure you.

Quite the reverse in fact.' I felt him turn his head to look at me but I did not meet his eye nor speak, which perhaps obliged him to explain further. 'You see, her own situation is quite unsatisfactory, her mother allows her very little privacy and is jealous of her friendships. She even reads her correspondence! And just now, has engaged her in tutoring some silly young girl who has moved into live with them, and is taking all her time when Jane had rather follow her own studies. I frequently send her parcels of the latest books to read, did I tell you?'

'You said that she regards herself as your pupil,' I said slowly. 'But—'

'Precisely!' Thomas nodded. 'In fact, though I do not wish to boast, I think it is only our correspondence that gives her some relief. For the brother of this young girl, one Dugald, has been a persistent courtier of Jane for some time, giving her much annoyance. And now he has a constant *entrée* to the household to visit his sister. And is much encouraged by Jane's mother besides.'

'Which is why you write to Jane often and at length?'

'It is!' Thomas was clearly relieved to have arrived at so satisfactory a resolution. 'For she is also often ill having been a sickly child, born some weeks too early her mother once told me.'

'And she is an only child and therefore glad to have you as a *brother*,' I added. I paused to allow Thomas' response but, none being forthcoming, changed the subject. 'It is good that Mr Irving takes such pleasure in his domestic situation,' I began.

'Oh that baby!' Thomas laughed. 'One would think there had never been one born before. Visit the Orator at any time and you will find him dry-nursing his offspring! Sometimes he attempts a hideous chaunt to it by way of lullaby! Ha!' He was about to laugh again but broke off abruptly. 'You are not amused. Oh forgive me, I let my tongue run away with me, for the sake of sounding—'

'"The *Orator*?"' I interrupted. 'Is he not your friend?'

'Of course he is! Good Irving! Dear Kitty, how good you are for me, you shall teach me to be kind and check my acid tongue. Truly, I am happy for Irving that he does find such comfort at home. As a refuge from his multitude of admirers. For I think, or rather I have observed, that in this liberal London, pitch your sphere one step lower than yourself and you can get what amount of flattery you will consent to.'

'It is rather what some people said of my brother when he married,' I said, intending to steer the conversation into safer waters. 'Meaning that his deformities made him wary of pitching his sight as high as he might with his fortune.'

'He seems happy enough,' Thomas opined, but did not await my response, which might have been more tempered. I did wish my brother had married someone more like us, someone of whom I could have made a true friend.

Thomas pursued another implication. 'In fact, visiting your brother made me wish, wish very much, that I could set up my own establishment.' He looked at me and the distress in his eyes entirely revived my sympathy. 'But my 'not' Schiller book – which now seems to me so wretched and commonplace – will make me a mere one hundred pounds when it is published, that is the bargain made. And nothing before that date and still I make slow progress.'

We had reached the corner of Middleton Terrace and Pentonville Road where cabs in plenty were to be seen, but Thomas did not immediately hail one. He took my hand and turned to me, his face barely visible in the gloom, only his eyes reflecting the occasional passing carriage light. I think I held my breath, unable to say what both of us knew to be true: that I had wealth enough for both of us.

'Oh Kitty, I wish we did not have to say farewell,' he continued. 'Where Irving blossoms inside his home, I shrink and stiffen and am full of self-doubt. Of course they are kind to accommodate me but – my heart sinks to think I must soon return there.'

His face mirrored his conflict as he spoke. I determined to voice, indeed name, what I believed its true causes.

'I wonder what Mrs Irving writes to Miss Welsh?'

Thomas dropped my hand as if it were aflame, but his eyes did not leave mine. He looked thoughtful for a moment, then nodded. 'You are right,' he said. 'Isabella Irving is no friend of Jane. If she could wound her I think she would. I must move, if only to a small rented room somewhere. Where none shall oversee my comings and goings.'

'And you will have space to write and quickly make your fortune!' I touched his hand and then signalled an approaching carriage. Thomas' expression was again bright and full of optimism as he waved me farewell.

He found rooms in Southampton Street, just off the Strand, very near the River and well-situated therefore for walks in every direction. No doubt there were occasions when he took a rest from his writing – which was again progressing – and walked alone while he organised his thoughts, but often he came to call in Fitzroy Square and then I accompanied him to Piccadilly, the West End, even as far as the Embankment where, like Wordsworth, we stood on Westminster Bridge and watched the great grey Thames slide ever seawards beneath our feet, battling the incoming sea in treacherous eddies and currents or effortless and benign at low tide.

'One could never tire of this river,' he observed on one such occasion. 'For it is never still, and never the same, yet ever patient and overcoming all obstacles. It is in fact a model for us all and I think I should always live near it. If I could afford my own house—'

'*When* you can afford your own house,' I amended.

He smiled briefly. '*Then* I should like it to be by the river.'

'Sometimes in summer we take a boat from the jetties here to Kew,' I told him.

'Then *when* it is summer I hope I may accompany you,' he replied and we both laughed.

He never did, for even before spring had arrived he was gone. But not so many years later he did move to a house in Chelsea near the river and he lives there still.

20

Portsmouth

'Look, Mother! See what a splendid view we have all over Portsmouth Harbour. I did not imagine it so huge. No wonder it is home to our great navy.'

Jolted from her reverie, Kitty sees that Emily and her new friend Georgina are already getting out of the carriage and calling her to follow.

'Such noble ships,' agrees Kitty. 'And so many.'

'And so close to shore they seem,' Georgina exclaims. 'One would think they would run aground.'

'It is for its depth as well as its breadth that the harbour is so renowned.' Mr Standfield has joined them. 'For it makes loading and unloading that much easier, with a short distance from shore for the tugs and barges to traverse. And it seems to me there is a deal of such activity underway.' He nods. 'As I had heard there might be last time I were here.'

The three women narrow their eyes to survey the scene more closely and see that he is right.

'Those skiffs and smaller yachts and ferries?' asks Georgina. 'There is such constant traffic hither and thither across the water one might expect some collision.'

Kitty has caught some particular meaning in their driver's tone, 'Why were you led to expect this increase in such activity? There are preparations for some further naval excursion? I thought our fleet to be already in the eastern Mediterranean. Did it not sail thence some months past? To act as a deterrent to Russian advances?'

Mr Standfield looks grave and taps his nose. 'There'll be war, ma'am, very likely. In the end. With the Russkies still hanging onto their conquests whatever our threats. So we'll have to be sending more ships. And troops. Folks around here get whiff of these things long afore the rest of us, afore the papers even.' He laughs grimly. 'To think that France and us'll be allies this time around, on the same side.'

Kitty sighs. 'And we shall be helping the Turks who have in the past been our bitterest enemies.'

Emily is aghast. 'Then James may have to fight, Mother?'

'If his regiment is called upon,' Kitty nods sadly. 'My son, Mr Standfield, he is in the army, the 60th Rifles. After our stay in Horsham we are going to London to see him. I only hope we shall be in time.' She sighs again. 'I did not want him to be a soldier but his heart was set, from when a little boy, wanting to emulate his father.'

Mr Standfield looks suitably sympathetic before suggesting they move on. 'I'll try to discover more what's a'happening,' he promises. 'This night in the inn.'

The Ship and Castle is perched on a narrow spit of land that juts into the southern end of Portsmouth harbour. Walking on the quayside, Kitty and the girls have a clear view back up the great waterway to the hill which they have just descended. Not far from shore frequent passenger ferries cut across the water and, less often, larger boats set out for or arrive from an island a few miles offshore. But it is the large ocean-going ships that take their breath away, for they pass so close to land.

'It is hard to believe the water can be deep enough at so short a distance,' Georgina marvels.

'One feels one might almost touch them,' adds Emily. 'Or that they might brush against us with the slightest miscalculation by the captain. Mother,' she points beyond the ferries towards a small forest of tall masts which indicates a dense mooring of large ships, 'do you think that is where you landed?'

'I think that is the naval dockyard.' Kitty shakes her head and then she laughs. 'Can you believe that after so long a journey we were put into a small rowboat and made our landing on a beach? Perhaps in that direction.' She points behind them away from the harbour to where the land curves round and out of sight. 'I guess my brother and I were carried ashore through the waves, together with the daughter of our guardian, Mrs Ure. But poor Mrs Ure, no one could have carried her I think, for she was rather large.'

'Was it customary to arrive in such a fashion?' Emily looks doubtful.

Kitty laughs again. 'In fact, I have been told since that it was something to do with customs. Avoiding the payment of customs. Or the confiscation of our valuables. Some bribery was involved. It makes me think perhaps my family was once not so respectable as now it appears!' Suddenly she shivers and clutches her shawl more closely to her. 'Should we go indoors? I think it time we dined.'

Kitty leads the way but overhears the girls' conversation as they linger a little, gazing out to sea.

'I wish I might visit India,' says Georgina. 'I might find myself a husband which here is so very difficult for a girl without connection or fortune.'

'One of my cousins went there some years ago,' Emily tells her. 'I do not know if it was for a husband, for our great-grandmother was then alive and she planned to visit her. But then she got sick and was obliged to return home. And then on board ship she met the man who is now her husband!'

'That would make a fine novel!' Georgina laughs. 'Of course one hears India is so much more civilised now that perhaps it would not be quite such an adventure as it was in your mother's day.'

***

Dinner is served to the three of them in the privacy of a small snug room overlooking the harbour whence they can see the lights of vessels criss-crossing the water and hear the occasional deep-throated warning blast of a larger ship nosing its way out on the tide. While they are waiting for dessert Emily holds up one of her new books.

'I tried to read this while I was resting before dressing for dinner,' she tells Georgina and frowns. 'But could not make way. The tone is too arch, the author too distant from her characters. I was very disappointed having greatly enjoyed Mrs Gaskell's earlier work.'

Georgina leans to read the title. '"Cranford". I have so been hoping to read it soon. What is it about?'

'Small-minded women living small lives in a small town,' says Emily and then laughs. 'But I told you I could not make much progress for it seems the author's intention is to mock not understand.'

'It sounds just the kind of life I have been living for longer than I care to think,' observes Georgina. 'A life of repetition, tedium, the greatest excitement being the arrival of new ribbons at the village shop.' She smiles but then looks sad. 'And yet now I find myself yearning for it.'

'Georgina is going to be governess to a family in Horsham,' explains Emily. 'Her aunt with whom she has been living died recently and there is no one else to give her a home.'

'Then you are understandably apprehensive,' Kitty reassures Georgina. 'But it is an honourable occupation and should allow you time to pursue your literary interests also.'

'Here,' Emily holds out the book. 'I brought it down to give to you, Georgina. You read it and if I like your opinion of it you may return it to me in Horsham. At the very least I shall be interested to know who is the narrator. The 'I' was not identified through all the opening pages which might have been interesting had I not been more generally irritated.'

'Perhaps you are too impatient,' Georgina observes.

'Oh and intolerant, I have no doubt whatsoever,' rejoins Emily gaily. 'Only there is so much to read I am reluctant to waste my time on undeserving material. Oh!' She puts her hand to her mouth. 'So I am asking you to waste yours! Give it back, I did not mean to so insult you.'

There is a brief tussle as Georgina insists that she wants to read the book and then turns politely to Kitty.

'Unless you wish to, of course, Mrs Kirkpatrick?'

Kitty shakes her head. 'I am afraid I am not as much of a reader as you girls all seem to be. Though I daresay I could find the time.'

Georgina looks at her thoughtfully. 'Perhaps it is because your own life, and that of your family, has been so eventful, that it is hard for you to find interest in the contrivances of fictional accounts,' she observes. 'I should love to hear more of your earliest memories of coming to this country which must have been so very different to your previous life. If it is not too impertinent of me to ask.'

There is something a little too forward, too contrived, in Georgina's manner, Kitty thinks, but she has long been accustomed to people's interest in her exotic origins, Thomas being neither the first nor the last to enquire, though he was certainly the most determined. So she obliges her daughter's friend a little.

'My grandfather's household was large and somewhat ramshackle, and very different indeed to the calm and quiet of my mother's house in India,' Kitty begins. 'There was always someone to play with, and many different activities and conversations continuing at the same time. It was not a usual family life at all, and at first quite confusing.' She pauses as a long-forgotten memory surprises her and shares it almost without further thought. 'I remember there was one little boy I particularly remarked for he looked rather like my brother, of darker complexion than our other cousins. But before I could befriend him, and quite soon after our arrival, he had gone.' She pauses again. 'I think he died. No-one said, though I remember my grandfather was very sad. I loved him very much, my grandfather, and I think myself fortunate to have been given so safe a haven. I do not think all children in my position were so fortunate.'

Kitty says this with some finality but Georgina looks thoughtful and before she can ask any more questions Kitty makes excuse of her tiredness to leave the two girls alone to their coffee.

Thomas also enjoyed the pleasures of my cousins' large households, she reflects, as she mounts the stairs to her room. He loved there being always some interesting conversation or activity in which to engage. His own manner became freer, less considered, more expansive, less serious. Perhaps he felt too free, took too many liberties, and too little care. Perhaps he thought himself already part of the family, licensed to speak as one of us, even on my behalf.

21

1824 London, December

There had been a slight frost on the grass and trees in Fitzroy Square every morning that week, the first that winter, and Julia had had a sudden wish to be in more rural surroundings. Shooters' Hill was too far for a day's excursion so she persuaded Edward to take a day away from work, invited Thomas to accompany us and, together with their two youngest sons, decided we would visit Isabella.

The further we drove out of town the thicker lay the sparkling frost even as the pale sun rose higher. It was as Julia had yearned to see and we were all in fine holiday mood. Thomas had been responding to Edward's questioning about his writing which, as he had hoped, was progressing more smoothly since his removal to Southampton Street. It was his Schiller collection, I believe, at the time he was receiving the chapters weekly from the printers. But his replies, while courteous, were brief. There was clearly something of more immediate import that he wished to tell and only I knew already what that was.

'I have had a most civil letter from Herr Goethe in Weimar,' he announced at last to immediate murmurs of interest and surprise from Edward and Julia. 'It is in belated response to the copy of *Wilhelm Meister* which I had sent him, together with some profoundly reverent note. I had not expected a reply and quite given up hope of one.' He took a single sheet from his inside pocket and held it out. 'He blames his great age for the delay and, as you can see, only the signature is his own, the rest, while short enough, is surely the work of some secretary or scribe.'

'But still a token of some esteem,' Julia passed the letter to Edward who nodded.

'Well done, Thomas. No doubt one day others will treasure your signature.'

We all laughed in a happy conspiracy of expectation. Thomas was young, but his future already seemed full of bright promise. The celebratory air was however dissipated by Edward's next question.

'Have you heard again from your young correspondent in Scotland? Kitty tells us she was once enamoured of Edward Irving. And that she is hoping to visit them shortly and stay awhile in London.'

I knew from the look that Julia gave him that this enquiry had been planned between them and I was perhaps grateful since I could not make it myself. But this did not prevent my embarrassment at Edward's revelation of what I thought had been said in confidence. (I had not mentioned the lock of hair.) Thomas however seemed little fazed.

'Oh I told her she could come if she can,' he said casually. 'For London is full of delights including your good selves. But it is not in my hands and she thought better of asking me to enquire on her behalf concerning the delay in Irving's promised invitation.'

'Which is scarcely surprising,' Julia murmured.

'And I wrote something of my difficulties in settling to work, I believe, much as I confessed to dear Kitty.' He glanced at me and I nodded. 'And Jane replied with much encouragement,' he continued. 'She has always been a good influence upon my work, questions of literature and philosophy having always been the principal subject of our correspondence.'

I do not think Edward was entirely satisfied with this reply but if he had wished to say more he was interrupted by Julia.

'But now you have removed to your own rooms you are working well,' she stated. 'And very happy we are to hear it.'

'Yes indeed,' said Thomas. 'I intend to make much swifter progress from now on. However,' and then he fixed his gaze on me for what seemed an eternity before looking back to his questioner. 'I have learnt, I am learning, that there is more to life than literature, which cannot constitute the sole nourishment of any true human spirit.' He spoke with increasing passion. 'It is a poor sort of man – or woman - who turns his back on Nature and has no household or social enjoyments. He becomes a hack, she a Blue-stocking. Life is no longer with them a verdant field, but a parched garden. No, literature is the *wine* of life, it cannot be its food.'

His face was flushed as he looked from one of us to another. His sincerity was in no doubt and I could see that Edward and Julia were surprised, but very reassured as to his motivation concerning myself. Their earlier troubled expressions had entirely cleared. As for myself, I had never heard Thomas on this subject, though it was surely not the first time he had thought of it. And it was difficult not to believe that his inspiration was myself, for I was certainly no Blue-stocking.

As we reached Kew Bridge Julia called out to the driver to stop. 'Let us walk from here,' she said. 'It is such a beautiful day.' The boys were hastily bundled deeper in wraps, and we all descended from the carriage.

Edward carried baby John, while Julia and I each held one of William's hands and encouraged him to run and jump between us. When we reached the middle of the bridge he allowed Thomas to pick him up so that he could look down over the parapet to the river beneath where a few keen oarsmen practised their skills. This far upstream there was little commercial traffic.

'Do the Bullers keep a boat?' Thomas enquired. 'It looks splendid exercise. I have only rowed on lakes.'

'I believe they do,' Kitty replied. 'For Charles and Arthur row at school. But in any case there are skiffs for public hire. It is a popular activity in summer.'

Thomas said nothing as we walked on but he nodded and was clearly absorbing the information for future use.

The ice on the pond on Kew Green was thick enough to provide a skating rink for the resident ducks, who would doubtless have preferred their customary method of traversing the water. Julia produced some stale bread from her pocket for the boys to throw to them and we all spent some minutes laughing at their inelegance. William had to be prevented from joining them and instead both children enjoyed sliding on some frozen puddles.

Sadly, our carefree mood did not long endure after our arrival at the Bullers. Even the news of Herr Goethe's letter did little to thaw the chill of our welcome. Charles was not at home and it was left to Isabella to convey the full force of their disapproval of Thomas' new status as a family friend rather than her sons' tutor, let alone as a potential suitor. She was sitting on a couch, a little removed from the large and blazing fire, while Edward and Thomas stood warming themselves with their backs to it. Julia had taken John to the old nursery for his morning nap.

Thomas soon began to quiz Isabella about the large Kirkpatrick family and its various ramifications. I think he was primarily pursuing his long-avowed interest in our 'exotic' heritage, but perhaps he contrived his inquiry also as an attempt to improve her opinion of him. I was a little preoccupied in playing with William, who for the first time had been entrusted with a fine set of his older cousins' toy soldiers, so did not pay Thomas and Isabella's conversation much attention. But soon after Julia came down and joined her sister on the sofa, it became apparent to me that Isabella was becoming upset by Thomas' relentless questions and that Thomas had not realised it. Finally she stood and, drawing herself to her full height, addressed him.

'Families have secrets, Mr Carlyle, and the older and larger the family the more they are likely to have. Most people make mistakes during their lives and there is no need for their children and grandchildren to know about or suffer from them – or people would never make progress in the world. I shall order lunch.' And with that she swept from the room, leaving Thomas gazing dumbstruck after her.

He roused at Edward's good-natured laugh. 'She is not to be added to your butterfly collection, Thomas. Perhaps you must refine your hunting methods. Although it is true that there are secrets she had rather not reveal too widely.'

'Edward!' Julia's voice was unusually sharp, but he was not to be deterred.

'Should not *good friends* favour one another with a frank knowledge of their history?' he challenged her. 'How else may they develop a proper trust and understanding of each other's character? And is it not better that any shameful secrets be shared honestly rather than discovered later by default?' He turned again to Thomas. 'Isabella's own father, Julia's too, was of illegitimate birth,' he began. 'Their grandfather, who of course was also Kitty's grandfather, was a handsome man and known for his dalliances. He was also loving and generous and not ashamed to recognise his offspring and supported them equally. And all of this was, I should say, widely known in Calcutta society. It was not a secret at all.'

Thomas was silent as he digested this information, while I pretended to be engrossed in little William's carpet soldiering which now surrounded me. I think I had known in some vague way of Uncle William's status for some years but as it was never talked about so it was never clarified. Now Thomas shook his head as if to clear it. 'And the career of William Kirkpatrick, Kitty's uncle, was every bit as successful as that of her father. I had not imagined British society could be so enlightened.'

'Not only that,' Edward warmed to the theme. 'And you must forgive me, my dearest Julia, and I dare speak only because I know in what affection you hold Thomas.' He went to stand behind Julia and rested his hands on her shoulders. 'Julia's mother did not die in childbirth as some of the family have been led to believe.' His hands gently caressed her neck. 'Maria left her four young daughters when Julia was seven and William had found her to be a most unsuitable mother owing to her - misconduct. She had resided in Bath with the girls for some years having left William in India. He then arranged for the girls to go and live with their grandfather. And Maria subsequently returned to India to live with another man. Very likely she still does. All this *was* less openly spoken of, I believe, perhaps in deference to the reputation of William and his family.'

Now Thomas did look shocked, in fact he quitted the fire and crossed the room to look awhile from the window. As yet no one had noted my own reaction. I stood, a little unsteady from my cramped situation on the floor, and went to sit by Julia. I took her hand.

'Dear Julia, can this be true? I had no idea of it. When did you discover she had gone to India?'

'Not long before my marriage,' said Julia. 'My father told me, thinking I would quite possibly discover it in India for myself.'

Thomas returned to his position in front of us and bowed low in front of Julia. He took her other hand. 'And what a model of wife and motherhood you have made of yourself, dear kind Mrs Strachey. I have often remarked it, never guessing the sadness and loss on which it has been based, which makes it so very much more admirable.' He raised her hand to his lips.

I think at this point I was wondering what secrets of my birth and upbringing might yet be in store for me, but was much reassured by Thomas' response to the news of Uncle William's parentage. I decided to tell him when it seemed appropriate of the doubts about the legitimacy of my birth but that opportunity never came. It cannot have been very long before someone told me that the little dark-skinned boy was my half-brother, born to another Indian woman who the family believed to have died, for there was no pension made for her in my father's will. My father had sent the little boy to live in his father's large and welcoming household just as, not much later, he sent us. No doubt I would have one day told Thomas this also, but I do not think I shall ever tell Emily. I fear she could not reconcile it with her romantic view of my parents' marriage.

22

Portsmouth to Horsham

'Do you know, Mother,' Emily addresses Kitty earnestly as soon as their carriage begins the journey up and out of Portsmouth the next morning, 'Georgina has almost no relations at all? Does it not seem unfair when we have so many?'

At the sight of her daughter's serious expression, Kitty restrains a smile. 'Why yes, if such things were a matter of the dispensation of justice. I suppose if one holds God to be omnipoten—'

'I am not challenging God, nor even making a theological point.' Emily frowns. 'I was only thinking how different would have been my own life without my brother and sisters, uncles and aunts, cousins and second cousins…without you and Father.'

Kitty hastens to make amends for her lack of understanding. 'Oh indeed, as I know only too well. As, if you remember, I said yesterday, I was blessed indeed to find such loving relations here in England.' She turns to Georgina. 'Have you really no one with whom to make a home?' She would rather hear the girl's tale from her own lips than those of her impressionable daughter.

Georgina shakes her head, setting her blond curls dancing. 'Distant cousins whom I scarcely know. My mother died when I was two years old in giving birth to my brother who also died. And my father was lost at sea soon after. His sister, my aunt, gave me a home but she died a few months ago and now I must make my own way. The parson was good enough to help me find this position of governess in Horsham.'

'Is it not quite tragic?' Emily's eyes are dark with emotion. 'So sad a tale.'

'Which nevertheless is common enough,' says Georgina quickly, perhaps perceiving Kitty's fainter concern. 'And I do not remember my parents so cannot be said to have grieved. Whereas you, Mrs Kirkpatrick, I can hardly bear to imagine a three year old child's mental condition on being taken from her mother. Never to see her nor her grandmother again.'

'It is not something one ever forgets,' acknowledges Kitty, wondering how much else Emily has confided. She looks away abruptly out of the window and catches a last sight of the harbour before the coach turns north and out of the city.

Emily breaks the long silence that ensues. 'But you did have some correspondence with your grandmother.' Her tone is tentative, perhaps a little placating.

'I did. And very lucky I was to be put in contact with her after so very many years.' Kitty smiles brightly at both girls. This she does not mind recalling. 'Would you like to hear how this occurred, Georgina? It is an extraordinary tale, is it not Emily? Depending on highly unlikely coincidence.'

'Oh yes, Mother, do tell,' Emily says eagerly. 'You told me once when I was much younger and I do not fully recall the circumstances.'

'I was visiting a childhood friend, a Mrs Duller,' Kitty begins. 'She lived, indeed lives, near Reading in the county of Berkshire. She proposed a visit to some neighbours who lived in a house called Swallowfield. I was curious to see this house for it was reputedly rather grand. But imagine my surprise when, on walking into the entrance hall, I was confronted with a very large painting of myself, my three-year-old self, and my five-year-old brother, painted thirty-six years previously in the last days before we left India. In fact, you must imagine my friend's and hostess' surprise also, for I was immediately engulfed in tears.'

Kitty speaks lightly but the girls are attending gravely her every word. 'This was a painting my father had commissioned,' she continues, 'intending it as a consolation to my mother while we were away in England. But he died shortly thereafter and she somehow lost its possession.'

'So how did it come to be in that house?' whispers Georgina.

'The owner of the house was a Mr Henry Russell, a retired India Company official who was once my father's assistant. He later held his position as Resident in the city of Hyderabad where I was born. And lived in the house where I had lived.'

'The British Residency,' Emily explains. 'A large official house, I have seen the drawings.'

'So the painting was hung in that house and this ... Mr Russell ...brought it to England with him when he retired?' Georgina appears satisfied with her own explanation and Kitty does not disagree although to her the sequence of events is not quite so self-evident. 'But what a very strange coincidence indeed that led you there!' Georgina exclaims. 'And where is the painting now?'

'It hangs in *our* entrance hall,' Emily says with triumph. 'So now we can all see it every day.'

'So Mr Russell returned it to you as surely its rightful owner.' Georgina nods with pleasure at this satisfactory end to the story but her smile fades as she sees Kitty's more quizzical expression. 'Or did you have to go to the law?'

'Neither of the two. And indeed Mr Russell himself was not present when I visited his house. He did visit me some time later in Torquay.' Kitty's voice wavers for an instant. 'It was a difficult visit. He was much embarrassed, I did not quite understand why but of course it made me uncomfortable also. I had hoped to hear some precious details of those childhood years which I was too young ever to recall. In fact, he later communicated with me through his brother, who was also in Hyderabad and also knew my mother. Anyway, Mr Henry Russell promised to leave me the picture in his will, and his family honoured this promise.'

Georgina nods. 'And he also put you in touch with your grandmother.'

'After a fashion.' Again Kitty corrects Georgina's assumption. 'But it was a little more complicated than that, involving another chance encounter about a year later with the wife of a newly appointed assistant to the Resident at Hyderabad, in Exmouth, which is a town near Torquay where in fact we once lived! How strange life is. In any case, between them all I was at last put in contact with my grandmother. And for six whole years, through interpreters, we were able to communicate and regain some of what we had been denied during the many many years that had passed.'

A long silence greets the end of Kitty's story. Georgina is the first to raise an objection.

'I don't understand why Mr Russell kept the picture once he knew you had seen it,' she says. 'Surely he knew it was meant for your mother? And a picture of someone else's children, however beautiful, can have little significance for someone who has no relation to them.'

Emily snorts. 'But it could have a great deal of *value* if the painter has subsequently become very famous! No wonder he was embarrassed when he met you, Mother. He was ashamed of himself. Or should have been.'

Kitty smiles, glad of her daughter's love and loyalty. And on the whole she thinks she is correct in her condemnation, while sometimes wondering that so rich a man could have so simple a motivation. 'Perhaps you are right,' she says. 'But even before the painting was returned to me the most important outcome was to find my grandmother after so very many years.'

Georgina nods. 'Of course,' she says. 'Only one wonders how it was that you had lost her. I suppose you could not read or write when you were little but surely someone else in the family...' She stops and waits in clear expectation that someone will enlighten her.

But Kitty has said enough. She closes her eyes and leans back in her corner in the coach as she remembers how Thomas tried to solve this very same mystery, acting, so he supposed, in her interests, succeeding in losing her for ever.

23

1824 London, December

It was the week before Christmas 1824 and I had been much occupied with gift buying and wrapping in preparation for our visit to Isabella's where we were accustomed to spend several days at this time of year. I was sitting at a small table helping Richard, who must have been eight as he was home from his first term away at school, and William make cards for their aunt and cousins. Julia was playing with baby John on the rug near the fire and I think young Edward was out somewhere with his father. Suddenly William looked up at me, his head tilted to one side, his expression quizzical.

'That is three times you have sighed, Auntie. Aren't you excited that it will soon be Christmas? I am!' he exclaimed.

Of course I rallied my spirits and made some bright response to satisfy him but Julia was not fooled.

'It is not for me to tell Isabella whom to invite,' she said a little later when the boys had all gone to bed. 'And I too am sad that Thomas cannot join us. But it is only a few days and I daresay he can spend Christmas Day with the Irvings. And then sometime in the new year no doubt she will relent in her opinion and again welcome him to her house.'

I said much the same to Thomas when we met the next day for a last walk before the holiday and he professed to believe me. Yet he was in sombre mood when we parted.

'I had not thought how much my life in London depends upon your family,' he said. 'It is a large and otherwise unfriendly city, where I am not much at home.'

His words struck through me with chilling effect. Was he considering a return to Scotland where he was better connected?

Where he had family of his own and the company of Miss Welsh to console him? But then, the very morning of our departure, I received from him a note.

'*I am to join you in Kew on the eve of Christmas,*' he wrote. '*Having received a letter from Mrs Buller. It seems my erstwhile pupils declared a strong desire, nay, need, to see me again. For they are returned as you will know for their holidays. Charles has a philosophy essay to write which he wishes to discuss, Arthur requires help with mathematics and Freddie wishes to re-enact the entire battle of Waterloo! I once, rashly it seems to me now, suggested that playing with soldiers would be a deal more edifying were one to attempt to replicate the strategies of some of the great generals. I have, as you will guess, accepted your cousin's invitation with great pleasure. Yours, in anticipation of a very merry Christmas, Thomas.*'

We made a large party with Isabella's three boys and Julia's four, together with my brother's two small daughters, all gathered around the table to eat or the tree to exchange gifts and sing carols. Only my brother's wife, Catherine, kept herself rather apart, taking her breakfast in bed and on some days remaining in her room until past midday. She was still feeding seven month old Emily and seemed constantly fatigued, which should not have occasioned comment since, at nineteen months old, her older daughter Catherine naturally also required much care and attention. But comment there was, if mostly well-meaning and sympathetic, and I knew my brother wished she would participate more in the family festivities.

Of course, there were many helping hands in that gathering including, I was surprised to see, Thomas, who appeared fascinated with the two little girls. I remember he took pride in having taught little Catherine to construct towers of bricks and was greatly intrigued by baby Emily's perpetual attempts to knock them down.

'All babies do that!' I overheard my sister-in-law assert.

But I could see that she was gratified by Thomas' attentions, the more so when he professed great interest in her observation, and wondered aloud if this behaviour were truly a basic characteristic of human nature and if so what it signified. I thought Catherine would be fazed by such a response but instead she laughed.

111

'I think you have not had much close contact with small children!' she said and, across the room, I saw William's surprised delight in her good humour.

Throughout the first few days there was no occasion for particular confrontations, no serious debates to inflame passion, and one felt on the best of terms with everyone without it being necessary to speak individually to each. I doubt if Thomas and Isabella did more than exchange greetings, yet it seemed that their relations were again amicable. There was also little opportunity for me to spend time alone in Thomas' company and in fact I took care to show him no special regard beyond an occasional exchange of glances. Only once did he seek me out when, coming to stand beside me, he observed cheerfully that we would have made a portrait of family life fit for a Christmas card. I smiled but perhaps without sufficient enthusiasm. Thomas was surprised.

'Are you not happy as I am?' he asked.

'Oh, I am always happy to be with my family,' I said. 'Only, especially when we are all together at times like this, I can't help thinking of those who are not here, who were deprived of such joy.' He was looking at me closely and I was encouraged to continue.' Sometimes I look at an empty chair,' I confided, gesturing to one nearby, 'And imagine that my father or my mother is sitting there, entirely part of the loving company.' And then I tried to smile more brightly. 'An idle fancy! And mostly, I assure you, I count my blessings, which are many.'

Thomas looked thoughtful and would surely have spoken but I forestalled him.

'Come, I have promised a game of hide and seek with the little ones while you, I believe, are to challenge young Charles in a game of chess.'

Thomas groaned. 'It will be no challenge. He is become much more proficient than I, having joined a club at Oxford with, he says, that express intention!'

It was a very merry Christmas and I was especially happy to observe Thomas in such good spirits. It was not until the last day of our stay as we were all returning from a walk along the banks of the Thames, that the spell was broken and the atmosphere irrevocably changed. Thomas had been lagging behind in earnest discussion with my brother, I supposed about poetry or some such. I was just in front of them, walking slowly with young William who kept stopping to pick up sticks to throw into the river. The rest of the party was strung out ahead in twos and threes, the footpath being not wide enough for more.

Suddenly Thomas raised his voice. 'I shall go and ask her,' he declared and hurried past me to catch up with Charles and Isabella. My brother joined me, his expression a little troubled.

'Thomas was quizzing me about our never being allowed to write to our mother and grandmother,' he explained. 'And was not satisfied with my replies. Now he's going to ask Isabella.'

I was instantly afraid. 'He must know he will upset her again,' I said. 'What makes him so determined?'

'Oh, he was making comparison between the fortunate situations of Julia and Isabella in close and loving company with their husbands and children, which he has had ample opportunity to observe these past few days, and that of your mother, alone and abandoned in India.' William paused. 'He has got it into his head that it was due to arrogance, an unwillingness to admit a person of another background into the family circle. The 'magic circle' was what he actually said.' He paused. 'He is angry with them, on your behalf, with Isabella and Charles that is, for he has only good to speak of Julia and Edward. He also said,' William's distress visibly increased as he swallowed hard before continuing, 'he said, just as they do not fully admit Catherine as one of them.'

'Oh William!' I dare not waste time saying more. And in any case knew it to be true. 'We must hurry after him. Try to stop him or at least temper his attitude. See, he has just reached Charles and Isabella.'

But it was too late. By the time we reached them, Isabella's face revealed her fury even while Charles was still blustering. 'Not at all, not at all, my dear young man, they were half-English after all...and it would have been different had their father still been alive...if he'd decided to bring their mother here then of course we'd have welcomed her to our bosoms.' He held his arms wide in illustration. 'As indeed we did when she came to Calcutta as a young widow. Isabella was very kind to her, weren't you my dear?'

113

He might not have spoken. 'As I told you before, Thomas,' Isabella said with icy disdain, 'there are matters that families are entitled to keep to themselves without being harassed for explanation by,' and here she paused for emphasis, 'outsiders. And if someone chooses to persistin' such untoward harassment, I think it should disqualify them from ever becoming a member of that family. I should also tell you that our family has done its best to avoid scandal over the years and will continue to do so. And I would remind you that it is a rare person whose conduct invariably meets the highest standards. You may or may not think that you are one such, but, bearing this general truth in mind, conclude that it is as well not to cast the first stone.' With this she turned and began to walk on along the path but then she glanced back over her shoulder: 'I do not expect you to leave my house tonight but do now bid you goodbye.'

She never did speak to him again and he did leave the house as soon as we returned, accepting my brother's invitation to stay the night at his home. Not wishing to openly defy Isabella, Julia thought it best that Thomas and I did not meet nor even correspond for a while. She was confident that the storm would blow over. I thought so too, especially as Julia had received a note from Thomas saying that he had written to Isabella giving his apologies for provoking her anger and Julia had then written to Isabella offering to mediate a meeting with Thomas in Fitzroy Square. I had not seen Thomas for almost a fortnight and Isabella had not yet replied to Julia's letter when, one morning, she burst into the sunny morning room where Julia and I were effecting some repairs to young Edward and Richard's school clothes before the start of the spring term.

'Isabella!' Julia looked up in surprise. 'You should have given notice!'

For the briefest moment my spirits rose but, when I saw Isabella's expression, I knew she was no harbinger of good news. She swept across the room to us, dropping her fur wraps into the arms of the maid who had admitted her and stood looking down at us as a queen over her underlings.

'Close the door,' she instructed the maid without turning her head.

'Do sit down, Izzie,' Julia said with some asperity, but I could see she was flustered and appeared as apprehensive as I was feeling.

'I prefer to remain standing while I deliver myself of this most shocking information,' Isabella said coldly. But then she looked at me and her face softened for an instant with pity and perhaps sadness, and I was really afraid.

'I have received a letter from a good friend in Edinburgh,' she began. 'As you know, the Scots celebrate the New Year rather more than they do Christmas. But, beyond seasonal greetings and other gossip, she gave me news of a matter that I daresay she also thought would be of but passing interest to me as it concerned my sons' former tutor.' She laid stress on the last two words and a sense of dread took hold of my heart. 'She could not know how closely it would concern me.' She paused to take breath. 'It seems there is a young Scottish lady whose mother is well-known to my friend, with whom Thomas has been corresponding these two years past, as it happens much against the mother's will.'

Isabella paused to allow us to absorb the full import of her revelations but, as one and in great relief, Julia and I laughed.

'Oh Jane,' I said carelessly, as if I knew her well. 'Yes, there was talk of her coming to London to visit him. She may stay with the Irvings. She knows them also.'

'Thomas told me she used to be his pupil,' Julia added. 'And he is happy to continue their correspondence for she is very intelligent but I daresay in want of continued direction. He says they regard each other as like brother and sister.'

At first our response had caused Isabella some apparent confusion, but Julia's final assertion entirely restored her offensive. She was brusquely dismissive.

'Do brothers propose marriage to their sisters? I do not think so, even in Scotland.'

Julia stood to confront her sister. 'What are you saying Isabella?' she asked quietly. 'Tell us quickly for you are causing much pain.'

I sensed her look down at me but my gaze was locked on Isabella as I willed her not to say what it seemed she must.

'Thomas has written to this girl asking her to marry him and live together on some farm she owns in Scotland. My friend has seen the letter.'

'How so?' I knew Julia no more wanted to believe her sister than I and questioned the second circumstance in hope that it might invalidate the first. But I knew how it might have occurred.

'Thomas once told me that Jane's mother often insists on reading her correspondence,' I explained, 'and could I suppose have shown it to her friend. But when was this letter written?'

This was what I could not understand, not reconcile with Thomas' behaviour towards me, his evident regard, his desire to spend ever more time in my company and that of my family. He had neither expected nor desired this rupture in our relations which had only been caused by his efforts to alleviate my sadness. I was certain he cared for me. If I were mistaken then, I thought, I shall never again trust my judgment in my relations with others. He must have written to Jane when he was so low in spirits just before Christmas. It was wrong of him, no doubt, to play with Jane's affections, for it was surely possible that his fraternal feelings may not have been as perfectly reciprocated as he intended. She was his junior, his inferior as a pupil, it was all too likely that she harboured a more romantic inclination towards him than would a sister.

'Last week I believe,' Isabella replied. 'Certainly after Christmas.'

Ah! I thought. Then it was written in the depths of his despondency when he believed he would never be allowed to marry me and had better remove himself entirely from London and my life. Again, it was wrong of him, or at best unwise, to propose marriage when not in his right mind. He, and therefore she, might so easily live to regret his haste.

'Although she has rejected him,' Isabella continued, 'regarding it as an entirely impractical project.'

'So he is not to be married?' I gasped and my relief must have been plain.

Both Isabella and Julia looked down at me, the one with incredulity, the other with sorrow and shaking her head.

'Not now at least,' Isabella agreed. 'But whether and when he may be married and to whom is surely immaterial.' Her eyebrows remained raised. 'To you.'

I jumped to my feet at this and, my hand clasped to my mouth to stifle my sobs, ran to the windowseat to hide my grief. Julia came to sit beside me and put her arms around me. 'You must see that Thomas is too undecided, too inconstant, too unreliable for you to continue your current relations with him,' she said. 'Other people will hear and talk about this other girl Jane, and they will wonder why we are allowing you to compromise yourself with a man who is apparently so committed to another.'

'So it is these unspecified 'other people' who are to decide my fate?' I pulled away from Julia in anger. 'I did not think you were so swayed by public opinion. I thought you loved Thomas.' This time I did not attempt to conceal my tears and I allowed Julia to again comfort me.

'Hush, hush,' she stroked my hair. 'I did and I do love him. I was happy to overlook his lack of fortune or steady employment. I still thought his prospects were good and if you cared for each other I was glad to help further your relations. You know that and so does Isabella. And, Isabella,' she insisted, 'these were *not* unreasonable expectations.' She released her hold on me and stood up. 'But this I cannot ignore. And it is not 'public opinion' in itself that sways me, Kitty. It is my concern for its effects on you, for your future happiness. And also, yes, Isabella I agree, its effects on the rest of the family. One cannot ignore the society in which one lives.'

'So I must say goodbye to him for ever?' I stood up determined now to maintain my composure. 'Or say nothing at all? Simply never see him again?' My voice wavered. I bit my lip.

'Hmph! A letter is more than he deserves,' said Isabella.

Julia was silent for several moments, considering. 'I will ask him here and allow you a few minutes to speak alone. But you must sever relations. If I thought we could not trust you to do so I would remain in the room.'

'You can trust me, dear cousin,' I whispered. 'I could not in truth continue to enjoy the company of one who has practised so much deceit, even if I excused it as a sign of immaturity or lack of self-understanding. Love cannot long survive without trust.'

And that is what happened. Thomas was duly summoned and I informed him that I could no longer receive him as a friend. So I kept my word though he must have known that it was against the wishes of my heart. But I did not stand back when he moved to kiss me for the first and last time. Julia tried to persuade him to remain in

London for the sake of his future career and I daresay she would have given him what assistance she could. As it was, when he left London she sent gifts after him including a fine writing desk which, if he used it, served him well. Perhaps Julia even harboured the hope that with recognition and greater prosperity Thomas would become the more dependable character that is desirable in a husband. Perhaps so did I, though I was less able than she to set my sights on so uncertain and distant a future. Perhaps had he remained in London it would have so come about. Howsoever, a little over a year later Thomas and Jane were married and for several years did indeed live on a farm in Scotland. At a place called Craigenputtock.

PART II

The Visit

24

1853 Horsham, October

Nur is reading the last of her sister Faiz's letters of which there is a small pile on the table beside her. They are of fine vellum but creased and yellowed with age, having been written more than thirty years ago in a language she has almost forgotten. From her chair by the fireside she looks across to the windowseat where Mary is sucking on a pencil as she frowns over a child's copy book. Though small and slight Mary is no longer a child but not having attended a school, has only recently begun to learn the alphabet. In a few years, thinks Nur, she will be a very pretty young woman with her dark eyes and black hair that needs no teasing to frame her face in a becoming halo of curls. So very like her daughter Ann except for the curls; Ann whom she can remember so clearly sitting in another window seat in just the same way with her books; Ann who was about Mary's age when she lost her. Can it truly be fifty years ago? Very near. She sighs.

Mary looks up at once and runs to her side, pencil and book discarded. 'Ma'am? Shall I fetch you summat? Some hot tea?'

'Thank you, Mary.' Nur attempts to blink away her tears. 'We will wait for our guests. I was only thinking…' She breaks off to wipe a recalcitrant tear from her cheek.

Mary nods. 'Of your son.'

'Yes.' It is almost true for Charles is never far from her thoughts. 'Had he not died so unexpectedly, you and I should have been in Chambery now, and have met my daughter-in-law and grandchildren. Seen the snow-covered mountains called the Alps. And the town to the construction of which Benoit, my husband, gave so much of his time and money. We should have seen his lonely effigy high on his column!' She sighs again. 'But I was thinking of other things also, other people. My sister, my daughter…so many people who are no longer here.' Nur reaches out to take Mary's hand. 'Oh Mary, how fortunate I am to have your company, these last weeks in particular. Without you I should surely have been crazed with grief or entirely lost in opium dreams.'

Mary tucks in more tightly the shawl round Nur's knees. 'And no wonder would it have been if you had,' she says firmly. 'If ever you needs your old pipe I've not forgot how to make it. But…' She bites her lower lip.

'What is it, Mary? Tell me.'

'Oh, 'tis nothing. Or rather, 'tis too late.' Mary's rosy cheeks flush more deeply. 'And any case not my business.' She turns away. 'I'll see 'bout laying the tea tray.'

'There is no need as yet,' Nur insists. 'Tell me, Mary, do. Come sit with me. I confess my feelings about our visitors are a little mixed.'

Mary takes her usual place on the hearthrug and leans back against Nur. '*I* fear these visitors, Mrs Phillips and her daughter, will be more'n upset than relief,' she says. 'Though they are obliging your grandson in coming and mean well I know.'

Nur rests her hand lightly on Mary's head. 'Do you know, now that I have read my sister's letters, I have come to think it is Mrs Phillips who may be the more upset. Until now I had quite forgot their content or perhaps not read them closely at the time.'

Mary glances at the pile of letters. 'I cannot fathom how anyone could read them.' She shakes her head. 'The ABC is hard enough. These seem but lines and squiggles. Though handsome to behold,' she hastily adds.

Nur laughs. 'It is Persian,' she says. 'I found it a puzzle at first, not having seen it for so long. And my sister wrote it much better than I ever did. But listen,' her face becomes serious. 'I would hear your opinion.'

Mary looks up, surprised.

'There are matters there that concern Mrs Phillips more than they do myself, indeed I think I cared little when my sister wrote of them, not knowing the personages concerned. For my sister met Mrs Phillips' parents and became a good friend of her mother – she was

121

with her when she died some eight years later - while I was far away in London and had just lost Ann.'

'So you told me.' Mary nods gravely. 'And Mrs Phillips and her brother were by then in England?'

'Yes indeed.'

'Then will it not be of comfort to her to have even so distant a connection as yourself?'

'Is it better to preserve one's childish memories or to discover some truths which may affect them?'

Mary frowns. 'Oh ma'am, tis a question I cannot answer without hearing more.' She hesitates as she considers. 'I guess it depends on the person concerned, upon their understanding.'

'Well said, Mary,' Nur regards her with admiration. 'So I must wait awhile before I judge. But I do not mean to tease,' she adds quickly. 'It only seems right that she should hear of these matters first.'

Mary nods. 'Of course, ma'am. S'no need for me to know. Though I do love your stories. But listen!' She cocks her head. 'There is a carriage approaching. It must be Mrs Phillips and her daughter.' She jumps to her feet. 'I must help Mrs Redford in the kitchen.'

'Their chamber is ready?'

Mary nods her head, setting her curls dancing. 'Mrs Redford said to put Mrs Phillips in the front room and Miss Phillips in the back.'

'But that is your room, Mary.'

'I'm to share with Mrs Redford. 'Tis fine, ma'am.' Mary assures her. 'I always share at my Gran's. So I've made up both beds. And lit a fire in each room.'

'Then show them up and ask if they want hot water. And bid them join me when they are ready. And then we will take tea.'

Nur's tone is calm, but her heart is beating faster, her breath is shallow and she casts frequent looks towards the door, whilst listening to the guests' arrival and ascent to their rooms. It is a very long time since she spoke with anyone who has any knowledge of her home and family. She has been Mrs Bennett too long. She takes several deep breaths then raises Faiz's last letter to her lips before placing it with the others. Reading them, it has been as if her beloved sister were speaking to her across the years and at last bringing her this visitor who cared enough to agree to make so long a journey to see her. She remembers being jealous of Faiz's preoccupation with this Mrs Phillips' mother, whom she described as her closest friend. For had that not always been herself? But it was not Faiz's fault, she acknowledges, if she barely referred to her younger sister's own sad abandonment for, in her letters home, she had herself tended to minimise its impact.

Now she wonders why. She had at first believed her principal reason was to spare their mother's suffering, for she had sent her an explicit message asserting her well-being through an early visitor from home. Later she had admitted to herself the part played by pride, for what else did she have to sustain her shattered sense of worth and public esteem? Then there had been the desire to protect Benoit's reputation, nay his feelings almost, for she still loved him and his new marriage to Adele d'Osmond had brought him no joy. Some of her friends had found her overly self-sacrificing, if not perverse, in always wishing him well, (Adele she detested), but they all acknowledged that she was dependent upon his charity and right to wish to preserve his relations with Charles and Ann. Who could have predicted the tragic consequence that was Ann's early death? Benoit blamed himself for being so impatient to meet his daughter after so many years that she was obliged to make the difficult journey more or less alone and uncared for, then barely lived to see him.

But nor would any have thought that Benoit would have been ennobled (partly due to Adele's influence with the restored monarchy, for she wanted a title despite rarely living with her husband.) Nor that he would have recognised Charles as his heir, since for some years he must still have expected to have children with Adele. And now her grandson Ernest, whom she would surely never now meet but who had procured her this visit, was the third Comte de Boigne. *God moves in mysterious ways* she whispers, finding, as ever, much solace in the words. She is still smiling when there is a tap at the door.

'Come in!'

25

Nur is instantly attracted by her visitors' appearance. Mrs Phillips is quite small though well-formed, her dress plain and modest, but her face and hair are striking. Her eyes are dark, almost black, her hair a wondrous shade of brownish red – auburn one might say - and with no sign of grey, her complexion is not dark but nor is it English. Her daughter also has remarkable colouring with the same shade of hair and though of lighter complexion surely bears more than a quarter's resemblance to her grandmother. Perhaps both could be from the Mediterranean. But they are not. It is odd to meet strangers and yet know so much about them, she thinks, even that, in Mrs Phillips' case, she must be kind or she would not have come. With the aid of her stick, Nur stands and advances upon her visitors, her free hand outstretched.

'Mrs Phillips! And Emily. So very kind of you to come so far. My dears, I am so very happy to make your acquaintance. Come!'

She guides Kitty to a small settee and indicates that Emily should take the seat that she has just vacated. She herself sits next to Kitty. She holds Kitty's hand and gazes into her face until Kitty, a little disconcerted, gives a low and pleasant laugh.

'I am happy to find you so well, Mrs Bennett. It is not as we expected.'

Nur drops her hand. 'Oh, you think you have been lured under false pretences. Please be assured that merely anticipating your visit has raised my spirits. And now that you are here—'

'Dear Mrs Bennett, we do not regret our journey, in fact it was enjoyable, with time to reflect on the history which has brought us together in so strange a way.' Kitty smiles at Emily. 'But I was worried that our visit might only be a burden.'

'Quite the opposite,' Nur assures her. 'And I should have said if I did not very much wish you to come.' She turns to Emily. 'I hope you have seen some interesting places along the way? I used to love to travel when I was young.'

But any response Emily might have made is precluded by the arrival of a tea trolley at which she jumps up to assist Mary in handing round cups, despite the younger girl's protestations.

'We do not wish to be a trouble to you,' Emily insists.

''Tis no trouble,' Mary replies quickly and bobs a swift curtsey. 'I shall be in the kitchen, ma'am. Summon me if you needs anything more.' She is gone so fast that her skirts and curls swing wide in her wake.

'Thank you, Mary,' Nur calls after her and glances at Kitty as Emily takes her own tea and sits back in her chair. 'I often tell Mary that she resembles my daughter,' she says. 'Ann was her age, fifteen, when she died. You have heard of it?' Kitty nods. 'And you,' Nur continues, 'Perhaps you are as Ann might have become.' She shakes her head in wonder. 'It is a miracle, the circumstances that have brought us together.'

'Indeed,' Kitty softly responds. 'I wish we had met when first I came to England and was so sorely missing my mother.'

'Which was very soon after my daughter died. I remarked the coincidence when reading my sister Faiz's letters.' Nur smiles at Kitty's quizzical expression. 'You came in 1805. You see, I know your history as you know mine.' Only perhaps I know more, she thinks, perhaps more than I shall ever tell.

'Tell me about the acquaintance between your sister and my mother,' Kitty begs. 'How they did meet, and when.'

''Twas more than an acquaintance,' Nur corrects her. 'It seems they had only to meet to become close friends. In fact,' she adds. 'Faiz once described her as her closest friend.' She sighs. 'Which made me envious, for once that was myself.' She drinks some tea, sits more straight and looks into the fire that seems to glow more brightly as she begins the tale.

'Faiz first met Khair when she and her husband Major William Palmer went to stay with your parents in Hyderabad. It was January 1802 and Khair was already five months pregnant with you. Her little son, your brother—'

'William,' Kitty whispers.

'He was one or two years old. My sister and brother-in-law had just left Pune, where he had been relieved of his post as British Resident after only four years following many years anticipating, and richly deserving, such a post. They were on their way to Madras where they were to take a boat to Calcutta and intended spending just one week resting at the Hyderabad Residency. But they enjoyed your parents' company so much that they eventually stayed three or four months! In fact, you were born the day after they left. However I am sure they made great claims on your parents' hospitality.' Nur smiles fondly. 'For my sister never did travel light. I remember when once they came to stay with my husband and myself, being astonished at the number of bullock carts, elephants, baggage camels, syces, sepoys, bearers and women servants that they brought with them. I guess many of these made camp in the grounds of the Hyderabad Residency as the house, though fine enough, was not so large that—'

'Does your sister describe the house?' Kitty interrupts. 'I should like to hear for I was only three when we left for England.'

'I believe she does...' Nur searches through the pages. 'Here: "*A fine entrance on the northern side up a flight of steps, flanked by stone lions through high columns to a splendid high reception hall within. And the most wonderful curving staircase beyond, up which one may ascend on the right or left, the whole illuminated by a large rose-shaped ceiling window.*'

'I remember that window,' says Kitty eagerly. 'Looking high up as I climbed, my hand always in someone else's for I was not allowed to climb alone, it being so high... what else does she mention?'

'*Khair also has her own much smaller but very elegant accommodation to which we mostly retire when there are official guests at the Residency. The Rang Mahal is set in a rose garden and is of lovely design ... oh, and I must tell you of the model house. Dear James had an exact replica of the Residency fashioned in stone in the garden. Little Fanny was especially entranced—*'

'Fanny?'

'Oh!' Too late Nur realises her indiscretion. 'A little girl who was adopted by my sister.' She glances quickly at Emily and is relieved to find that her attention is at present directed upon the letters, no doubt like Mary marvelling at the strange script. 'My brother-in-law's natural daughter,' she says quietly. 'I remember how shocked I was to read this, for I always envied Faiz her loving husband and happy circumstances and wished for the same myself and could not then understand how she could accept this child into her family.'

Kitty looks surprised but does not comment, perhaps not wishing to discuss it further in Emily's presence. Instead she observes: 'I guess the Palmers discovered much in common with my parents.' And then she asks: 'Why was Major Palmer required to quit his position?'

'For being out of sympathy with the aggressive British policy introduced by the new Governor, Wellesley,' Nur explains. 'My brother-in-law had spent his career forging friendships and agreements between the local Indian rulers and the British, thereby greatly assisting the development of trade and therefore profits for the Company, the East India Company. But you know,' she interrupts her narrative. 'Until recently even I was scarcely aware of such matters. I discovered my sister had written of them in several previous letters but to me then it was all so distant, as in another world...what is it Mary?'

Mary is hovering in the doorway, clearly hesitant to interrupt. 'Dinner's ready, ma'am,' she replies quickly. 'You asked for it to be early today. Will I tell Mrs Redford to serve?'

'Thank you, Mary, yes. I am sure our guests are hungry and have waited long enough. Mrs Redford is my landlady,' she explains to her guests. 'Though being long-acquainted I regard her more as a friend.'

26

During dinner Nur encourages Emily to describe the journey from Devon. She is especially interested in Emily's account of fossil-hunting in Lyme and of the newly-ordained clergyman who had accompanied her.

'So this Reverend Mohun Harris—'

'His first name is Walpole.'

'Walpole. He is a friend of Richard Astley, the new curate of our parish church? Who is a very pleasant young man, assiduous also for he has visited me more than once and hopes I may be persuaded to attend his church.' Nur laughs. 'And perhaps I may, for Catholic or Protestant, it matters little to me.'

Kitty looks surprised. 'You remain a Mahommedan? My brother and I were baptised when we came to this country.'

Nur considers a moment before shaking her head. 'I do not know how to answer you. I have not *practised* the faith of my ancestors since coming to this country, when my husband arranged for me and the children to be baptised as Roman Catholics. Helena, my Christian name, is the English version of his mother's name which was Helene. When I have attended church it has been the Catholic one here in Horsham. But now I find myself beginning…perhaps under the influence of my sister's letters….' She falls silent. *I do not know what I believe,* she thinks, *and it is time I did.*

'Many people are now questioning their faith, Mrs Bennett,' observes Emily gravely. 'On account of the fossils and other scientific discoveries. I discussed it with Walpole.'

Nur is surprised at Emily's serious turn of mind. 'Well then, you may care to continue your discussions with Richard. I find him most – enlightened. And I daresay he will call once he learns you are here.' She turns to Kitty. 'Mrs Phillips, do you know your birth name?'

'Noor,' Kitty answers. 'Noor-un-Nissa. The Light of Women. Though I cannot remember being called that. Why do you smile?' she adds quickly.

In fact, Nur is almost laughing as she tells Kitty of the coincidence in their names. 'Although if I call you Noor I think we will become quite confused,' she says. 'For I should like you to call me Nur.'

'Then please call me Kitty.'

'Shall we retire to the parlour? I would like a more comfortable seat.'

She leads the way and Emily chooses a window seat where she takes up one of her new novels and Nur and Kitty continue their confidences sitting on either side of the fire.

'My father also suffered the hostility of the East India Company to his marriage,' says Kitty. 'And this attitude was, I have been told, due as much to the fact that he wished to treat fairly with the Nizam, the local ruler, while they wished only to exploit him. And his marriage was seen as proof of his overly sympathetic, even treasonable relations with the Hyderabadi regime and people.'

'It is no wonder Faiz and your mother became such friends, their situations being so similar,' Nur reflects. 'Though I do not think the British objected to my sister's marriage.'

'Yet your brother-in-law was never promoted as he should have been and then not for long.'

'You are right,' Nur says. 'I had not thought of that being a reason. And moreover,' she continues, 'I have discovered anew from Faiz's letters how quickly British attitudes changed after I left India. Including to the children of marriages between Indians and Europeans. They became the object of increasing discrimination, the young men no longer being accepted into the Company's service. And this I did take note of, for it affected my dear eldest nephew, another William, named after his father. Instead he found employment in the Nizam's troops. In fact I believe your father had some hand in the matter.'

'And it was through this William Palmer, whom I now know to be your nephew, that my grandmother and myself were brought in touch after so many years!' exclaims Kitty. 'Which is yet another story,' she quickly adds.

129

'Oh but Mother do tell Mrs Bennett, Nur,' Emily interjects. 'For it is a wonderful tale and one which you did not fully relate this morning in the coach. And since it does concern Nur most closely...'

'I should certainly like to hear anything favourable of my dear nephew,' Nur interrupts. 'For it is a very long time since I had news from him...of course he is almost as old as myself, though it did not seem so when he was a child ...but only if your mother wishes to confide it,' she adds hastily.

'Of course I do,' Kitty assures her and outlines the events which she had recounted that morning to Emily and Georgina, how recognising the painting of herself and her brother at Henry Russell's house had eventually led to her reunion with her long-lost grandmother. 'And,' she now adds, 'it was a letter from your nephew, William Palmer, of whom at the time I knew nothing, to Mr Henry Russell that enabled the connection to be made. Mr Palmer had been supporting my grandmother for the past twelve years since, the British having confiscated her, or perhaps I should say, our family's property, she was living in poverty. Mr Palmer's circumstances also being much reduced due to his banking business having collapsed, he wrote to suggest that Mr Russell, who had once known her well, should now assist. Which he did, as subsequently did my husband and myself. While I was blessed with six precious years of correspondence with her. Could one invent such a tale?'

'Indeed not,' Nur agrees and wonders how much she should add to it. But she is interrupted by an indignant Emily whose opinion of Mr Russell seems a great deal less benevolent than her mother's.

'But Mr Russell only gave back the painting of my mother and her brother in his will so she only received it when he died last year,' exclaims Emily. 'I am sure he could have found her and returned it as soon as he came back from India and certainly as soon as he did discover her after she visited his house. Is that the action of an honourable man? I don't think so.'

'Oh my dear, one should not speak ill of the dead,' Kitty demurs. 'And I wished only to give Nur the pleasure of hearing such good news of her nephew.'

Her tone is apologetic but Nur does not immediately respond. She has been greatly disturbed since the first mention of the name Henry Russell, about whom she has heard much more from her sister. And much worse. Some of it she knows she will relate to Kitty later, when they are alone together. But just now she cannot resist one revelation which, though scandalous, will cause her no pain.

'But Emily is correct,' she says. 'Henry Russell was far from honourable. For, as I have learnt from my sister, he was once close friends with my nephew and a secret business partner in his bank, from which he made most of his fortune. It was secret because illegal for a Company official to be compromised in his duties by such personal interests. Eventually, rather than be discovered, he put such restrictions on the bank that he caused its collapse and ruined my nephew. He left India shortly after, under a cloud but with his own fortune intact.'

'A thorough-going scoundrel!' pronounces Emily in outraged satisfaction at her opinion being upheld. She might have said more but is diverted by the distant ring of the front door bell and the subsequent sound of hurrying footsteps to answer it. They all three listen in silence, until there is a knock at the door of the room where they are sitting and Mrs Redford, plump and motherly in her widow's dress and old-fashioned mob cap, enters, a little breathless.

'It is the Reverend Astley,' she says. 'He says he has news for you, Mrs Bennett, or he would not have called at this hour.' Mrs Redford casts a proprietorial eye around the room, plumps up the cushions on the window seat and goes out to fetch their guest.

'Mrs Bennett, ladies,' the Reverend Astley bows at the doorway. 'Forgive me for this late disturbance.' He is a tall, slim, clean-shaven young man with straight brown hair that he wears a little long and a fine-boned pleasant face.

'I thought your curiosity to see my guests would soon bring you here.' Nur beckons him closer. 'Mrs Phillips, Miss Emily Phillips, the Reverend Richard Astley. I am afraid my wagging tongue has preceded this formal introduction so that you all know something of each other. But we have discovered a surprise for you, Richard, a pleasant one I daresay. Shall you guess?'

'Richard' scratches his head in a fine display of puzzlement. 'Could it concern a coincidence in acquaintance?' he asks and then laughs. 'I have a surprise for you or I should not have come so late. Your acquaintance,' he nods to Kitty and Emily, 'and my good friend, Walpole Mohun-Harris, now the Reverend Mohun-Harris, as

131

he says I must constantly remind him, is to pay me a visit. And he arrives tomorrow!'

'Oh!' Emily exclaims and exchanges a glance with her mother. 'So soon!'

'Then you must bring him to renew the acquaintanceship and meet me,' Nur says firmly and, whilst unsure that Emily entirely welcomes the news, adds: 'It will surely be agreeable for you all to have some diversion other than the company of a very old lady who is already a little weary and ready for her bed.' She stands. ' You will forgive me,' she addresses them all before turning to Kitty: 'And do order some refreshment as you wish.'

***

When Mary has helped her undress and left her for the night, Nur again leafs through her sister's letters until she finds the place, the time, when Faiz next met Khair. She wants to remind herself of some of the particulars, to find those that will most please her guest, those that a three year old child would not remember, that perhaps no-one but herself knows or can tell. But she also wants to reflect on how these matters may bring to light others which are certain to distress Kitty, however they are described. And it is important how they are described for how she hears the story will surely make all the difference to whether the adult Kitty condemns or condones her mother, pities her or loves her the more. But first she, Nur, needs to understand events that took place so far away and so long ago in a world that once was hers but which she was obliged to forget. Perhaps it may help, she thinks, if she writes out an account in English. Which she can give to Kitty to read if the telling proves too difficult. She picks up the first letter and begins to write.

Calcutta April 1806
My dear Nur,

Well, here we are in Calcutta again and not in the best of spirits as you can imagine for we are on leave from a very dull posting at Monghyr which is not at all of the rank which your brother-in-law deserves. But he has a promotion! In name at least and certainly not *before time. Yes, he is now <u>General Palmer</u>. And takes some comfort and pride in being so addressed by Calcutta society.*

Not that there is a great deal to respect in Calcutta society. The city itself, as I daresay you recall for it will not be much changed since you were here, is grand and beautiful. 'The City of Palaces', 'St Petersburg of the East'. I do remember you were much impressed by the cleanliness of the streets and the paved sidewalks which do not become muddy. And by the number of grand houses which, I am told, is rare to find in England. We are staying with my husband's son John whom you will certainly recall and who sends you his best wishes. It is a fine mansion only spoiled by the prevalence of mosquitoes which do not bother me much but John tells me his European lady guests are forced to wear thick stockings as protection when they come to dine!

But there are still few respectable women here and therefore little society for me to enjoy. And besides, many of the Europeans hardly venture from the city and have therefore no knowledge nor interest in our country, our customs, our art and music. It is not at all the equal of our dear Lucknow (wherever could be?) and Hyderabad appears the height of civilisation in comparison.

I am however awaiting the arrival of my dearest friend Khair of whose sad losses I have written you. Because of the season she has travelled much of the way by land from Hyderabad, only taking ship at Masulipatam. It is now more than nine months since her children were sent to England, (indeed they must have arrived by now,) and almost as long since her husband died in the house of his niece, Isabella, who had been recently married.

Isabella is quite the most beautiful English woman I have seen and very quickly found a husband. Buller his name is, Charles Buller, who though young has already an important Company position. James was to have attended the wedding (as was Khair herself) but in the even the was too late. By the time he did reach Calcutta he was so ill even my husband could not visit him, though he did attend his burial. I am glad to say this was with full military honours, but there were present no others of those who loved and admired him.

How very different for all of us the situation could have been, for the return of Cornwallis as Governor in October promised the restoration of the just relations between the British and our Indian rulers that James and your brother-in-law had laboured so hard to preserve. In fact

133

Cornwallis had summoned James to Calcutta and met with your brother-in-law to discuss such a programme. But the good Lord saw fit to take Cornwallis too when he had just begun (and a matter of days before dear James' own sad demise.)

I shall write again when Khair arrives.

Your loving sister

Faiz

May 1806

Khair has brought with her the most wonderful painting of her two dear little children whom she misses beyond telling. It is full life-size and had to be transported on elephant back before being loaded on the ship. It is quite the talk of the town. People come to their lodgings to ask to view it! She and her mother have taken a large house together with some of her Hyderabadi relations. It is quite near to us. But I have not as yet seen much of her for she and her mother are almost all the time grieving at James' graveside. I believe she intends fulfilling the entire period of mourning there...

June 1806

At last Khair is beginning to revive her relations with those who care for her. Did I tell you she had sent Isabella a wedding gift of a splendid set of opal jewellery? Well now she is constantly commissioning from Hyderabad the purchase of fine materials or readymade outfits for her friends amongst whom of course I am counted. Truly she has the most generous nature and there seems no trouble too great, no length to which she will not go to obtain such gifts once she has determined her choice...I gather that James' one-time loyal assistant, a Mr Henry Russell (the son of the Chief Justice here, Sir William Russell) whom of course we met when in Hyderabad was it three? four? Years ago, is much engaged in pursuing such errands, requiring his younger brother (another Charles) to arrange the purchasing and transport from Hyderabad. He is also a Company servant at the Residency and one might think too much occupied to find time for such tasks. But once dear Khair has decided on a course of action she has always shown great determination in achieving her ends.

27

Nur joins Kitty and Emily next morning when they have just finished taking breakfast. She is tired after her efforts the night before but eager to continue her conversation with Kitty and not sorry therefore when Mary comes in with a note for Emily.

'Is it from Walpole?' Kitty frowns. 'It seems a little forward of him to write so soon and to you alone.'

Emily looks up and laughs as she passes the note to her mother. 'I thought you liked him, Mother! But no, it is from Georgina as you see, and she invites me to meet her in town to help her with some purchases. To assist her in her tutoring. May I go?'

'You may, only how will you find your way?'

'Let Mary accompany you,' says Nur. 'I am sure Mrs Redford will also have some errands you can run for her.'

***

As Nur had hoped Kitty is delighted to read these descriptions of her mother and laughs at the thought of her bringing the portrait so far on the back of an elephant.

'I didn't know she had it there. Almost as if we were with her. I have often wished we had made a similar portrait of our children.'

'As have I,' Nur agrees. 'Their childhood years pass so swiftly in the best of circumstances. I daresay you are also happy to know that your mother was to some degree recovering her spirits in the company of her friends and family?'

'Oh yes, for how else should she survive? Though I might not have understood it then. Do you know, I have *never* stopped missing her. My own last memory is of her utterly distraught and tearing at her hair when we were taken from her. Of course I knew that she

135

spent some time in Calcutta but I have never been able to imagine her there.'

'I expect that you received letters which were read to you but were too young for them to evoke any strong impression?'

Nur's question is almost rhetorical and she is surprised to see Kitty's face fall. 'My brother and I were not allowed to receive my mother's letters,' she replies and looks away as tears come to her eyes.

'Oh my dear,' Nur begins, her suspicions being somewhat confirmed but not enough for her to know how to respond further. But then Kitty continues.

'And I have never really understood why. What I know is what I was told by my family. By Isabella in particular.'

'Isabella was your—'

'My cousin. My father's older brother's daughter. My Uncle William's daughter. When my brother and I were young we used to stay with him and his family in Devon, in Exeter, where he had a house. And then later sometimes we lived with Isabella, after our grandfather died. Isabella died some years ago. She was still very beautiful.'

Nur is only half-listening as she tries to make sense of what she has learned. It does seem likely that Kitty is entirely ignorant of her mother's later fate, in which case she herself must think carefully as to how and how much to tell her of what she knows.

'And you must also be glad that your father was honoured at the last,' she suggests. 'Most particularly by the new Governor.'

Kitty nods. 'I did not know of that,' she says. 'To think that all his life's work was not to come to nothing. Although the hurried journey to Calcutta cannot have improved his health. He was delayed in Hyderabad you know, by his duties, by his health and by the weather and my mother would otherwise have been with him on the journey. She would have taken better care of him. And they would have first arrived in Madras in time to see us once more before we sailed to England.' Kitty sighs deeply. 'I should like to tell my daughter of all this, to show her these copies of your sister's letters, if I may. She thinks the story of my parent's marriage a true romance. Though surely it became a tragedy which one would find it hard to invent, so dependent is it on chance and circumstance.'

'Of course you may,' Nur says. *But,* she thinks, *I wonder how much more you will wish to relate of what I have to tell you.*

'And perhaps it may improve her opinion of Mr Russell who seems to have acted towards my mother like a faithful servant!'

***

Emily comes home in time for lunch, her cheeks flushed with the excitements of her morning. She has barely sat down at the table before beginning to tell of her doings.

'Georgina and I had just finished our purchases (for I bought a piece of close work thinking I might need occupation here other than reading) when who should accost us in the street but the Reverend Astley! He insists we call him Richard and indeed we are all now on first name terms, quite in the modern way. I hope you do not think it inappropriate, Mama?' She does not pause for Kitty's response. 'And Walpole was with him, newly arrived from Lyme. So we had a fine time strolling around the town together and partaking of a hot chocolate in some hotel. I confess I did not have high expectations of Horsham – forgive me Mrs Bennett – but I am most pleasantly surprised. Georgina also.'

'Is Walpole to stay here long?' Kitty enquires, and Nur thinks she detects a note of anxiety in her voice. And guesses why, at least in general terms, for Emily is most certainly at the marriageable age and very pretty, one might say beautiful, besides. There seems to be more than a quarter of her grandmother in her appearance, she thinks and, she recalls from one of Faiz' letters, Khair was renowned for her beauty.

'He has found a position as curate in a parish down in the west country somewhere,' Emily is telling her mother. 'Somerset I believe, but is come here for a holiday before taking up his duties.'

'Such a fortunate coincidence for you young people,' says Nur, hoping her disingenuity is not too apparent.

Emily looks at her sharply. 'It is no great coincidence,' she says. 'For he expected to find us here. In fact I think, on having met in Lyme, he may have changed his plans accordingly. And I am very glad of Georgina and Richard's company for a party of four is altogether more enjoyable.'

137

Ah, thinks Nur, she has as yet no romantic attachment to this young man, whatever he feels for her.

'And they, Georgina and Richard, already seem to enjoy each other's company greatly.'

Kitty changes the subject. 'Mrs Bennett, Nur, has been showing me her sister's letters,' she tells her daughter. 'Or rather translations of them which she has made. And you may care to read.'

'Oh yes indeed,' Emily's eyes are again lit with enthusiasm. 'Of what do they tell?'

'Of your grandmother's stay in Calcutta where she renewed her friendship with my sister and her husband,' replies Nur. 'And began to regain her spirits after her bereavement and loss of your mother and her brother.'

'And of the great assistance rendered her in all her tasks by Mr Russell!' Kitty laughs at Emily's surprise. 'Perhaps we have judged him too harshly. Come, let us eat. We will talk of this later.'

***

Nur is lying on the couch with her eyes closed and she knows that Kitty and Emily think her asleep from their whispered conversation and that Emily has just read the letters.

'Why do you think Mr Russell was so very helpful to your mother?' asks Emily. 'Does it not seem strange to think of him running all her errands, especially since they concerned such feminine preoccupations as the choice of dress material and trimmings! Imagine Papa being sent to buy lace! What would he come back with?' She laughs.

'Hush,' Kitty cautions. 'I think Mr Russell was perhaps acting according to established habits of loyalty to my father. On the one occasion we met he told me how much he admired him. He was not at all one of his detractors. When he himself became Resident some five years later here instituted many of my father's practices and on occasion wore his Indian style costumes. And besides, I am beginning to think my mother may have been a little – imperious in her ways. Faiz Palmer implied as much do you not think?'

'But his brother too!' Emily smothers another laugh. 'It is so amusing to think of two young Englishmen at her beck and call! Of course,' she adds, 'she was young too, even younger perhaps.' She pauses. 'I think they were a little in love with her, the elder at least and the younger accustomed to doing as his brother demanded. Oh Mother!' she exclaims. 'I have just remembered. Richard has invited us to visit his church. He said Mrs Bennett might like to accompany us. I should have mentioned it before she fell asleep.'

Nur makes a pretence of waking. 'Did I hear you mention my name?'

'Mrs Bennett!' Emily is contrite. 'I have disturbed you. Only I should have said before that Richard – Reverend Astley– suggested we might all like to visit his church and he included you most particularly.'

'Did he indeed!' Nur smiles. 'He is persistent. And then no doubt he hopes I shall attend a service. But perhaps I shall come with you, for an outing would be pleasant though I fear we must take a carriage as it is far for me to walk. Almost two miles,' she explains, 'which not long since I could have accomplished without thought. But first I should like to take some tea.'

Emily jumps to her feet. 'I will go and ask for some,' she says. 'And for a carriage to be sent.' She runs to the door. 'And to send a message to Richard that we shall be coming – within the hour?' The door bangs shut after her.

Kitty shakes her head. 'My daughter is impetuous,' she apologises. 'Perhaps she takes after my mother in more than appearance.' And then she adds in explanation: 'We were just speaking of my mother's apparent expectation that the Russell brothers should serve her.'

'I heard you,' Nur says. 'And it is therefore I who should apologise for eavesdropping. But I was interested to hear your daughter's opinion, as I have found it hard myself to imagine the...' she pauses, 'the manner of their relations. For, you know, your mother lived more or less in purdah, more than did my sister or myself. But as you will read when I have translated the rest of the letters, in one of them my sister writes that your mother even removed her veil for Mr Russell. Thus treating him as one would a brother.' She stops abruptly at the sound of voices outside the room. 'We will talk more later, when we shall not be interrupted.'

28

'How pleasant it is to ride in a barouche after being enclosed in a coach for so long.' Emily looks out eagerly from side to side of their carriage as they travel the mile or two to the church. She has insisted on sitting with her back to the driver while Nur and her mother share the opposite seat and are bathed in the deep gold light of a sunny autumn afternoon.

'It is very good to be out in this fine weather,' Nur agrees. 'Very soon the days will be too short for outings in the afternoon.' She is extraordinarily happy to be out of doors and in such agreeable company, and resolves to return to her old habit of taking daily walks as soon as her visitors have left, with Mary for company and assistance. But suddenly she has an idea and leans forward.

'Stop at the end of The Broadway,' she calls to the driver. She turns to Kitty. 'From there it is only a few minutes' walk to the church and a more pleasant approach. I daresay you will enjoy a little exercise after sitting with me all morning, and whilst I do not doubt that Torquay is a great deal more picturesque, you must enjoy what few sights we have to offer.'

'But this is most elegant,' exclaims Kitty after they dismount. 'Quite like Exeter in fact, the area around the cathedral, where my uncle had his house. Do you not think so, Emily?'

Emily looks along the row of fine houses that line one side of the wide paved roadway at the end of which a small church spire rises above some trees. 'Indeed,' she agrees, then frowns and bites her lip as she hesitates. 'Though to be sure, it is rather smaller,' she amends. 'But then again one could almost think oneself in Bath,' she again corrects herself.

Nur is amused at these signs of conflict between honesty and the desire to please, and even more by the resolution. She takes Emily's arm with a feeling of great affection. 'Now there, my dear, I feel you may be going too far. Come, help me hobble this short distance for I fear these weeks of inactivity have stiffened my old bones more than I had recognised.'

The Reverend Richard Astley is waiting for them at the lychgate whence he escorts them up the path to the main door. The churchyard is nearly full of gravestones, Nur observes, some of them clearly very old, their inscriptions illegible. The church itself is the oldest building in the town, Richard tells them, built in 1247 on the site of an even more ancient building and largely unchanged since, giving it an unusual coherence of architectural style.

'It is also notable for its proportions,' he continues. 'The nave being of the same width as the chancel. But you must see for yourselves.' He leans his weight against the heavy wooden doors, which open slowly with much creaking of their hinges and indicates that the visitors should precede him inside.

They are at first silenced by the sight that greets them for, despite its generous width, any view of the nave is obscured by heavy wooden box pews, each with a family name affixed to their entrance .In like manner, the upward gaze is everywhere blocked by hanging wooden galleries, each reached by a narrow winding staircase. The overall effect in fact is to depress spirits that have been raised by the building's attractive outward appearance.

'It is a wondrously high roof,' says Kitty at last. 'And the eastern window is accordingly of magnificent proportions. In the morning it must admit a great deal of light and...' Her voice trails off.

'But it is in poor repair,' Richard responds. 'As indeed is the whole building. In fact my superior, the Reverend John Hodgson, tells me he has long been concerned as to the safety of the congregation, with so much superstructure– ' he indicates the galleries, '– that could collapse at any time.' He sighs deeply. 'Yet we do need their seating space for it is a very large parish and we regularly have congregations in excess of five hundred.'

'It could be so beautiful,' Emily enthuses. 'Imagine that window filled with stained glass, some depictions of the life of Christ perhaps... with His birth in central position and His mother holding him.'

'I too imagine it often,' Richard smiles at her enthusiasm. 'For as Mrs Bennett may recall, the full name of the church is 'St Mary the Virgin'. He turns to Nur. 'Quite Catholic is it not?'

Nur laughs but in fact from the moment she stepped inside and despite the gloom, she has felt very much at home, in communion with the many centuries of souls who have worshipped here.

'And there is a further fact of which you may not be aware,' he regards her with fond amusement, 'a recent incumbent, the Reverend Rose, was a prominent Tractarian who regarded the Church of England as part of the Church of Rome and was very much opposed to state interference in its affairs.' He smiles. 'And we are still quite high church.'

'You see the strength of theological pressure he deploys upon me,' Nur appeals to her companions. 'But it is all a pretence. What he really wants is for me to contribute to the fund-raising efforts of some of the lady parishioners to restore the fabric of the church.'

Richard continues to smile but does not refute her accusation. 'Reverend Hodgson made it clear to me at my appointment that he regarded this as an important part of my duties,' he tells them. 'Mrs Bennett is renowned in Horsham for her generosity to the poor over many many years. I am merely suggesting other ways in which her charity may be exercised.'

Kitty and Emily smile back at him in appreciation at the news of Nur's benevolence but Nur's mood changes as she considers his proposal.

'We shall see,' she says at last. 'Now that I must sell my home and my remaining family is certainly in no need ... but tell me,' she rallies, 'are you sure you have room for me in your churchyard? And shall I be welcome? A Muslim turned Catholic? For it cannot be long before I shall need some such resting place.'

Her tone is light and it is the turn of her companions to be sober and fall silent. Richard takes her arm and, while Kitty and Emily walk further into the church, leads her back out into the slanting sunlight of late afternoon.

'How about there?' He points to a place at the side of the path not far from the churchyard wall. 'Could you rest in peace there?'

Nur looks long and hard at the spot indicated and attempts to imagine herself lying beneath the grass that covers it, a mound where at present the ground is flat. 'It is hard to contemplate one's own death,' she says thoughtfully. 'Perhaps it depends on one's view of the afterlife. And perhaps it matters little where lie one's physical remains.' Richard is clearly about to respond, but Nur continues. 'I greatly appreciate your concern for my spiritual welfare,' she says lightly touching the hand that still supports her elbow. 'And it is very probable that I shall seek your counsel in the weeks to come. Once my visitors have gone I must search my soul before it is too late. Ah my dears!' She turns to greet Kitty and Emily who have emerged from the church porch.

Richard also turns to greet them. 'Mrs Phillips, Emily, I was beginning to fear you buried in some ruinous collapse of stone or woodwork! When I had am hoping you will take tea in my apartments. Reverend Hodgson and his wife have very kindly given me rooms in their splendid new vicarage. It is a temporary arrangement while some repairs are made to enable me to live in a much older building, which apparently was described as dilapidated over a hundred years ago! Will you join me?'

Nur feels suddenly very tired and old. She wishes to go home but not to impede the others' enjoyment. 'Could you perhaps send a request to the carriage driver to come round to the other side of the church to collect me?' she suggests. 'And you two may walk or take another carriage later?'

Kitty will not hear of this. 'No no, I think we have all been out long enough. But we must certainly call the carriage nearer.' She turns back to Richard. 'I hope there will be another occasion.'

'Meanwhile you should come to dine with us,' Nur says on impulse. 'And we shall also invite your friend whom I am eager to meet. Shall we say tomorrow?'

'Then may we invite Georgina to complete the party?' enquires Emily.

'Of course of course. If she is at liberty to leave her charges.'

'Thank you.' Richard bows. 'That will be most enjoyable.'

His tone is matter-of -fact but Nur sees the sudden flush in his cheeks and the slight evasion in his glance. Well, she thinks, I am happy enough to be the facilitator of romance, if only the object of his interest is worthy. I wonder what is Kitty's opinion of this Georgina. That will be something else to talk about later.

***

Nur has an early opportunity to make her own observations for, on returning home, they surprise Georgina in the act of leaving a message for Emily. Nur suggests Georgina stay for supper, which invitation Georgina accepts instantly, her evident pleasure transforming her pale narrow features into fragile prettiness.

'How are you enjoying your new position?' enquires Kitty when they are seated at the supper table.

Georgina smiles. 'Oh I like the children very much. There is Master Philip who is five and already learning his multiplication tables, and Miss Augusta – Gussie –who is seven and likes nothing better than to bury her nose in a book. Really I could not ask for better charges. There is also a baby but for her there is a nursemaid, although one day I suppose she will join us in the nursery...if I remain in post that is...' Her voice trails off and her smile fades as she looks away.

'You are not entirely happy?' Kitty asks.

Georgina hesitates before making a careful reply. 'I find itis hard being in a position of subservience,' she says slowly. 'Not that I am badly treated. Indeed, Dr and Mrs Wright are quite civil and at times even amicable. It is just that one never knows, I never know, how to respond. If I am amicable in return I feel them retreat; if I state an opinion, for example, concerning the children's progress, there is a silence, even a frown, before they reply.' Georgina is again silent for a moment. 'I believe it to be a matter of inequality of status, a situation with which I am unfamiliar but with which fact I cannot argue. I must not complain,' she adds quickly. 'I shall become accustomed to it, I am sure. I am very lucky to have been taken on at all with so little experience.'

Nur has been watching this exchange and sees Kitty's expression soften from one of cool appraisal to understanding and sympathy. But she is surprised at the bitterness in her tone when she responds.

'It is early days,' says Kitty. 'Although in some cases there is no such resolution.' She frowns and bites her lip. 'I had a friend in similar situation. A person of such excellent intellect that he has become famous for his writing and opinions. If anyone deserved to be treated according to his merits it was he.'

'Mr Carlyle,' confirms Emily with a nod.

Georgina appears a little surprised at Kitty's confidence. 'And did he not persevere in his position? I guess with such abilities it was easy to find alternative employment, while I fear I have little choice.'

'He did not find it easy at all,' Kitty replies. 'He endured several years of comparative poverty before making his way. Of course his wife had some property...' It is her turn to leave her speech unfinished.

Emily reaches across the table and takes Georgina's hand. 'And you may find a husband similarly able to support you. You shall, I am determined.'

Georgina releases her hand with some impatience. 'I must make my own way, Emily. I cannot assume any such outcome, having no fortune nor family connections. I must concentrate my energies on improving my tutoring skills and knowledge. Which is my duty and which shall be its own reward.'

Nur is convinced by the determination in Georgina's voice and, so she soon sees, is Kitty.

'What you say is both true and admirable,' Kitty tells her. 'I am happy that Emily has you as a friend.'

'And it could even be your passport to travel if you find a position abroad,' urges Emily.

'As in "*Villette*"?' Georgina raises her eyebrows.

'Perhaps not quite,' agrees Emily.

'Villette?' enquires Kitty. It is apparent that Nur does not understand the reference either.

'The new book by "Currer Bell",' Emily replies. 'One of those I bought in Southampton. And about which there is so much speculation as to the identity of the author. The heroine goes to teach in Belgium and falls in love with a professor. Only he is married so of course that is not a good example to follow.'

'I am not sure you should even be reading it,' responds Kitty promptly. 'You must let me have a look at it later.'

***

Emily and Mary escort Georgina to her home, it being but a half hour walk for which Emily declares a need despite the lateness of the hour. While they are gone, Kitty and Nur sit at either side of the living room hearth where a small but welcome fire has been lit.

'So,' says Nur. 'You think Georgina a worthy object of Richard's affection?'

Kitty nods. 'I do now. And am glad you gave her the opportunity this evening of doing herself such credit. I was not earlier convinced of her sincerity, or depth of character. She seemed a little too - forward – in her conversation.'

'But now?'

'Now I think perhaps it was because she was suffering, in the same way that she finds with her employers, from an uncertainty of status, a feeling of inferiority to us, to me. For clearly we are more fortunate than she in our station in life. But whether she will secure Richard's affections, or even desire it, I cannot say.'

'No indeed, the affairs of the heart are never straightforward.'

'No.'

Kitty says this with such conviction that Nur is emboldened. 'This – Mr Carlyle whom you mentioned. Your friend. You were to some degree close to him at the time of his unhappy experience as a tutor?'

Kitty looks sharply up at her. 'He was tutor to my cousin Isabella's sons who loved him,' she replies. 'But he was regarded and treated by the Bullers as more a servant than household member. And he did not like it. No more did I. But he was to blame also, in presuming too much too soon.' She hesitates, thinking how good it would be to confess her secrets at last 'As,' she continues, 'was I.'

'It is hard to understand one's own heart, let alone another's,' Nur says carefully. 'For my part, I have doubted if my husband ever loved me or if I simply suited his needs at the time. And I don't think he knew either.'

Kitty has been following Nur's words intently. Now she nods. 'I came to the same conclusion concerning Thomas – Mr Carlyle. But I think he might have remained true to me had he not alienated some of my family. It is quite a long story but I can tell it if you wish, for time and circumstance have reduced its power to hurt any of those concerned.'

So Kitty tells Nur of those few glorious months when she had come to believe she knew where her future happiness would lie, but how the combination of Thomas' duplicity and uncertainty about his future and therefore ability to support a wife, had proved fatal to her hopes.

'But you did find happiness, with your husband,' Nur states, not daring to make it a question. 'For you there was a happy ending.'

'Most certainly,' Kitty's response is immediate. 'And I have never stopped counting my blessings that I found a husband who has continued to love me. But, you know, the heart does not quite forget its earlier pains. It may recover, even increase, its capacity and yet be scarred for life.'

Nur looks at the younger woman in admiration, finding her words an accurate reflection of her own experience. Surely her life and the nature of her love for Benoit was overshadowed by her earlier marriage, from which she had been released only by the death of the elderly Nawab to whom her parents had promised her as a child, before, praise be to Allah, he could call her to his bed. It is not the time to tell Kitty of all this, though she would like to, but she is now assured that she can reveal to her the full circumstances of her mother's later life and death, sure that the mature Kitty will understand what many would surely condemn. But not now. She yawns.

'I am tired, my dear, forgive me. We shall speak again in the morning.'

***

Mary is helping Nur into bed.

'Leave the lamp lit, my dear, I must translate these before morning.' Nur holds up a handful of Faiz' letters. 'I have promised Mrs Phillips she shall know their contents tomorrow.'

'Are you not over-tired, ma'am? Can you not read them to her in the morning?'

Nur shakes her head. 'It is better she read and appraise them for herself. I had rather not be the messenger of bad news.'

'Is it so bad?'

Nur hesitates. 'I am not sure how she will respond though I have tried to imagine. She will certainly be distressed on her mother's account, whose life ended in such sadness. I hope there will be no stronger feelings of condemnation, shame, anger.'

Mary shakes her head. 'Well ma'am, I trust you will not stay awake long as last night. 'n any case there's but an hour's worth of light in this candle, though I can bring another if you wish.'

'Thank you , Mary, it will suffice. And I shall like to tell you the whole sad tale one day soon, to have the benefit of your judgment, which no doubt will be as wise as ever.'

29

Nur and Kitty are again sitting on either side of the living room fire, while Emily and Mary have gone out furnished with a list of purchases for the evening meal. It is a blustery day and Kitty has made this her excuse for not accompanying them. Nur delays no further in giving her some pages on which she has written passages from several more of her sister's letters. She looks again at the miniature of Khair-un-Nissa that Kitty has shown her and which she holds in her lap and then, as Kitty begins to read aloud, gazes into the fire and imagines that it is her sister's voice.

'November 1806, Monghyr
My dear sister,
As you can see we have returned to this dull place, a posting which is so inferior to that which your brother-in-law deserves. If only Cornwallis had lived what preferment might have been ours! I daresay you remember when we visited you in Aligarh that I could not imagine how you could bear to live in such a remote town. Well, now I have to. As you know Calcutta is far from being my preferred place but now when I receive news from thence it is as water to a dying man in a desert.
However the latest news of my dear friend Khair has caused me considerable concern. I think I told you that she had unveiled for young Henry Russell and received him in her apartments as if he were her brother. She now plans to return to Hyderabad in his company and the opinion is that it is not as a brother that he accompanies her.'

Kitty takes a sharp intake of breath but does not glance up before continuing, a deepening frown the only indicator of her distress.

'In fact, not finding much favour with the acting Resident in Hyderabad, Mr Russell had decided to seek some position in

Calcutta or elsewhere, this having been his principal motive for coming to the city. Hence his sudden change of heart itself raised suspicions as to the nature and degree of their attachment.

I do wish I had been there to advise her of the need for more caution. Henry Russell is not James. He is very young and I have heard that his attitude to his bibis has been quite lacking in responsibility. Khair herself told me that he was angry when his present girl reported her pregnancy and quite uncaring when the baby soon died. I fancy Khair was more distressed than he since, missing her own children so very much, she had offered to adopt the little girl. However, your brother-in-law says he is less surprised that Mr Russell has decided to return to Hyderabad, since under the new acting Governor he would have had little chance of preferment. So let us hope that Mr Russell's intentions whatever they may be are honourable.

December 1806

My anxiety on Khair's behalf was sadly justified. It became known that Henry Russell was attempting to purchase a zenana next to his bungalow in the Hyderabad Residency where Khair was to live so that, he said, he could give her his protection. However, one gathers that no-one is in any doubt as to the nature of this protection and the Governor is now attempting to prevent Khair from ever returning to Hyderabad. Meanwhile the Resident has offered her official protection rather than let her return to the Residency. He says this is to prevent her from finding herself in a very inferior condition compared to that which she enjoyed as James' wife. But this course has fallen foul of the Nizam's Prime Minister thereby threatening relations with the British authorities.

I will not trouble you with the details, suffice to say that longstanding rivalries in the Nizam's court are at play and the Minister has not long returned after a period of exile on the grounds of corruption and is perhaps now bent on revenge. Khair has written me of her fears. She told me that Mr Russell has made strong protest to the Governor General saying that he has no right to prevent Khair's return to Hyderabad since she is a citizen of the Nizam. It is a veritable hornets' nest and I fear there can be no happy outcome.

January 1807

Good news! Khair and her mother have been allowed to leave Calcutta together with Henry Russell and their household. The Governor General agreed to this on condition that she live under the protection of her family and not of the British Government. The party appear to be travelling very slowly perhaps because they are apprehensive as to their reception, but, one hopes, also because Khair and Mr Russell are happy to be in each other's company away from prying eyes and critical opinion.

Kitty's hands fall to her lap still holding the pages. She sits in silence for several minutes and Nur does not disturb her. At last she looks up, her face pale and drawn and takes a deep shuddering breath.

'I never imagined... perhaps because I was a child... I thought my mother died because she never got over her grief at losing my father and us. Now I don't know what was in her mind. So soon after my father's death.' Kitty's voice falls to a whisper. 'But I do understand why my family would not let us communicate with her. At last.' She sighs.

Nur chooses her words very carefully. 'Do you think that she was attempting to ensure that her future life in Hyderabad would be as it was before? As much as possible, that is. In which case you were right to believe her still grieving and desperately missing you all.'

Kitty smiles sadly. 'Perhaps. She was ready after all to adopt Mr Russell's baby by another woman in order to have a child to cherish again. For she was such a wonderful mother.' Tears fill Kitty's eyes as she continues. 'What I really do not understand is why Henry Russell did not tell me that he loved her, that they lived together despite such opposition on all sides.' She glances down at the papers in her lap and frowns. 'I guess there is more I must know. Would you read it to me?' She passes the pages back to Nur who part reads, part gives her own summary.

'In March 1807,after twelve weeks of travel, they had not arrived in Hyderabad and my nephew wrote to his parents that they had made camp at only a week's journey from the city. Their worst fears must have been realised when they received a letter from Charles Russell telling them that '*both the Resident and the Prime Minister have decreed that all contact between you must cease once you return to the city, the Resident describing the Minister's objections as natural enough when the customs and prejudices of the Moossulmen respecting their women are considered.'*

'But then in April,' Nur turns to another page. 'The Minister told the Resident that Khair-un-Nissa was a disgrace to her family and would not be welcome back in Hyderabad. This was of course the very worst news and not what Henry Russell had expected. But on discussing the matter with Khair and her mother they reluctantly agreed that they should make their home in the town of Masulipatam, also in the Company's territories, at least until the controversy had died down or the Minister had died. And Henry Russell asked his ever faithful brother to convey the news to Khair's grandmother in Hyderabad without revealing the true causes. It was due to some whim on Khair's part seems to have been the message, though the old lady surely must have wondered at her granddaughter's decision for the town of Masulipatam was small, very rundown and notoriously unhealthy.'

'So Henry Russell leaves them there?' Kitty's tone is incredulous. 'And himself returns to Hyderabad?'

Nur nods. 'Quite soon,' she agrees. 'And according to my nephew, putting a most matter-of-fact appearance on the situation. William found him heartless in the extreme, my sister said, appearing relieved to have arrived at a solution to the problem.'

'He could have married my mother,' Kitty says with scorn.

'It seems he was not willing to risk his career as your father had.'

'Which then went smoothly, I guess, since he later became Resident.'

'Although not before he had served elsewhere and suffered to some extent,' Nur interjects. 'But this will not greatly enhance your opinion of him. After a few months back in Hyderabad he found a position in Madras where he was able to make a new start and very soon began to enjoy himself tremendously.'

'With a new 'girl'?' asks Kitty bitterly.

Nur extends a comforting hand though she cannot reach to touch Kitty. She is sad to have caused her so much pain. She wonders briefly what Khair's mother, Sharaf-un-Nissa, had thought of Henry Russell and whether she had counselled her daughter against the relationship. Clearly, though not surprisingly, she had not written of it to Kitty.

'I daresay,' she acknowledges at last. 'But the real reason he was happier was that he had more European company than ever before and it was not long before he met a girl whom he did want to marry.'

'And did he never visit my mother again?'

'Once at the beginning it seems, but after that he relied on his brother to convey messages.'

Kitty gasps, 'He is worse than I or even Emily thought. Was worse,' she amends.

'Except that he did not live happily ever after,' says Nur, unable to withhold the satisfaction from her voice. 'Let me tell you the rest of the story.'

She opens her mouth to continue but then stops abruptly at the sound of Emily's voice outside the room. The door opens and Emily enters and pulls up a seat between them.

'Brr.' She rubs her hands together and holds them out to the fire. 'It certainly feels like autumn today. Have you enjoyed your morning? I daresay you have had some interesting conversations.'

Her tone is light but she glances at the letters and notices the miniature as she speaks and Nur knows that she is as interested in Khair's story as is her mother and that Kitty will need to decide how much of it to tell her. But for the present, it seems, Emily is preoccupied with the events of the day.

'Mother, I have said I wish to help in the kitchen this afternoon,' she announces. 'I hope this is acceptable to you, Mrs Bennett?'

'I should advise you, my dear Nur,' Kitty interrupts. 'Emily is entirely without experience of cooking.'

'I am sure I can prepare vegetables and such like, with a little instruction,' Emily reproaches her mother. 'Anyway, it will be good to be occupied and I do like Mary. She is very - *sensible*, as the French say, sensible too of course. One would not think her so lacking in schooling.'

Nur is very happy to hear this appreciation of her onetime kitchen maid. Since her son Charles' sudden death and their removal here, giving Mary some formal instruction in reading and writing has been her principal delight. But Mary is not simply a project on which she has embarked, she is her closest companion and she dearly hopes she will remain so, and that Mary's grandmother will not require her return.

'Rest a little now,' Nur suggests. 'Until lunch. You may help all you wish this afternoon. I was about to tell your mother of a part of Mr Russell's life that may affect your opinion of him.' She breaks off as she notices the expression of alarm on Kitty's face. 'You may even feel a little sorry for him.' She sees Kitty relax.

'I shall never quite forgive him, however,' Emily says firmly, 'for withholding my mother's portrait for so very long. When it can have meant so little to him, aside from its monetary value. And he was rich enough from his ill-gotten gains as you have already informed us.'

Nur smiles at her determined expression and wonders if Kitty will ever tell her the full truth of her mother's ill-fated attempt to rebuild her fortunes. Perhaps when she marries and has children of her own, she reflects, when she understands better the complexities of life.

'Where were we?' she wonders aloud as she tries to recall the last part of the story that Emily heard.

'In Calcutta,' Emily reminds her. 'With the two young Russell brothers running errands for my grandmother.'

'So we were.' Nur smiles. 'Which continued for several months until Khair and her mother, Sharaf-un-Nissa, decided it was time they returned to Hyderabad where Khair's grandmother had remained alone all that time. By this time it seems that Mr Russell had given up on his attempts to find a position in Calcutta or elsewhere so he was able to escort Khair and her mother on the long and arduous journey home. According to my sister who heard it from Khair, it took him several weeks even to organise the caravan, so many possessions had they all acquired whilst in Calcutta.'

'Including elephants to carry them?' asks Emily.

'Oh indeed, and bullock carts of various kinds, camels perhaps; I gather they made very slow progress until, after some months, they were within a week's journey of Hyderabad. But then Khair took it into her head to go and live in a small town on the coast instead of returning home while Mr Russell, having secured her accommodation, went on alone.'

Nur stops, seeing that Emily has become thoughtful. She hopes that there will be no difficult questions for she is trying very hard not to utter too many untruths.

'I suppose my grandmother did not want to return to her old life as it was before she met my father,' says Emily at last. 'Which is entirely understandable, under any circumstances, but especially, perhaps, since she had enjoyed some freedom from the constraints of her family and upbringing. One gathers that in Mahommedan countries women's lives are closely restricted.'

Nur sees the surprise and admiration writ clearly on Kitty's face as she regards her daughter, and herself wonders where Emily has learnt this. From reading? Discussions with Walpole and Richard? The young are full of surprises, she thinks, and how we do need them to advance our own understanding. In any case it is a credible account which Emily may never question. Yet so very far from the truth.

'So then what happened to dear Mr Russell?' Emily enquires, her voice full of disdain. 'He prospered, that much I know.'

'After a few months in Hyderabad he found a position in Madras, which you may know is one of the East India Company's three largest settlements, the others being Calcutta and Bombay,' replies Nur. 'And though not as large as Calcutta, there were many more Europeans there with whom your "dear Mr Russell" soon felt quite at home and, for some reason, many more English women than in Calcutta. It was not long before he met one particular young woman, a Miss Jane Casamajor. In short, he fell in love and wished to marry her.'

'English?' Emily enquires doubtfully.

'Half English, half Portuguese,' Nur clarifies. 'In fact Faiz heard from her son that Jane's somewhat mixed parentage was for some time a hindrance to the romance, for she had a great-grandmother who was a Malay. Henry's father had made publicly known his abhorrence of mixed race relations saying that he would never let any of his children marry anyone *contaminated by one streak of black.* So Henry did not dare to reveal his desire to marry this Miss Casamajor—'

'Ah, this is the man I recognise!' Emily interrupts.

'And Miss Casamajor broke off the engagement in consequence.'

'I am delighted to hear it!' Emily laughs. 'I certainly would not deign to marry someone who was reluctant to declare his love for me on such an account, which could indeed one day be the case.'

'But somehow Henry and Miss Casamajor did make up and were married,' Nur continues. 'But most tragically, she died within two months of some sickness and the heartbroken Henry, for whom one must surely at this point feel some sympathy, went home to England for a year to recuperate. It was on his return that he was made Resident at Hyderabad and reinstituted many of your grandfather's customs. And by this time Khair and her mother were also living back in the city.'

'So were they again on close terms?'

Emily's question is entirely innocent but it silences Nur, and she sees that Kitty too looks agitated, no doubt wondering how she will respond.

'Oh no,' she says at last. 'I do not think that can have been possible, it was not like Calcutta, not at all. It would have been quite improper. But my sister writes that he did invite Khair back to live in her old house at the Residency, near the end of her life. She died there you know, with my sister and her mother at her side.'

Emily is entirely satisfied with this story and she is willing to accord Henry Russell some credit. 'That was kind of him,' she acknowledges. 'I am glad to think that my grandmother's tragic life ended in a place where she had once been so happy.'

'And I,' agrees Kitty softly. But her face is troubled and it is clear that for her there remain many unanswered questions which she will not ask in Emily's presence.

Nur wishes she were close enough to take Kitty's hand. Instead she reaches for the bell. 'It is time we took lunch' she says. 'Which will be in the morning room for I believe Mrs Redford has been busy preparing the dining room for our supper party.'

***

The sun has moved on from the east-facing room where they had breakfasted some hours before. But there is a warm fire and the dimness of the light and smallness of the room seem to make it conducive to confidences.

'It is so like a novel, the tale that you have told us,' Emily muses, her full plate as yet untouched in front of her. 'I thought so before, even more so now I have heard the rest of my grandmother's story. She risked so much for the sake of love and when all those she loved were taken from her she lost the will to live. One might cavil at the simplicity of this conclusion were one to read it in a book.'

'Perhaps you should attempt to write it,' Nur suggests, toying with the small amount of food to which she has helped herself. She has never needed to eat much. 'And in the process you may discover how much one has to omit or invent in order to please the reader and make credible the story.' And, she thinks, perhaps prepare yourself for the less simple account which you may one day hear.

'Oh...' Emily waves her fork in protest, while she chews and swallows a mouthful of bread and butter. 'I do not have such talent,' she responds at last. 'And besides Walpole says I waste my time in reading novels when there is so much that is factual to read, so many new discoveries to learn of and theories about them to understand.' She pauses but, before anyone else can dispute this opinion, rises to her own defence. 'But I think that to learn of other lives is just as important, to compare and relate them to one's own, to broaden one's perspective, to give one the impression of having lived in other places, other times. Even if the accounts of those lives are the products of an author's fancy.' She cuts decisively through a thick slice of cold lamb.

'Bravo!' Nur smiles. 'It is I believe why Mary wishes to learn to read, for she loves my stories and knows how small her knowledge of the world. But I say again, why do you not attempt to write? It has become much easier for a woman to be recognised as having such capabilities. Do take some fruit, Kitty.' She indicates a large bowl full of new apples and ripe Victoria plums.

'Thank you.' Kitty selects and begins to peels a succulent Russet. 'Perhaps, Emily, Walpole would be more satisfied were you to read works of biography? No doubt one may take similar lessons from these besides factual information of an enlightening nature, the subjects of biography being invariably chosen for their having attained some importance and influence on the events of their time.'

'But even biography is selective I am sure and their authors have a particular prejudice whether in favour of their subject or not,' objects Emily, pushing aside her empty plate. 'Or they are very dull. But I am sure you and Walpole are right, dear Mother, and I should be more serious. But then,' she continues with renewed determination, 'What of the unimportant people whose lives may have had as much value and significance and interest. They will not be chosen for any biography but they can appear in novel form, if in part or in some other guise.'

'Like your grandmother.' Nur aligns her knife and fork side by side on her plate. 'At whose death there was, my sister wrote, more public display of mourning in Hyderabad than anyone could remember yet she surely will not appear in any history book. Do you know,' she sits back in her chair. 'it has just occurred to me that I am related to two very successful writers though I have only read the one. *Confessions of a Thuggee*, do you know it? It did cause quite a stir some years back. My son sent me a copy, which you may borrow Emily if you wish.'

'Philip Meadows Taylor.' Kitty nods. 'I found it too full of violence myself but James was fascinated. As was our Queen as I remember! Which perhaps helped its rapid success. We have it at home Emily if you do not read it here. But, Nur, what is your relation to him?'

'He was married to my great-niece, my sister's granddaughter Mary Palmer, daughter of William, the one-time associate of your Mr Russell. Mary died young many years ago and he has not remarried.' Nur shakes her head sadly and, not for the first time, thinks how much she would like to have known Mary and her cousins and siblings. So large a family there where here she now has none. 'Nor has he written other works of fiction, I think, though he remains in post in India, in the employ of the Nizam. I fancy he would have much liked your father, having a similar sympathy with India, its customs and its people.'

Emily's eyes are wide and dark with wonder. 'Another tale awaiting the telling,' she exclaims. 'And full of strange coincidence besides. But who was the other?'

For a moment Nur is puzzled. She frowns. 'The other? Ah! I meant my husband's second wife, a Frenchwoman and therefore very likely unknown to you. Adele d'Osmond, the writer of many popular novels and celebrated in artistic Paris circles I gather, where her position was enhanced by my husband's title. And his fortune.' She cannot prevent the note of bitterness from entering her voice. 'But that is yet another tale!' She forces a smile and pushes her chair back from the table. 'Come, let us return to the sitting room where I would rest a little and you, Emily, may read whatever you choose! Before you go and help cook our supper if you are so determined.'

30

Later that afternoon Kitty and Nur are walking in Mrs Redford's pleasant garden behind the house. The wind has dropped and they are sheltered by a high old brick wall which, they have agreed, must be responsible for the late blossoming of so many flowers. There are dahlias of every hue and both double and single-petalled varieties, high-reaching blue agapanthus and yellow sunflowers, a few remaining spikes of orange montbretia under the apple and pear trees and, in and around it all, purple Michaelmas daisies, no doubt defying the gardener who will surely have attempted to control their self-seeding spread earlier in the year. Indeed, as Kitty has pointed out, many of its heads are again in seed waiting for the slightest breeze to disperse next year's plants and flowers to every corner.

'Our gardener at home would root them out before they have finished flowering if we didn't keep an eye on him.' She laughs and then sighs. 'How the years fly by!' She sits down on a low stone bench in a corner, leans back against the wall behind her, closes her eyes and raises her face to the last rays of the rapidly setting sun. 'Somehow I do not feel ready for winter this year though I have no particular reason for melancholy. Unlike you, my dear Nur,' she adds quickly. 'I am so sorry, I spoke thoughtlessly. Such a year you have endured...'

Nur holds up a hand to stem Kitty's apology and sits beside her. 'I was going to say,' she says, 'that unlike me you should have many more springs and summers to look forward to. And don't feel sad for me,' she continues before Kitty can protest. 'For I have been in this world long enough. You will feel the same I daresay if God spares you to so great an age.'

'I hope so.' Kitty is silent for a few moments. 'So now do please tell me about my mother's last years after Mr Russell abandoned her in that town. Did she ever see him again, until those last two weeks before her death? Was there any contact between them or did he just leave her?'

Nur takes some pages from her pocket and spreads them carefully on her lap.' Henry Russell wrote to your mother from Hyderabad every two or three days,' she begins. 'Though his letters were short and matter of fact and not of love or of missing her. But after eight months, when he obtained the post in Madras, he travelled via Masulipatam and stayed with her for some weeks. This is what my sister wrote.

"Khair is overjoyed, and having found more comfortable housing is in more optimistic mood. She also believes that Henry will intercede for her return to Hyderabad but I fear that is unlikely, for the scandal surrounding them is only beginning to die down and he will not wish to compromise his new position.

"He is more likely to oblige her in securing the return of the painting of her children whom naturally she misses so very desperately. She says she begs him constantly to intercede with the artist in Calcutta. Apparently Mr Chinnery had 'borrowed' it, claiming it required repair or some such. Besides this, Khair is glad that in Madras Henry will now be nearer to Masulipatam and able to visit her more often. But I fear he will not. "'

'And did he?'

'He did not. Ever again. Not in Masulipatam. And he wrote less and less and finally deputed his faithful brother to do so on his behalf, blaming the lack of a Persian scribe in Madras. He tells Charles to enlist the help of an old servant whom he says Khair will remember.'

Kitty is astounded. 'Whatever did the servant think of helping a foreigner to write personal letters to a Muslim woman of high birth?' she says. 'Henry Russell's insensitivity would shock me had I not long since had personal experience of it.'

'When he failed to return to you the very same portrait.'

'Strangely enough,' Kitty agrees. 'But do go on.'

Nur takes up another of Faiz' letters.

"'Khair's mother, Sharaf-un-Nissa, has gone to Hyderabad herself to plead her daughter's case to be allowed to return to the city. She has been gone near a month and Khair is desperately lonely. If only I could visit but it is so far that I would have to stay

longer than your brother-in-law would wish me to be away from him. Besides there is the great expense of the transport of myself, some attendants and our various baggage and the Lord knows best where has gone our earlier wealth. "'

Nur picks up another page. *"'Sharaf-un-Nissa has returned to Masulipatam but with empty hands. There is to be no reprieve. Could Khair's situation be more desolate? I fear the answer is yes for she added a postscript with the following devastating news. "Mr Charles Russell has paid us a visit which under any other circumstances would have been a welcome relief of the tedium of our lives for he is a pleasant young man. However he brought with him news with which Henry entrusted him thinking a letter inappropriate. Which is certainly true. Henry is to be married!!Oh my dear friend how I need your support and sympathy. God be praised I have my mother's company once more. Though I need no-one to tell me that I must give up all hope of regaining Henry's love. But what then is to become of me? I am twenty-three years old and it seems my life is over. Your unfortunate friend, Khair-un-Nissa."'*

Nur takes some time smoothing the creases in her sister's letter and replacing it with the others, allowing Kitty to ponder these long ago words of her mother. Words which Khair cannot have guessed would ever reach her daughter's ears. Kitty jumps to her feet and walks a few paces away from Nur before turning, her eyes full of tears.

'But within – two months was it? - the new Mrs Russell was dead. I wonder how my mother felt then?' She paces up and down, both hands clasped to her heart, apparently heedless of a nearby blackbird which, perched in a small cherry tree, seems to be pouring out his soul in thanks for the passing day.

'Neither she nor Faiz make comment except in the most general terms,' says Nur. '"*Mysterious are the ways of God*" and "*even the mighty are not safe from sudden illness and death".*' She listens admiringly as the blackbird invents two more refrains, each repeated only the once, and speaks more brightly. 'But the next year, 1809, fortune of a sort at last smiled upon Khair and her mother. For the hostile Prime Minister died and they were allowed to return to their home in Hyderabad. And then the following year Henry returned to the city as Resident after his year of mourning in England.'

'Raising my mother's hopes again?' Kitty asks, hopefully. 'Did she at least see him before... before she died?'

'There was *some* communication with her household,' Nur is searching through the letters as she speaks. 'Mr Russell had apparently promised to repair a locket containing a lock of your father's hair but he manages to lose it and – this is the letter. "*Khair is distraught to have lost this precious memento. And both she and her mother were shocked beyond words at Mr Russell's lack of understanding. He has offered to make another locket – if they can send some more hair*"!

Nur gathers up all the letters. 'Let us walk a little,' she suggests. 'I am stiff from sitting.' She takes Kitty's arm and they set off down a path which is already in deep shadow.

'What a scoundrel he was.' Kitty takes a deep shuddering breath. 'And what happened then?'

'Nothing Khair wrote of to Faiz that Faiz thought worth the repeating to me,' she says. 'But after about two years when my brother-in-law retired from his position, my sister went with him to Hyderabad where they lived with William, their eldest son.'

'Whose daughter married Mr Meadows Taylor?'

'Yes indeed. William was by then very prosperous and lived in a large mansion opposite the Residency. No doubt my brother-in-law and Mr Russell would have met sometimes, and I suppose enjoyed each other's company, having in common their love of your father, in fact it may have been in this way that the business relationship between William and Mr Russell developed. Faiz writes only of how very sad Khair remains and how she spends as much time as she can with her at William's house or her own. So I am quite sure that the only time that Khair was in Henry's company was in 1813 when he invited her and Faiz to the Residency to meet a visiting Scots lady at that lady's request to meet some Hyderabadi women of rank. I will read of this to you.'

They have reached the top of the garden near the house. Nur holds the last sheets of Faiz's letters to a shaft of dim light escaping through the yet uncurtained kitchen windows. '*"Lady Hood was clearly impressed by my poor friend's gracious manner and spoke long with us about our life in the city. I think she must have known something of Khair's history, though whether of Mr Russell's part in*

163

it I do not know. Dear Khair roused herself so far as to determine on making her a dress which Mr Russell then spent some weeks in facilitating. As of old in Calcutta. But this time there are no meetings between them, he communicates only through others or in writing."

'So my mother developed no hopes of a reconciliation?'

Nur sighs deeply and reads on. ' *"I think if she had any such hope it was but a brief flutter, a faint recall of those earlier days. By this time she cared much more about the loss of her children and she and her mother wrote many letters to England begging that they be sent back to her."*'

'No-one told us,' whispers Kitty. 'They should have told us.'

Nur nods in sad agreement. ' *"I think that it was her pride that gave her the strength to return to the Residency to meet the Scots lady,"'* she continues, ' *"but soon after this her condition weakened still further."'*

'So perhaps her hopes had been raised again only to be quashed for ever?' Kitty's normally soft eyes flash and her nostrils flare with anger. She paces up and down the paved terrace behind the house. 'Anyone but Mr Russell might have foreseen how inappropriate was his invitation, when the purpose was only to gratify some English curiosity. Scottish curiosity. He treated my mother and your sister like freaks in a circus show.'

'You will be even more angry to hear also that he did finally have your painting in his possession but had not returned it to your mother. Never did return it, I guess, or you would not have discovered it in his house so many years later.'

'So she never saw it again?' Kitty stops pacing. 'Oh, but you told me that she did return to the Residency, just before she died. So she could have seen it there.'

'Yes. Your mother wrote to Mr Russell telling him she was dying and he invited her back to live in her old house, the lovely Rang Mahal in the Residency gardens.' Nur shivers. 'It's getting chilly, let us go back into the sunshine.' She leads the way to the one corner of the garden that is still bathed in golden light where they settle on a seat large enough for two. She finds a page amongst those in her hand. 'This will make you a little happier,' she says and again starts to read.

164

' "*Every day for the following two weeks Khair lay on her bed, which was the very same bed as that on which she had given birth to her daughter Noor...* "' Nur looks up briefly to see that Kitty has understood before continuing,' "*... and gazed at the great painting of her children as if she could never see enough of them. Finally, one evening as the sun set, she gave a great sigh, turned her face to the wall and passed away from us. Sharaf or I were with her throughout this time and both of us were there at the end. It is my only solace and I hope it was of some comfort to her.*"'

'Oh my poor mother!' Kitty wrings her hands. 'It is of great comfort to me that our portrait was with her at the end. Only it makes my heart almost break to consider her lying there. Rejected by the family in England, knowing she will never again see us in this life. I do think they were cruel, that they need not have treated her quite so badly. When Henry Russell had also abandoned her.'

Nur holds up her hand. 'Wait, I was about to tell you. They did relent a little. Unknown to her they commissioned and sent her two small portraits of you and your brother.' She stops, surprised to see that Kitty is nodding.

'But they arrived too late. Six weeks after my mother died. My grandmother told me this when we began our correspondence so many years later. Which, I must remind myself, was thanks to Mr Russell. And how overjoyed *she* was to have them. I was eleven, my brother thirteen at the time.' Kitty smiles sadly. 'I guess they are still there. I hoped someone would send them to me when my grandmother died.' She takes Nur's hand in her own and they sit in silence as the sun finally sets behind the neighbouring rooftops.

'We should go in, my dear,' says Nur. 'Our guests will soon be here.'

They stand as one and retrace their steps slowly towards the house.

31

Arm in arm with Richard, Nur leads her guests into supper. Kitty follows with Walpole and the two girls bring up the rear. Nur has noted the beginnings of some attachment between Richard and Georgina. There have been smiles exchanged, a special attention on hearing the other speak, a glow of happiness on Georgina's cheeks, the eyes of both bright. It is also apparent that Walpole is only too conscious of Emily's comparative lack of interest in him. He does not fire her heart , she thinks, however worthy he may be, and Emily is young and free to look around and choose her mate. How customs have changed in this country, thinks Nur, since she came here fifty, sixty years ago. And of course there is no comparison with her own youth in India when she expected to marry whomever her parents selected, although in the event she was married to the aged Nawab whose power overrode even their wishes.

Mrs Redford has truly excelled herself .The table is adorned with a fine arrangement of flowers from the garden set between two large candelabra. The silverware shines, the fine glass catches the light turning it into small rainbows and there are more candles on the sideboard. She has clearly brought out her best china over which the ladies exclaim as Mary helps her hand around bowls of lightly spiced parsnip soup.

'Mr Redford liked to entertain.' She smiles with satisfaction. 'And he always said if a thing's worth doing, it's worth doing well. But we have Emily to thank for the flowers, and it was she and Mary who worked up such a shine on the cutlery and glasses.'

'I enjoyed being useful,' Emily says quietly and Nur notices the surprise on Walpole's face. It appears to be a quality in her he had not yet noticed. 'But I confess I am glad you have employed another to assist with the washing up.'

'For which I must thank dear Helena,' replies Mrs Redford. 'As indeed for the spices which make a fine addition to the soup. Which Mary made.'

Richard lifts his glass of Madeira wine. 'May I presume to propose a toast? To our hostess and to Mary for their hard work in looking after us all.' They all raise their glasses before Richard continues. 'And to Fortune, though I had rather say the Lord God, for bringing us together, for which I am sure we all give thanks.' As they clink their glasses, Nur notices what seems an especially lingering look between him and Georgina.

After the soup plates are cleared, Mrs Redford and Mary bring in the next course: a large leg of lamb on a platter, its crisply browned skin giving off the heady aroma of rosemary, dishes of new carrots and runner beans and a large tureen of buttered potatoes. When everyone has been served and Mrs Redford and Mary have returned to the kitchen, Emily turns to Georgina. 'I have just started reading a new book, Georgina, set in quite another country and culture. Mrs Bennett has lent it me. It is called *"Confessions of a Thuggee"*.

'Ah!' Walpole interjects. 'The novel that caused such a stir when first it was published.'

'It may be a novel, Walpole,' responds Emily. 'But it has the most serious intent for in the foreword Mr Meadows Taylor says that he wishes to inform those abroad of conditions in India and also to help improve those conditions. And it is based on facts which he was in a very good position to know for he was in the employ of an Indian prince.' Emily's conclusion has the triumphant air of a challenge.

Walpole flushes but is too polite to pursue what is clearly an on-going disagreement.

Nur considers telling the company how her husband, who was also in the employ of an Indian prince, tried to improve conditions in India by importing practices from his European experience of soldiering and organisation. But Kitty speaks first.

'And, as Emily and I discovered earlier today, he was married to Nur's, that is Mrs Bennett's, great-niece Mary Palmer whose family have been in India for several generations.'

'Was he not *The Times* correspondent on matters Indian, at least until recently?' Richard enquires after the various exclamations of surprise and interest have quietened.

Nur does not know but Kitty is nodding. 'Indeed and my husband read out every one to me to the extent that I think they are perhaps my own memories! For,' she hastens to explain, 'the Indian prince to whom Emily referred was the Nizam of Hyderabad in which city I was born. And the accounts were always so vivid. But recently he stopped, having become an employee of the East India Company.'

'And therefore no longer free to report his observations,' Walpole concludes. 'Let us hope he retains his freedom of spirit however and does not lose his Indian sympathies. It seems to me that too many of the British now hold themselves aloof and are entirely certain of their moral right to govern. I have even read of the use of the word "nigger" in referring to the native people, which is not only intentionally disparaging but entirely inaccurate.' He stops abruptly, glances quickly at Nur and Kitty, blushes scarlet and covers his confusion in mopping at his chin with his table napkin.

To Nur's surprise, the ensuing silence is broken by Emily who reaches across to, though does not touch Walpole's hand. 'And *I* hope he writes more novels instead,' she asserts, which makes everyone laugh.

'I suppose the best writing involves a compromise between fact and imagination,' says Richard thoughtfully when everyone has finished eating. 'It is perhaps why I liked Carlyle's history of the French Revolution so much. It made one feel as if one were there so real are its descriptions, its attention to small details, which is not at all commonplace in books of history. The *'whiff of grapeshot'*. I truly felt I could smell it for myself.'

'Not my subject,' Walpole admits, a little ruefully. 'Though I have attempted and indeed learnt from his essay on Mohammed. I had not realised how rapidly the new religion spread in so many countries, or that now there are an estimated 150 million Mohammedan souls in the world.'

'Which perhaps accounts for the hostility of Christian nations, which might rather be termed fear,' observes Richard.

'My mother knows Mr Carlyle,' offers Emily. 'She visits him occasionally. when we are in London.'

There is a murmur of interest from the two young men.

'Oh, he was tutor for a while to two of my nephews.' Kitty's tone is dismissive but then she throws caution to the winds. 'I once travelled to Paris with him,' she says proudly though quickly adds: 'Together with my cousin's husband, Edward Strachey and of course a maid as female companion.'

Nur notes Emily's surprise, though she says nothing and Kitty quickly continues.

'And I am fairly sure that our brief trip, for it lasted but twelve days, was the inspiration for his books on the revolution, backed up I daresay by a great deal of research in libraries.'

'He is deservedly famous and much admired,' begins Walpole, 'attracting the great names of our times to his lectures and I guess private discussions. Only—'

He breaks off, embarrassed, and takes a drink of water.

'Only— ?' Richard prompts.

'Oh, you know, the recent controversy, over his assertion of the need for strong, I should say, dictatorial leaders. And the so-called Nigger Question, which in this case *is* about Negro people, the sugar plantation workers.'

'Poor downtrodden people, forbidden a true family life,' comments Georgina sorrowfully. 'What is Mr Carlyle's position? Surely he takes a similarly sympathetic approach?'

'Well no, as a matter of fact,' Richard corrects her. 'He argues that they have a duty to work hard to supply people in colder parts of the world like us with sugar - for our puddings!'

He ends with a laugh and a sweeping gesture towards a splendid example of the type which has just been brought in by Mary, almost staggering under its weight. Everyone turns to admire the great pie, which is topped with a pastry bird and spills out a rich mixture of berries when it is cut.

'Sometimes,' says Nur when all have been served, and feeling that Kitty's friend's reputation deserves some restoration, 'sometimes, people become a little contrary as they grow older, a little tired of the same old habits and opinions of the company in which they find themselves. I know I have. So I think if one were famous and much praised, one might tend to court a little criticism as a corrective to too much blind adulation which must be tedious, not to say stultifying.' Nur stops abruptly, surprised at her own eloquence. 'Anyway, ' she continues. 'I have long been grateful to Mr Carlyle for his translations from the German of my beloved Persian poetry, my own Persian having become too rusty for its proper appreciation.'

'You mean translations from Herr Goethe?' Richard nods.

'Yes,' says Kitty. 'Mr Carlyle was a great admirer of his, thinking him only second to Shakespeare as a writer in the European tradition. He was very proud when once, while he was still himself very young and almost unknown, Herr Goethe sent him a letter.' She smiles a little sadly.

I wonder what it is that she is recalling thinks Nur, and sees that Emily too is regarding her mother quizzically. 'I should like to hear some of that poetry again,' she says quickly. 'I have a book of Goethe's translations from the greatest Persian poet of all, Hafiz.'

Kitty rouses. 'I should like to read it,' she says. 'For I have long wished I had learnt more of my mother's culture, to which my father was also so very close. Sometimes I think I am only half the person I could have been. In appearance I may be 'hybrid', but in my mind I am almost entirely English.'

'Oh Mother!' Emily looks stricken. 'Is that really so bad?'

She might have said more had Nur not spoken. 'I too sometimes feel cut off from my origins, uprooted and still not entirely transplanted. I will find my books and we can make some study of them together tomorrow.'

'And I should like to join you,' Emily says quickly. 'For by your reckoning, Mother, there is a quarter of me, if not more, that lacks nourishment.'

She is not entirely reassured, thinks Nur, and is glad when Richard speaks out.

'I believe all of us would be better for a greater knowledge of other people and cultures,' he says. 'And look forward to future conversations with you on the subject, dear Mrs Bennett.'

Nur laughs. 'And to make a thorough convert of me I daresay!'

'Do not let him, Mrs Bennett,' Walpole interposes. 'He will tell you that it was not an angel dictating the words of revelation into the Prophet's ear, but a pigeon trained to find there grains of corn.'

'You do me a dishonour,' Richard protests. 'And that story is discredited.'

'I spoke in jest, dear fellow,' Walpole apologises before turning to Nur. 'Nevertheless, be warned Mrs Bennett, Richard can be most persuasive as I have cause to know. I believe,' he looks pointedly at his friend, 'I believe Christianity would be the better for its admissions of the truths of other faiths, which all must have some common roots. Not to mention assisting the furtherance of peace on earth of which we are sorely in need.'

'But then you are in danger of being accused of heresy!' responds Richard. 'Like my illustrious predecessor in this parish. You with all your fossils and their challenge to the Book of Genesis. I would think that, like most good English Christians these days, you should be more enthused by the notion that today's civilisation is directed by steampower, as Bentham would have it, rather than by divine revelation and wonder at God's marvellous Creation. Which was a comparison made by Carlyle in favour of Islam,' he explains to the rest of the company.

Walpole brushes this aside and speaks with increasing passion. 'But what if it is in our common roots that we will find the questions that only God can answer and science cannot? Most seriously I believe that to be the case and perhaps to be necessary for the survival of our religion, if not religion itself. '

'Oh Walpole,' Emily is the first to break the silence which follows his outburst. 'I do not know whether to call you an optimist or a pessimist. But if your strength of conviction could alone be sufficient to achieve such an end then it surely will be achieved. And I doubt there can there be any greater prize than peace on earth.'

She turns to address Nur, apparently unaware of the effect of her little speech on her admirer. Walpole looks, thinks Nur, already taller and stronger and prepared to slay any dragons if it would win his ladylove's hand. And she has remembered something, the truth of which seems suddenly very appropriate.

'"The world, my brother,' she declares, 'will abide with none
By the world's Maker let thy heart be won. "'

And everyone is momentarily silenced as they make sense of this each in their own way.

32

The next day after breakfast Emily has gone out with Mary, while Kitty and Nur are again strolling in the sunlit garden.

'Is it better to have continuing grounds for hopes which may slowly fade or to have them abruptly dashed?' Kitty muses aloud.

'There is a third possibility,' Nur holds up a hand to emphasise her point. 'To have continuing hopes without much basis which slowly fade away.'

'You speak of yourself?'

Nur nods. 'Some years after he left us, which was almost without warning, my husband proposed that I should return to live with him in France, taking the children, or at least my daughter with me. Our son was to remain at his school,' she says. 'It did not happen and when my daughter died, Benoit abandoned the plan so I think he perhaps only wanted me as her guardian. But for several years, while he was attempting to obtain our passports, which he could not do since there was again war between England and France, I never doubted that it was what I wanted to do. So I suppose in some way I had always hoped he would come back to me despite the fact of his marriage. I wonder what your daughter would think of such lack of pride and spirit! I should not make much of a heroine in her book I think.'

Kitty does not smile at this distraction. 'I thought I was to marry someone else,' she confides, 'as he had led me, and others in my family, to believe. We had spent so much time in each other's company and travelled abroad, as I told everyone last night. And even when he had offended my family, Isabella in particular, I believed that our relations would soon be restored.'

'You speak of Mr Carlyle?'

'Yes. But then one terrible day I discovered that he had proposed to another with whom he had been carrying on a compromising correspondence, despite assurances to my family and to me that it was only in the capacity of friend or tutor. And that was the end of it, even though she initially refused him.'

'And did you stop loving him ?' Nur stops and turns to face Kitty. She finds this hard to believe.

'No, I was ready to forgive him!' Kitty replies. 'When I heard she had refused him, I would have made every excuse for his conduct. But my family forced me to renounce him. So I knew there was no hope. And I did come to understand their concern to protect me from the scandal which might have ensued had his entanglement with another become widely known.' She reaches for the remaining petals of what has been a large and beautiful pink rose. 'If only someone had better protected my mother from Mr Russell.' She holds the petals to her nose and inhales deeply. 'But it was several years before I was ready to give my heart again, which was when I met my dear James.' She pauses for a moment in contemplation, crushing the rose petals in her hand, and then her face is transformed by a fleeting smile. 'Even though I heard quite soon that the Carlyles' marriage was not a happy one. They have no children, so you can imagine the conclusion that some drew.' She lets the petals flutter to the ground.

'Exactly as in my husband's case!' exclaims Nur. 'He even wrote me of his unhappiness. And his wife publicly denounced him and acted in ways that shamed him. She was certainly very different to me.'

'And I to Jane Carlyle,' says Kitty as they walk on. 'Many people have said that she is as clever as Thomas, so I know I could never have been the stimulating hostess that she is, attracting so many famous people to their house. But I am ashamed to say that I do take a little satisfaction in knowing that she has not made him very happy. Do you feel similarly?'

Nur stops. They have reached the back entrance to the house. 'Perhaps,' she concedes at last. 'But I should certainly have liked the chance to make him happy once again. Although then I should never have developed so full and independent a life as I had until recently. Benoit was very... fond of me, that I do know, and I suited his life in India very well. But perhaps he was never in love with me as he said he was with Adele.'

'And I don't know how deep were Thomas' feelings for me,' admits Kitty. 'But – I must tell you this before Emily returns. He did regret the ending of our relationship for I was the heroine of the only work of fiction that he ever published: *'Sartor Restartus.'* It is generally taken to be almost an autobiography if in very fanciful form and tells of a hero who loses his love, Blumine, to another. I was his Blumine, the Goddess of Flowers. His "Rose Goddess". The first time we really met was after he saw me in my cousin's rose garden.'

Nur smiles. 'The village people, where I lived until recently, called me "The Black Princess"! Though it is more inappropriate than your fond designation.'

Kitty frowns. 'I once heard myself described by Mrs Carlyle as "the Hindoo Princess". I believe she did not realise I could overhear.' She sighs. 'It is because we are strange to most people in this country. Certainly those living far from large cities and towns. The colour of my skin always goes before me, do you not find similarly? Until one is known for oneself, as an individual. Thomas was fascinated from the start by my hybrid family. In fact, that was what so alienated Isabella, his constant questioning. Why I could not understand except that he had been her children's tutor and therefore hitherto in an inferior position. Of course she knew how much the family wished to hide.'

Nur nods. 'Which then you did not.'

'And not only concerning my mother, which you have told me.' On sudden impulse she throws her arms round Nur and kisses her on the cheek. 'I will tell you all another time. I should like to tell you. For I feel you are my closest friend ever though we have but recently met. And which is so very unexpected since I came here to solace you.'

Nur returns her kiss and then takes a slim volume from her pocket. 'I have found one of the books I wanted to show you. Shall we sit here a moment?' She opens the book at a place marked by a strip of ribbon. 'My son brought it for me this year. It is a new translation of Hafiz's *"The Gulistan"* by another celebrated poet, Sadi.'

'"The Gulistan"?'

'It means the Rose Garden,' replies Nur and laughs at Kitty's surprise, 'Quite a coincidence is it not? But listen, I think you may like this particular story. Won't you read it aloud?'

Kitty takes the book and clears her throat. *"A devout personage had bowed his head on the breast of contemplation, and was immersed in the ocean of the divine presence. When he came back to himself from that state one of his companions sportively asked him – 'From that flower-garden where thou wast, what miraculous gift hast thou brought for us?" He replied, "I intended to fill my lap as soon as I should reach the rose-trees, and bring presents for my companions. When I arrived there the fragrance of the roses so intoxicated me that the skirt of my robe slipped from my hands."*'

'*Wah, wah!*' says Nur, and Kitty opens her mouth to make some observation but she is interrupted by Emily who bursts from the house bearing a copy of *The Times* and closely followed by Walpole.

'Forgive my intrusion so early in the morning, ladies,' he says, 'but I met Emily in the town having learnt news which you should know and she said I must come with her to tell you.'

Emily holds up the newspaper to show its headline. '"*BRITISH FLEET ENTERS THE BOSPHORUS!*"' she announces and then passes the paper to her mother.

'Then Britain is preparing to engage?' Kitty scans the front page.

'There will be negotiations,' replies Walpole. 'Backed up by our naval presence.'

Kitty looks up, her expression tense. 'And I see there may be need of land forces.'

'And so James may be called to fight,' Emily states.

'And you may wish to hasten your departure for London in order that you may see him in case of that,' Nur responds at once.

Then Mary comes into the garden. She is holding a letter. 'This has just been delivered, ma'am,' she tells Nur. 'For Mrs Phillips.'

Kitty takes the letter and slits open the seal. 'It is from my husband James,' she says at once. 'I had not expected him to write.'

'What does he say, Mother?'

'He enquires when we plan to depart for London,' she says. 'He hopes it is soon. I shall reply instantly. And then we must make our arrangements.' She turns to Nur. 'Though I shall be so very sad to leave you.'

'So shall I,' agrees Emily. 'Very sad indeed. I must make note of these books for future study. And I should write to Georgina. Though I hope there is time to say farewell in person to her,' she adds. 'And to Richard.'

'Oh, we shall all make our way to the coaching inn if at all possible,' Walpole assures her. 'There is a carriage at two o'clock, Mrs Phillips. I took the liberty of making enquiry. Would you now have me make reservations?'

'Thank you, Walpole. That would be most kind.'

***

In the late afternoon, not long after Kitty and Emily's departure, the house seems unnaturally quiet and empty but Nur is not as sad as she had expected. It is good to sit again by the fireside with only Mary for company.

'Shall you read these books to me, ma'am?' Mary is leafing through Nur's books with careful respect. 'Until I have the skill to do so myself.'

'I shall,' Nur promises, 'for I know you will appreciate them. But first,' she pauses and her voice takes on a teasing note, 'do you not want me to tell you a story as I promised?'

Mary looks up from her preferred position on the hearthrug in front of Nur's chair. She frowns, not at once comprehending.

'The true and tragic story of great love between a man and woman born into such different civilisations that one might say they came from different worlds.'

'Of Mrs Phillip's mother and father,' Mary remembers, and leans back contentedly against her mistress' knees.

PART III

Reunion

33

1853 London, November

The barouche swings into Eaton Place, Belgravia, an imposing terrace of four and five storied white stuccoed residences of classical design.

'I always forget how grand is Maria's neighbourhood,' comments Emily. 'But I would miss our wide sea view if I should stay here for long.'

'I should not care to live in London either,' Kitty agrees. 'But I think you will find other compensations, and indeed hope you will. There are altogether more distractions and entertainments which ought to be much to your liking now that you are eighteen and able to participate.'

'Oh I know, Mother, I am sure I shall have a wonderful time and am very grateful to Papa for arranging our visit. And cousin Maria of course for accommodating us all. Look,' she points a little further along the street. 'There she is, awaiting our arrival.'

They come to a halt at the porticoed entrance to Maria's London residence and Maria, wrapped in a shawl, comes down the steps to greet them. Kitty is struck by how aged she appears, whether due to the cold light of a grey autumn evening or because she is seeing her in a different setting. How soon she may also depart this life, she reflects, as have Isabella and Julia within the past few years, whilst instantly thinking how cruelly cut short was her mother's life who, born the same year as Maria, could still have been alive. She feels a rush of affection for this cousin to whom she has never felt quite so close despite for some time now being near neighbours in Devon. Maria was soon married after her own arrival in England and then frequently living abroad with her naval officer husband.

Maria's driver hands her down from the carriage and she steps forward eagerly hands outstretched.

'My dear Maria,' she exclaims, kissing her on both paper dry cheeks. 'It was exceedingly kind of you to send your carriage to the coach station to await our arrival. I did not relish the thought of competing for a hansom with passengers from so many other recently arrived coaches.'

'As I thought,' smiles Maria. 'Without James there to assist you. He is coming soon I gather. Emily,' she steps aside to embrace her, 'I shall be very happy to have your young company and that of your sisters. My own girls do not visit often enough despite being nearer to here than to Torquay. Come in, come in.' She ushers them up the steps ahead of her to the entrance, where her housekeeper bobs a curtsey to the newcomers and awaits instructions.

'The baggage, please, Mrs Potts,' says Maria. 'And then some refreshments.' She crosses the spacious hall, indicates where Kitty and Emily should leave their wraps and leads the way up the first flight of wide carpeted stairs that climb to the very top of the building yet are well illuminated by a large domed skylight. 'I'm giving you the whole third floor,' she explains, 'but while your bags are being taken up I thought we would have some tea.' She turns at the first landing and leads them into a large sitting room which stretches across the whole front of the house and has high windows from floor to ceiling. A small fire burns brightly and a candelabra is already lit on a side table next to a couch where a discarded embroidery frame suggests that Maria has been sitting. She indicates the candles that flicker as they approach.

'This house is not well-positioned to enjoy the afternoon sun,' she explains. 'But in winter it matters less when the days are in any case short. I think we came too early to town this year and should have preferred to remain a little longer in dear Devon. But the Admiral wished to be *au courant* you know, not trusting the newspapers to tell the truth about this war. I daresay he is right!' She subsides onto the couch, indicating that Emily should sit next to her while Kitty takes a neighbouring chair. She takes Emily's hand in her own. 'What a lovely girl you have become!' she says. 'The young men will be falling over themselves to become acquainted.' But then she again addresses Kitty. 'John is at his club now in St James',' she tells her, 'gathering what information he may of the progress of the fleet. While I care only about the safety of my son. I do not think I could survive the loss of another. My only other.'

'No indeed,' Kitty shakes her head sadly. 'You have heard from William?'

'Only what the world knows, that they are close to Turkish shores awaiting the outcome of the fighting on the Danube and in the Caucasus. But tell me of your mission. Was it a success despite being cut short? Was this other bereaved mother comforted by your visit?'

'She was certainly appreciative,' Kitty begins. 'Though in truth I was as much the beneficiary with such news of India that I had never expected.'

'OH? I daresay that was very welcome to you,' Maria says but without interest.

Kitty knows that Maria played little or no part in the family conspiracy of silence concerning her mother. But she cannot resist telling of what still seems to her such a miraculous coincidence. 'Mrs Bennett's sister and my mother were close friends,' she says. 'As were their husbands who were both English and Company officers besides holding similar views concerning British relations with the Indian population and its rulers.'

She speaks lightly and is not about to enlarge on these points but Maria gives a, possibly exaggerated, shudder. 'The less I think of India the better,' she says. 'Since our darling Thomas died there. And despite its being my place of birth. I know we all owe the most of our fortunes and positions to the colonies and should be appreciative of the fact, but I am only thankful that I shall not have to visit any of them ever again.' There is a soft cough at the door and a very young maid enters hesitantly, carrying a heavily laden tray and clearly anxious that she spill none of its contents.

'Ah! Tea! Thank you Millie. Put it on this table,' Maria indicates. 'And you may leave us. Perhaps you would pour, Emily, and we may continue our conversation.'

Millie withdraws, very nearly colliding with the Admiral whose large person and enthusiastic entrance oblige her to shrink against the doorframe before making a rapid escape back downstairs. Sir John Louis, the 2nd Baronet Louis, advances on his guests with arms outstretched. After some years on half pay following Trafalgar, he is only recently retired from his last position as Superintendent of Devonport Dockyard when he was promoted to the rank of Admiral. He has had a successful if not illustrious career. His father was only a Rear Admiral. Kitty finds herself smiling as soon as she sees him.

'My dears, my dears! Wonderful to have you here, eh, Lady Maria? Wonderful!' He bends to kiss each on the cheek and then stands and surveys them all with his back to the fire. 'Getting nippy out there,' he observes. 'Journey alright, Kitty? You've made quite a trek of it by all accounts. Trust it was as hoped and intended.' Pleasantries exhausted, he plays with his moustache and looks thoughtful.

'Well?' Maria prompts. 'What news? We are all agog for who knows if young James may also be drafted.'

'Ah!' Sir John's ruddy face breaks into a satisfied smile. 'Russkies not doing as well as they hoped it seems. Bit inconclusive as yet on the Danube but in the Caucasus the Turks are holding up rather well.' He walks to the window, cocks an imaginary telescope and peers south eastward as if he might be able to see this for himself.

'So we won't have to become involved?' Maria asks.

'Early days, early days,' responds her husband, returning to his position by the fire. 'So far the Sultan seems to be in charge. But then it all depends on what the Russians do next, whether they go on the offensive. We've reserved the right to act if they get aggressive. But meanwhile your son is safe.' He wanders back to the window and again gazes out, though this time in contemplation. 'Lucky fellow,' he adds.

'He means lucky fellow for being in the thick of things,' Maria interprets. 'Never mind what danger may be in store.'

'My James is just the same,' smiles Kitty. 'And he is much longer retired.'

'Uncle John,' Emily speaks up. 'I do not understand the terms of our engagement. Is not all fighting 'aggressive'? In which case should we not already be assisting the Sultan?'

Sir John laughs and slaps his thighs. 'Ha ha! Out of the mouths... Well but we are, we are. He is deeply in debt to us, or else he could not afford these operations. But still we do not wish him too much success.'

'We don't?'

'No no, bless you. Do you not think we welcome the weakening of the Ottoman Empire? I suppose you are too young to know how unlikely this once seemed.'

'So we are glad if the Russians fight them for us?'

Sir John becomes serious. 'Up to a point, up to a point.' He frowns and walks to another window and, hands behind his back, leans and peers in the opposite direction. 'Need to get ready though, ships and men, just in case.'

'Oh do sit down, John.' Maria's tone is peremptory. 'You are making me nervous. I am sure they are doing just that, even without your valuable assistance. And Emily please give him some tea.'

'I think Emily and I should go and unpack,' says Kitty. 'And change our clothes. I must say it is a relief to know that we shall not again be soon moving on.'

***

'Mother! Did you hear the doorbell?' Emily runs to the window of her mother's bedroom where she is helping empty their trunks. 'Oh I cannot see for the porch obscures the door.'

'We shall know soon enough,' Kitty observes but it is to an empty room for Emily has run out. She is leaning over the banister.

'There is a helmet on the hall table,' she exclaims. 'I do believe – oh it is! Oh James!' She races down the stairs and flings herself into his arms. 'James, James! It's been so long! I do believe you have grown even more. To think I was once the taller!'

Kitty watches lovingly as James swings his sister round before setting her down. He does look even taller than the last time she saw him, though it may be partly the effect of the close-fitting green jacket and dark blue trousers of his uniform. He plants a kiss on Emily's forehead. 'And you will never catch me up!' he tells her. 'Uncle John!' He turns to shake hands with the Admiral who has come out to greet him.

'My boy!' Sir John claps him on both shoulders. 'Your aunt says you must go straight up and see your Mother who has made such haste to come to London to see you. Needlessly by all accounts.'

'Oh?' James looks briefly puzzled but then he catches sight of Kitty at the top of the stairs, a great smile of gladness lights up his handsome face, and in three bounds he has joined her.

'Oh my darling!' She reaches up and takes his face in her hands as he bends to kiss her. 'I do believe army life suits you.' She stands back to admire him, then reaches up again to feel the width of his shoulders while he continues to smile down at her. 'Come and tell me all your news.' She takes his hand and leads him into her room. 'Can you stay for dinner?'

'Sadly no.' James flings himself down on the bed, his boots just hanging clear of the grey silk coverlet. 'It's some regimental anniversary tonight. Oh I say,' he bounces a little on the bed. 'This is very comfortable after my iron bunk in the barracks! But I have leave tomorrow and in fact have a good deal of leisure at present. So I may escort you around some of London's many sights and entertainments. I say, Emily, I did think we might go riding in the morning in the Park, you know, Hyde Park? If you have not forgotten how. And if Mamma does not mind. I know where we can get you a mount and I daresay Aunt Maria can find you some sort of habit. Mama?'

'Of course you may,' Kitty smiles. 'And I'm sure your father will like to join you one day, though I daresay he will make it an opportunity to regret your not following him into the cavalry.'

James' face clouds. 'Oh Mother, does he still grieve? You know I wanted to make my own way. And I am rather a good shot, though I say it myself.' He raises an imaginary rifle to his shoulder and points it at his sister. 'Bang! You see?' For Emily has obligingly fallen down silently beside him on the bed, where he leans over and tickles her until she giggles and rolls away.

'Children, children!' Kitty's reproof is not serious and they know it.

'And I do have some fine Hussar friends to whom I can introduce my little sister if she will not be too overwhelmed.'

At this latest provocation Emily sits up, takes a pillow and proceeds to beat him around the head with it until Kitty finally calls a halt.

34

It has been a cloudy morning with a wind strong enough to dislodge a steady cascade of leaves from the plane trees that line the street. They join earlier falls in a soggy carpet on the pavement. There was some rain during the night but none seems imminent and Emily could not be dissuaded from the proposed ride with James. The Admiral has taken himself off to some coffee place in Piccadilly to read the newspapers and since breakfast Kitty has been sitting with Maria, making occasional conversation about their respective families, Mary's wedding preparations and their plans while they are in London. She was at first glad of the prospect of a restful day but soon becomes restless. She tells herself it is due to her need for exercise, as opposed to travel, but there is one place that she particularly wishes to visit. When finally the sun makes a hazy appearance, casting a faint shadow of the window frame across her lap she makes up her mind. She could set out in another direction and turn back as if on impulse but she will feel less guilty if she does not dissemble.

'I should like to call on Mr and Mrs Carlyle,' she announces. 'It is two years since I saw them. Won't you come with me?'

Maria looks up from her needlepoint, her expression inscrutable. She knows of Kitty and Thomas' ill-fated romance although her opinion was never consulted. Perhaps for this reason, she has never questioned Kitty's desire to see him on her infrequent visits to London. Indeed she enables it and has never yet accepted the invitation to accompany her, however curious she might be to see him now that he is famous. She shakes her head.

'Thank you, dear Kitty,' she says. 'There are a few household matters which require my attention, James and the girls being soon expected. Tomorrow, I believe?'

She speaks casually, without especial emphasis but Kitty feels herself blushing and busies herself with putting away her own needlework in its bag. She stands. 'I shall be an hour, an hour and a half at most,' she says brightly. 'Back in good time for lunch.'

***

It is not warm outside but Kitty's spirits lift as gusts of wind ruffle her hair and whip up flurries of yellow and orange leaves around her hurrying feet. She lifts her face to the dappled sunlight and sees it will be some time before the next scudding cloud obscures it. She smiles. She had forgotten the attractions of autumn. When she turns down towards the river the air becomes altogether brisker and she is forced to hold on to her bonnet and battle the hundred yards or so to the Embankment.

As ever she feels a deep pull of attraction to the river and has always thought that, were they to live in London, it would have to be within sight. It is not so much the busyness of it, the comings and goings of ferries and tugs, the coal barges going up on the tide to its highest point at Richmond, the flat-bottomed skiffs rowed by white-trousered and shirted Cockneys plying for trade and every bit as stylish as their Venetian counterparts, she thinks. She and James have been to Venice and a few other Italian cities besides as well as the Lakes and mountains. It was a trip that had started from the sorrow of Julia's death, almost exactly six years ago she realises, but become a sort of honeymoon being their first holiday without the children. No, what she finds so thrilling about the Thames is its vital connection with all the waters of the world, which when near she feels herself.

Walking along the banks of the Thames also always reminds her of those many long ago walks with Thomas, when he had confidently looked forward to boating trips together, to the future together in general in fact, or so it had seemed. However, his eventual reasons for choosing this location had been much more practical, he said, the cost of the rent being a great factor. Nearly twenty years ago it had been, she calculates, and, the last she heard, they were still paying the same amount, despite the great improvement in his fortune. Then Chelsea had long fallen from its pinnacle as home to royalty and become unfashionable (though '*genteel*', Thomas had said)but there were in consequence plenty of large and well-built old houses. It was quiet and almost rural, their own house backing onto the fields and avenues of what had been a bishop's pleasure ground.

But it had changed, and not for the better as Thomas had told her on more than one occasion. He had always needed peace to work. The Embankment itself, once a quiet place to stroll, is now lined with coffee shops and eating places attracting people and their vehicles in droves, at least on summer evenings. Kitty can hear his complaint: '*How many parrots, dogs and dandy carriages do continually announce themselves!*' And there were street musicians such as organ grinders who, he had once claimed, he often paid to go and play elsewhere. But it is quite quiet today and she is almost tempted to escape the wind for a while and stop for a coffee. Instead, she crosses the road and turns up Cheyne Row, '*pronounced Chainie Row*'.

The street is lined with biennially pollarded lime trees. '*Beheaded*', Thomas once described them as, '*giants with tawtie wigs on*', which Scotticism Kitty could not understand though she had no doubt that it was apt. There are also iron railings all up one side of the pavements to prevent passers-by from falling into the half-sunk basement storeys of the houses. Kitty half expects to find the road dug up yet again for the installation of water or gas or sewer pipes. If one believed Thomas it was never without a team of workmen digging holes and trenches.

There is certainly noise of some sort of construction being carried out but it is further up the street. Banging, hammering, the clanging of metal, the shouting of men directing their joint activity … as she draws nearer to number five she sees the source of this disturbance and almost laughs aloud. For it is Thomas' own house that is being assaulted. It is without a roof, that is a proper slated roof, for there are tarpaulins stretched across timbers to keep out the rain, and its front is encased in a cage of wooden scaffolding connected by ladders up and down which clamber men carrying lengths of timber, hods of bricks, buckets of something that is heavy on the ascent, sand or cement perhaps. And further horror, the front door of the house is propped open and other men are going in and out carrying similar materials.

He cannot be there, she decides with disappointment, he could not bear such an uproar. The slightest repainting of the house he always refers to as '*an earthquake*', sent not by Nature but by Jane whose exclusive job it seems to be to keep order in the house. Kitty has seen enough of his impatience with such intrusions to have felt a moment or two of pity for Jane, who surely only has his ultimate comfort at heart. No more than a moment or two however for, whenever she visits, Jane always makes her feel like just another intrusion on Thomas' valuable time. *What does Thomas tell her?* she wonders. Does she know how his face brightens when he sees me, how much we laugh together, whilst neither of us intending any disloyalty to our lawful spouses. She is fairly sure of this. But today, she resigns herself, she will have to put up with only that icy stare and curt response. She will have to leave her card and visit another day. Unless Thomas has been sent away by Jane on a long holiday as he sometimes is. She is a good selfless wife, Kitty firmly tells herself. Then she stops suddenly and steps quickly behind a tree as both Jane and Thomas come out of the house, cross the road to step into a hansom which she had not noticed waiting on the opposite side and are taken off in the direction of the King's Road.

Kitty steps from her hiding place and considers. Surely both of them cannot be going out for long leaving the house so open to strangers and besides, as far as she could see, there had been only one small piece of luggage. Perhaps Thomas is going on a short holiday while the worst of the building works are completed, such as the roof replaced, and Jane is only going a short distance with him, to a train station very likely. Even Thomas will be glad for once of the invention of trains which will take him far away from all the chaos in a very short time. Otherwise, she knows, he does not like them, the dirt, the forced proximity to strangers – oh Thomas, she thinks, how did you become so ill-tempered? Rather than pursue this thought, Kitty hastens up the road, rings the bell and, as no-one answers, steps in and herself places her card in the brass dish on the hall table. Then she hurries back to Maria's.

***

187

Emily and James are back before her, seated side by side on a couch looking through what must be an early edition of the Evening News. Maria still sits where Kitty left her earlier in the morning. Emily has changed out of her riding habit and her hair is tidy but her cheeks are still flushed from the morning's air and exercise. Her eyes are bright as she looks up to greet her mother. It is perfectly clear that she has had a good time.

'Oh Mother,' she jumps up to give Kitty a hug. 'You can't imagine how exciting it was in the Park. So many soldiers marching about and galloping up and down, I swear it was like a re-enactment of Waterloo. Without the guns, of course.' She falls back on the sofa next to her brother while Kitty sits near them on a chair and unpins her hat.

'Hardly,' James laughs. 'There were a few platoons of foot soldiers drilling. Otherwise it was just mounted parties like ours out for pleasure.'

'Oh but did we gallop! I quite thought I should fall off!' exclaims Emily but hurriedly continues. 'Not really, Mama, mine was a very steady horse, I do hope I may borrow her again.'

'She belongs to our Colonel's daughter,' explains James. 'Who is away at school. So I am sure we may go out again.' He looks sideways at his sister. 'Although if it is only soldiers Emily wants to see there are other places besides.'

Emily slaps his arm in protest. 'We are trying to decide where to go this afternoon, Mother. What do you think? A matinee? A carriage ride around Westminster to see James' barracks? Shopping?'

'I should go to the theatre,' Kitty replies. 'For your father will want to see the barracks and the girls, at least Mary, will certainly want to go shopping. But tell me,' she enquires casually. 'Were there others in this 'party' of yours?'

'Three or four,' Emily shrugs.

'Making six altogether,' her son clarifies. 'My best Regimental colleague, Uniacke, another good Devon man, Norman Fitzgerald Uniacke to be precise, and not yet eighteen but a good strong reliable fellow. He came with me to fetch Emily's horse. And three fine Hussar friends we met by chance on the way'.

'Riding the most splendid great black horses,' Emily puts in, suddenly enthusiastic. 'So full of spirit, you could tell, the way they tossed their heads and flared their nostrils—'

'She means the horses,' James helpfully explains, returning to his newspaper.

'Oh so witty,' his sister responds. 'But they were from the 8th not the 7th, their uniforms were different to Papa's—'

'She means the men,' says James, without looking up.

Maria exchanges a look with Kitty and raises her eyebrows.

'Stop it, James,' Kitty says firmly. 'I hope your father and I may meet some of these new friends of yours. I should like very much to form a clearer impression of your life here.'

'What did you do this morning, Mother?' enquires Emily after a short pause. 'Stayed in and talked to Aunt Maria I daresay?'

'No, when the weather improved I went out for a walk and on impulse called in on the Carlyles.' It is Kitty's turn to dissemble a little. 'Only I just missed them.'

'James,' says Maria before anyone else can respond. 'Do please invite anyone you like here. I am sure your father would be very interested to speak with them, whatever regiment they may be from. Don't you agree, Sir John dear?'

The Admiral has just appeared at the door, home from his morning's excursion. He crosses the room and, rubbing his hands, stands warming his back at the fire. 'I always agree with you, My Lady,' he says fondly.

'James' friends,' explains Maria. 'He should invite them here, should he not?'

'Oh yes, splendid, capital, army fellows are a fine lot, don't mind meeting'em at all.'

'Thanks Aunt, Uncle,' James replies. 'I'd like to.' But then his voice again takes on a teasing tone. 'Even though they are a junior service, Uncle?'

'What's that? Oh most certainly, young man. Can't beat a fighting man, army, navy, cavalry, infantry, you know where you are with them, straight up, plain-speaking, it gives you backbone you see, the discipline, being with other men…' his voice trails away and he appears for a moment lost in thought. Then he comes to with a start and hastily regards his present company. 'Not that we don't need the ladies too. I'm sure I do.' He looks at his feet, and rises up and down once or twice on his toes until there is a soft tapping at the door at which he looks up with an expression of relief. 'Lunch ready, Millie?'

'Very near sir.' Millie replies so softly it is hard to hear her. 'There was a caller sir, only he wouldn't come in, for Mrs Phillips.'

Sir John is confused, Emily and James are again immersed in the newspaper, only Maria and Kitty turn to see that Millie is holding a silver salver on which there is a note. Kitty stands and goes to take it. 'I should just freshen up before lunch,' she tells the company in general. 'I shall be down in a few minutes. Thank you, Millie.'

She waits until she reaches her room before she unfolds the small piece of paper and reads: '*Greatly regret missing you. Do come this afternoon if you can. Jane is on her way to Scotland. T.*'

35

Emily and James have gone to see a play which is finishing its run this week. Kitty has sat for an hour after lunch with Maria and John.

'I told you that note I received was from Mr Carlyle?' she reminds them. 'I think I shall go now and visit him but take a cab, having already walked there once today. Won't you come, Maria?'

'Thank you but no, dear. A friend might be calling in. But as Mr Carlyle is on his own, perhaps you would like to invite him here to supper one evening? I should like to see him again, after so many years .'She does not consult Sir John who is gently snoring, his head lolling sideways in his chair. 'I will ask Mrs Potts to send someone to find you a cab.'

'Oh I can walk a short distance,' Kitty insists. 'I'll find one in the Square, won't I?'

Within a quarter of an hour she is at Thomas' front door which is now closed. In fact all is quiet, there is no sign of activity whatsoever. She rings the bell and a maid whom she does not recognise leaves her waiting in the hall while she goes off to find Thomas. 'Likely he'll want you to join him in his study,' she says.

Kitty looks around the hall which is surely darker than it had been. Where she remembers pleasant old-fashioned pine-panelled walls, now there is paper darkly varnished to resemble wood. The lamps have not yet been lit and the only light therefore comes from the far end where a partly glazed door leads into the garden. A creak on the stairs alerts her to the maid returning and behind her descends Thomas. Before either can reach her however a small white and black spotted dog slithers down the steps past them and, tail wagging furiously, jumps up against her.

'Down, Nero, down,' Thomas admonishes him fondly.

'I had forgotten you have a dog.' Kitty rubs its head. 'Or maybe you did not when last I visited. And the hall looks different.'

Thomas grimaces. 'One of Jane's less successful projects. I was rather fond of the old wainscoting but I suppose one has to keep up with the times, keep up appearances, with so many visitors...' He takes her hands in his and looks her up and down, appraising, and she feels her heart miss a beat. There are lines of fatigue round his eyes which have lost their youthful intensity and their colour has faded to what one would surely now call a light blue. But his bearing is still light, his movements vigorous, his manner purposeful. 'Still blooming, Kitty,' he observes softly. 'And still the same wonderful tresses with not a grey hair in sight. You are well. 'It is not a question.

'You *have* changed, Thomas,' Kitty observes, disengaging her hands and stepping back a pace as if the better to survey him. 'But it is not for the worse. You are certainly not grey...'

'Perhaps it is the beard?' Thomas suggests. 'Another concession to fashion about which I am unsure, though it saves a little time in the mornings.'

'And very handsome it is too!' she exclaims.

He flushes, looks gratified for an instant, then frowns and Kitty returns to less personal a topic.

'What is this current project of which there was so much evidence earlier when I called? And what has become of all your builders? This morning it was a hive of activity.'

Thomas grimaces again. 'They are scoundrels, the lot of them, and as it is Friday afternoon, I daresay they have extended their lunchbreak in some public house. Besides taking advantage of Jane's absence. She being better than I at keeping them up to the mark.'

'She is gone on holiday?' asks Kitty doubtfully.

'Oh no! Her uncle is ill, dying I fear. And she is very fond of him, having long lost her father.'

'Oh I am sorry,' Kitty murmurs. 'Then you do not know how long she will be away.' She observes a respectful moment or two of silence before continuing. 'And this project? You are having a new roof?'

'More than that.' He sighs. 'A new room. An attic room. A new and larger study. If it is ever completed. Come, I will show you. Nero,' he picks him up, 'you must stay in the parlour.' He carries him, protesting, into a room that opens off the hall and closes the door firmly, then leads the way up the solid old broad staircase. He stops on the first floor and opens the door to what has always been his study but which now appears in a state of flux. There are piles of displaced books along one wall and the desk has been moved to one corner to make room for several new pieces of furniture, currently swathed in white cotton dustcovers. 'This is the other part of the plan,' says Thomas. 'It is to be our drawing room, it has been enlarged, to accommodate our entertaining. We were becoming a little over-crowded down in the parlour.'

'Oh but it is charming,' Kitty exclaims, stepping inside. 'And that is the screen Jane made.' She tries to keep the false note from her voice. I think she had just completed it last time I came. How many pictures are affixed to it?'

'Four hundred.' Thomas' tone is curt. 'It kept her busy awhile.'

Kitty smiles, too broadly. 'Oh it must have.' She gazes around. 'Surely the windows are different also? Taller?'

'Yes indeed. We shall be very grand.' Thomas stops abruptly. 'Though surely not as grand as your cousin's house.' He pauses. 'Nor your own, I have no doubt. I daresay your Captain has built you a palace. Come.' He proceeds up the next flight of stairs and stops at the foot of yet another which is in the process of construction.

'Actually, being of Italianate design my house is more like a *palazzo.*' Kitty cannot let this slur on James go unchallenged. 'And Maria wishes to invite you to supper,' she remembers, her voice sounding strained to her own ears. She is a little breathless from the climb. 'The day after tomorrow. Shall you come?'

He looks at her doubtfully. 'Will all your family be there?'

'I daresay,' she replies as lightly as she can. 'One daughter is with me. My husband and the other two girls arrive tomorrow. And my son is presently stationed in London. Maria said she would very much like to see you again after so long. With Isabella and Julia gone I think she feels she is now the family's representative.'

He inclines his head briefly to one side. 'Then please thank her. I should be glad to come. Now take care, hold to the wall side,' he indicates, 'for the banister is incomplete.'

There is also as yet no door and they step straight into what will be the largest room in the house if lower-ceilinged, when there is a proper ceiling. It is presently draughty and dusty and Kitty cannot repress a sneeze but Thomas beckons to her to follow him across the unvarnished floorboards until they are beneath a rectangular opening in the roof of the house.

'Here,' he says proudly pointing. 'This is the whole reason for the upheaval.'

Kitty peers upwards. 'So that you will not be distracted by the view?' she asks doubtfully.

'No no,' Thomas replies. 'Look here.' He points to the window surrounds. 'There will be two panes of glass fitted double with a space between and also,' he walks to the far wall, 'there are double walls.' He taps the wall and cocks his ear in satisfied expectation of the echo which proves his point. . 'You see? There is a space between. An air chamber. To prevent the transmission of sound. It was my idea.'

'So it will be quieter?' Kitty understands at last. 'You will have more peace in which to write. As well as more space.'

'Exactly. You have no idea how much noisier Chelsea has become. No sooner had the pianist next door moved – you remember the pianist? - than the neighbours took up chicken husbandry. In London!' Thomas' tone is a mixture of outrage and disbelief. 'It is all the craze I gather, keeping fancy foreign bantam cocks.'

'Oh dear, how very distracting.' Kitty taps what she now knows is the inner wall and again hears a somewhat hollow reverberation. 'It is certainly ingenious,' she acknowledges.

'But you wonder if it will function?' Thomas frowns. 'So do I when I consider the despicable workmanship I have observed. Why, the other day five Irish workmen fell through the downstairs ceiling bringing cartloads of dust with them as you can imagine and narrowly missing poor Jane.'

'My goodness! What a shock she must have had!' Kitty stops, suddenly uncertain as to Thomas' mood for there is a glint in his eyes and a humorous curl to his lip. 'But five!' She blinks in disbelief and bites her lip to prevent a smile.

'Five!' Thomas gives a short bark of laughter before becoming again sober. 'Of course it could have been a tragedy.'

'Yes indeed.' Kitty shivers. 'Where do you work now there is so much upheaval in your home?'

'Oh,' Thomas sighs. 'I have begun a new and very great project which fortunately requires me to visit libraries and other places of research. But come, you are cold, let us go and sit in the garden where there should still be some sun and I will tell you.'

***

It is warm enough at the foot of the narrow garden where the shadow of the tall house has not yet reached. There are two wooden seats and a small table on which the maid has placed a tray. Kitty pours cups of tea for both of them and hands one to Thomas.

'I am going to write a life of Frederick the Great,' he tells her. 'Last year I even made a trip to Germany and you know how I dislike travel.' He stirs his tea vigorously.

'I rather thought you found it gave you inspiration.' Kitty finds herself unwilling to permit what seems to her this perverse misremembering. 'As when we visited Paris?'

'Ah! Paris!' He flushes before adding, as if in explanation: 'We were young.'

There is a moment or two of silence and Kitty changes the topic. 'I see you have yet another new maid,' she observes. 'Is it so unpleasant a position? With only the two of you to care for?'

'Oh.' Thomas fumbles in a pocket and brings out a pipe. 'I daresay between Jane being too particular, though she hardly descends to the kitchen, and me being too intrusive, for I always smoke a last pipe there at night—'

'Really?' Kitty finds this odd.

'It is warm down there,' he explains. 'And the maid makes my night-time porridge and so does not have to bring it up to me.'

'So what happened to the last maid? And how long did she stay?'

'Less than a year. She ran off with one of the workmen. Despite our having just had gaslight fitted in the kitchen.'

Thomas's voice rises with indignation at this betrayal and Kitty cannot prevent herself from laughing aloud. 'Oh Thomas,' she says at last. 'And wasn't there one who actually gave birth in the kitchen without either of you being aware she was pregnant?'

Thomas busies himself filling and lighting his pipe. 'Maybe,' he acknowledges eventually and then he smiles. 'I do so love your laugh Kitty, even when it is directed at me. I always did.'

'And you work too hard,' she says softly. 'Don't you think?'

But this he will not acknowledge. 'It is my life,' he says simply. 'And it is my duty. For, once I have conceived of a subject I cannot let it go. Once it is in my mind, it has to be written.'

Kitty finishes her tea and replaces her cup and saucer on the tray. She notices that the shadow of the house has almost reached them and stands. 'I must go,' she smoothes down her gown. 'Sadly the days are becoming short and the sun will soon be setting.'

Thomas stands also. 'I will come with you and find you a cab,' he offers. 'But might we not have time do you think to walk a short while? By the river?' His tone remains light but he regards her with sudden intensity.

'I should like that,' Kitty agrees. 'I always enjoyed our walks by the river.'

36

Nero is ecstatic at this additional outing and pulls Thomas along the embankment beside the river where there are evidently many interesting smells, from the investigation of which Thomas is frequently required to pull him.

Kitty looks ahead at the looming structure of Battersea Bridge silhouetted against the darkening western sky.

'Perhaps as far as the bridge?' she suggests. 'We could walk out a little way over the river. I have missed being near water these last days.'

Nero is less enthusiastic, indeed he is afraid and baulks at trusting himself to the ancient wooden structure through the slats of which the river can be seen. Thomas picks him up and soothes him.

'I have told him I am sure he could swim if he did happen to fall in,' Thomas says fondly. 'But his mind is made up that it is a dangerous place and in some ways he is correct.'

'The poor woman whose throat was slit whilst crossing, some years ago?'

'Oh I had forgotten that. I was thinking rather of the frequent collisions of vessels with the bridge's supports and resulting drownings which the design of the bridge has caused.'

Kitty stop and peers over the balustrade at the wooden pillars encased in wooden struts that hold up the spans of the bridge at frequent intervals. 'It is certainly not the most elegant,' she observes. 'Not at all like the bridge at Kew.' She pauses a moment to see if Thomas will comment on that long ago occasion when they had walked together across that bridge on their way to visit Isabella and he had first upset her with his questioning about their family, but, since he does not respond, continues. 'Though painters such as Mr Turner have deemed it worthy of a portrait.'

'While navigators detest it,' Thomas responds. 'The supports are overly large and close together,' he indicates, 'so that it is difficult to pass through safely, particularly in a swift tide. But also it is too close to the bend in the river.'

'Oh?'

'Have you never observed? Come.'

He takes her arm and leads across the road where the view upstream is soon curtailed indeed by the Thames' sudden southward curve. Kitty watches as the two crewmen of an approaching barge swiftly lower its main mast and red-brown sails to pass safely beneath them. Her gaze is then arrested by the rapid illumination of rows of small lights in an area of trees on the northern river bank.

'Oh look, Thomas. How pretty that is.'

'Cremorne Pleasure Gardens?' His tone is full of disdain. 'A principal attraction responsible for bringing such crowds to this once peaceful area.'

'Amongst them my family I fear, my children were delighted by it.' Kitty smiles at the memory. 'We came some years since, by road so I had not at first recognised its location. It is truly a most attractive place with lakes and walkways and pleasure pavilions where music plays, the so-called Crystal Platform...'

Thomas shrugs. 'We have never been there,' he says, 'preferring more natural pleasures, though hard indeed it is to find them in this restlessly growing city.' As if in similar protest, Nero makes his own restless movements in Thomas's arms. 'Come, we should go before it is quite dark.' Thomas begins briskly to retrace his steps towards the Chelsea embankment where he sets down the little dog. Kitty hastens after him.

'I too love natural pleasures,' she observes. 'But surely the one need not exclude the other?'

'In my opinion,' replies an unsmiling Thomas. 'Insofar as I have observed, a delight in artificial pleasures is a sign of an immature or uneducated mind. As you said, your children were delighted.'

'*And I delighted in their enjoyment*,' thinks Kitty and reflects that Thomas has never known such pleasure. He will not know quite what he has missed and yet, she realises, he may regret the lack of offspring. His tenderness towards Nero might suggest this. Perhaps in addition the gossips were wrong about the lack of relations between Thomas and Jane and some other circumstance was responsible for Jane's infertility, in which case she feels considerably more sympathy towards her than she ever has before.

'Nevertheless I was not averse myself to strolling in such pleasant semi-cultivated surrounds,' she asserts. 'For a paved path is certainly preferable to a muddy track, particularly in winter. Most particularly if you are encumbered by skirts as are half the population. Perhaps you would be happier in a smaller town or city whence you can access open countryside more easily? Although you would lose the benefits of well-stocked libraries, besides the company of other educated, cultured minds. The social life in small towns is limited , we are often quite dull. And you meet constantly with so many celebrated personages, not to mention the fact that I am sure they are mostly your devoted admirers which must give you considerable encouragement.'

Thomas grunts. 'Too much admiration is bad for the soul,' he observes. 'Remember poor Irving.'

'Nevertheless,' Kitty insists. 'I believe you must in general enjoy your many visitors, else you could discourage them, like your recent neighbour, Mr Turner, who I have heard became quite a recluse in his later years.'

Thomas smiles briefly. 'And went by the name of Mr Booth. Wherein, I daresay, lies half your explanation, that he was not married to the woman with whom he lived so long.'

'Perhaps,' Kitty acknowledges. 'But my point remains. You need not receive so many visitors if you do not wish to.'

'Oh,' says Thomas and passes a hand across his forehead as if to clear his thoughts. 'Do you know sometimes I think our company would be just as great were I to withdraw for Jane is equally able to sustain debate on a variety of subjects. In fact, very often it is she who steers the conversation, fashioning balls which she throws to me to play with.'

They have reached the King's Road where eastward-bound cabs are plentiful at this hour of the day having transported passengers from their West End occupations and excursions. Thomas hails the first and helps Kitty in, retaining her gloved hand a moment longer than is necessary.

'Until the day after tomorrow.' He bows and stands away to allow the carriage to move and when Kitty looks back to wave to him he is already striding away, Nero trotting rapidly behind him.

In the short drive to Maria's, Kitty has time to reflect on the bleak and mechanical vision of his social life that Thomas has conjured which, if accurate, seems to her as far removed from natural human discourse as Cremorna Gardens from uncultivated countryside. She also realises that she did not tell him what brought her to London this time and in particular that she has discovered why her family were so determined to prevent communication between her brother and herself and their mother, which once he had been so determined to discover.

37

'Oh my darling!'

James leaps to his feet to greet Kitty as she enters the sitting room where Maria is suddenly entirely preoccupied with her sewing. Sir John is dozing, a newspaper lying on the floor at his feet.

'How long it seems since we parted.' James embraces Kitty with a passion she has forgotten.

'Oh and I have missed you. So very much.' She kisses him quickly on the mouth then stands away.

'And how was Thomas?''

'Ever more crotchety! He is just embarked on another magnum opus.'

'Maria tells me he is invited to dine.'

'Oh yes!' She turns to her cousin. 'Maria, he was most gratified and accepted at once. She turns back to her husband. 'His wife is away.'

'So I gather.'

'Where are the girls? Upstairs I presume?'

'Repairing their *toilette* or some such.' James smiles. 'Is that what one says? One does feel quite dirty after a long train journey.'

'I must go up and see them,' says Kitty but before she can move there is the sound of rapidly approaching footsteps, the door bursts open and Bertha runs in. With a shout of joy she throws herself into her mother's arms and is followed more sedately by Mary who kisses her mother on the cheek. Sir John contrives to slumber on undisturbed.

'I am very happy to see you, Mother,' says Mary. 'I hope you have had a pleasant time.' She checks and corrects herself quickly. 'If pleasant is the correct description in the circumstances.'

'It was, it is, thank you. If surprisingly. Mrs Bennett and I discovered we had a lot in common. Bertha, you are throttling me.'

Kitty disentangles herself from her youngest daughter and leads both girls to a settee where she sits between them, an arm around each. 'But I am very glad to see you again.' She hugs them both closer and casts a happy glance upwards to include James who is standing with his back to the fire and smiling at them. 'Emily and James have not yet returned?'

'They may be delayed in traffic,' Maria suggests. 'It is the disadvantage of attending a matinee.'

Bertha reaches both hands up to hold her mother's face and forcibly turns it toward her. 'Can we go to the theatre? Can I?' she begs.

Kitty looks down into the astonishingly blue eyes of her youngest daughter who, since she was a baby, has always thus demanded her attention. 'I daresay it depends upon the nature of the play,' she replies. 'What does Papa say?'

'Papa says we must discuss all our plans together, because there will be no satisfying all of us all of the time.'

The three adults laugh which finally wakens Sir John who is momentarily taken aback to find himself in so much company. 'Sorry, m'dears.' He busies himself picking up the discarded newspaper and folds it carefully before putting it on a small table next to him. 'Never used to drop off like that. No offence intended.'

'None taken,' James assures him. 'It's warm in here, I'm feeling quite sleepy myself. I daresay we shall all sleep well tonight after our journey.'

'We shall dine early,' Maria declares. 'So that you are well refreshed for tomorrow's excursions wherever you decide to go.' She stands. 'I am going to dress for dinner. In one hour? I am assuming James and Emily will by then have returned.'

***

Dinner with all the family together has always been a lively occasion and today the more so due to their long separation. There is much to catch up on, to enquire about, to discuss. Frequently, Kitty finds herself an amused onlooker, the conversation being so fast-moving and intense. She has forgotten how much she enjoys her children's company and it is a delight to see them enjoy that of each other. She basks in her good fortune and exchanges contented glances with her husband who is also often silent.

When finally they are alone together in their room she gives an exaggerated sigh. 'Our children are exhausting are they not!' She is sitting at the dressing table unpinning her hair. 'But how wonderful it is to be together with them again. They make one feel truly alive.'

James comes and stands behind her, winds her hair around his hands and lifts it up so that he can kiss the back of her neck. 'Which only seeing me does not?'

'Don't be a tease,' she admonishes him. But his eyes are sombre, she sees, he needs reassurance, perhaps the more so since she has visited Thomas at the first opportunity. She had thought to do so, she tells herself now, before he and the girls arrived in order to be done with it, to free herself of further obligation. But on re-examination her motivation is less transparent. She wanted to see Thomas again, she admits, to enjoy that feeling of his continuing regard for her, however much she doubts whether their marriage would have been a happy one. She stands and turns to James, puts her arms around him.

'You gave me a new life,' she says carefully. 'What I meant is that young people being less mindful of the past, live more in the present. They understand it better than we do. And they are also the future which means that through them we too will have a part in the future, even after we have gone. Life goes on, I suppose that's what they make me feel and that is good. But,' she begins to unbutton his shirt, 'there are other ways in which I can feel more alive.' She nuzzles his now exposed chest and helps him remove his jacket. 'Which only you understand.'

Some time later when they are lying contentedly in each other's arms, and she is very nearly asleep James stirs. 'I haven't asked you about your visit,' he says. 'Mrs Bennett was happy to see you I gather. And you are glad you went to see her?'

'Oh most definitely. Much more than I imagined. She read me letters, from her sister, about my mother, one letter even quoted my mother's exact words which it was marvellous to hear as you can imagine. They were very close friends in my mother's last years and I was so glad to know my mother had others to care for her, besides her mother of course. Only...' Kitty sighs deeply.

'Only?' James prompts.

'She was so very sad. I think she died of sadness. And now I know why.'

'Because she had lost you and your brother.'

'And perhaps blamed herself.'

'Really?'

'Yes, that's what I have discovered.' She takes a deep breath. 'Less than a year after my father died, when she was in Calcutta, she became increasingly close to another Company officer, who had been my father's assistant in Hyderabad.'

'The one who had your picture all those years? Henry something?'

'Henry Russell. Yes. They became lovers. And it was a great scandal. But worse than that, he soon abandoned her and married someone else, though the lady died a few weeks later, and for some years my mother wasn't even allowed to live back in Hyderabad.'

'Phew.' James gives a low whistle. 'What a story. No wonder indeed that she was so very sad. And I suppose it does explain why your family broke off relations.'

'They certainly couldn't tell us the truth when we were children,' acknowledges Kitty. 'Just as I have not told Emily by the way. Nor ever shall I think .'

'No. Though Russell is as much to blame.'

'Oh James!' Kitty exclaims. 'You are wonderful.'

'Hmm. That's good to know.' He kisses her forehead. 'And later? Would you have wanted to know? One would imagine that sometimes they may have felt tempted to tell you, to improve your opinion of them, Isabella in particular.'

'That's true,' Kitty says thoughtfully. 'Isabella, the principal keeper of the family secrets. And it was all to protect me. To prevent my reputation being tainted also. So as not to deter potential suitors.' She hugs him. 'I might never have secured you.'

James kisses her again. 'I wouldn't have been deterred for a moment. Once I had set eyes on you.' He raises himself on an elbow to blow out the candles on both sides of their bed. 'We'd better get to sleep if we are to keep up with our youngsters tomorrow.'

38

It is a fine autumn morning, a good day to go for a drive in a comfortable carriage but Emily is out of temper having been outvoted in the choice of the day's activities. She had at first been an enthusiastic supporter of her father's proposal to visit the site of the Crystal Palace where the Great Exhibition had been held two years previously and she had successfully persuaded him that after this they could make a larger tour of Hyde Park.

'It is a great pity that James is engaged in exercises all day,' she had said. 'But I am sure there will be plenty of other riders out, military and otherwise. Why, you might even see some from your old regiment.'

James had smiled at his daughter's apparent thoughtfulness but Kitty, a little alerted by her son's teasing remarks the day before, had suspected that Emily was being devious. She wondered whether she had actual intelligence that some of James' military friends would be there and even whether there could already be one particular young man whom she hoped to see. But then Emily had discovered that the Crystal Palace had in fact been removed from its old site and was presently being rebuilt south of the river near a place called Penge.

'It's practically in Kent,' she grumbles as they rumble over Westminster Bridge. 'And a very long way to go to see a building site.'

'Oh do stop complaining,' Mary snaps, setting her black ringlets jangling with her irritation. 'This is our first day together for such a long time. And it's not as if you have seen the Palace before. One would have thought you would be glad of the opportunity to obtain some idea of its grandeur. Why, the Queen liked it so much I heard that she visited it five times in the first month.'

Emily sniffs. 'It was not my choice not to visit the Great Exhibition. You left me behind. To look after Bertha. While a third of the British population did go to see it in all its glory.'

Kitty reaches across the carriage to pat Emily's hand. 'You know that Bertha had been unwell and we thought the expedition would be too strenuous for her. There were ten miles of exhibits and crowds and crowds of people. Perhaps we were wrong. But do look now, there is a fine view of the new Parliament buildings across the river. It is certainly a splendid building though I confess I still miss the old one and am happy some of it was saved from the fire.'

'And I read that it is still not finished. There is to be a very tall clock tower at the right hand side.' James gazes from the carriage window until they begin to enter less scenic suburbs south of the river. He turns to Mary. 'What do you remember most of our visit to the Exhibition?'

Her smooth forehead creases briefly in thought. 'Oh I think the enormous diamond,' she says. 'Lit from beneath by gaslight it seemed to be the source of a million rainbows. Quite dazzling. Was it not from India?'

'The Koh-i-Noor,' confirms James. 'Presented to our Queen during the Exhibition by a nine year old Maharajah who had lost his kingdom to the British.'

'Only nine!' gasps Bertha. 'And so noble to make so precious a gift. I should have wanted to keep it, especially if I'd already lost my kingdom.'

'I am afraid that I very much doubt if it was his idea or if he had much choice in the matter,' James replies but before Bertha can question him further Mary again responds to his earlier question.

'And I remember the beautiful fabrics, silks, velvets, lace,' she continues. 'And food in tins and French daguerreotypes of which I had previously seen very few. But mainly I was struck by the great size of the so-called Palace! And how light it was, on account of the glass ceiling and walls. One felt one was more outdoors than in.' She turns to Bertha who is frowning as she apparently tries to imagine this so-called palace. 'It was like an enormous conservatory, Bertha, like Papa wants to build on the end of our house. Indeed it was on one such that it was modelled as I recall.'

'Well-remembered,' her father is pleased. 'By Sir Joseph Paxton in Derbyshire, wherein to grow a giant waterlily for which there was no space at Kew Gardens. Bertha, you might remember seeing a drawing of his little daughter standing in the middle of its pond on one of its enormous leaves?'

Bertha nods doubtfully.

'I must confess I remember the toilet facilities with some affection, flushing toilets that cost a penny a time,' says Kitty. 'I do not know what I should have done without them. But I thought you would remember the elephant, Mary, you were very struck by it at the time. A huge stuffed elephant, carrying a *howdah,* a big canopied seat which in this case was of precious materials highly decorated with gold embroidery and pearls. '

'Like your father might have ridden on,' interjects Emily. 'I remember you saying. Except unfortunately it was an African elephant on loan from a museum in Bury St Edmunds. And in any case you won't see it,' she tells Bertha. 'Nothing like it. There will be nothing there. Not even the toilets. It is all dispersed whence it came.'

Bertha appears about to weep, whether with disappointment at the disappearance of all these reported marvels or hurt at her sister's unkindness. Eyebrows raised, mystified, James looks at Kitty who is now sure of her intuition. 'Do cheer up,' she reproves Emily. 'And don't be mean to your little sister. You have been such a considerate companion these past days. And perhaps we may still take a turn around Hyde Park on the way home, may we not, James?'

Emily brightens a little at this prospect and it soon transpires that she is in any case not entirely correct in her predictions, for the reconstruction works have made sufficient progress to give a very fair idea of the final outcome. James and Kitty walk up the slope of Penge Peak with the three girls close behind and reach a viewing platform beyond which onlookers are not allowed. They gaze up in admiration at an enormous glass building with a barrel-vaulted roof, bisected by a high transept with a further transept at either end .There is a notice explaining that it will be even bigger than its predecessor and will provide space for concerts and other events and house permanent arts and science exhibitions. James begins a conversation with a well-informed Scottish neighbour who also had visited the

Great Exhibition and who reveals himself to be a fellow enthusiast of all things mechanical. In particular he extols American inventions that were exhibited such as typewriters, automatic harvesters and sewing machines, and reckons Britain to be the beneficiary of the display of such ingenuity.

James is more patriotic. 'But do you not remember the hammers, the ploughs and reapers, the spinners and looms and the washing machines, all driven by steam, all British ?' he counters.

'I do!' responds his new acquaintance. 'But most of all I was impressed by the building itself, its rapid construction and relatively low cost—'

'The fact that it was designed entirely around the standard size of its thousands of plate glass panes so that each unit could first be assembled and then fitted readily with its neighbours!' James continues.

'The glass had to be made in France and Belgium,' points out the Scotsman.

'But what of the thousand iron pillars!' James counters. 'The tallest ever made. They were made in England.'

'Aye. So they were. And somehow the vaulted transept was made high enough to accommodate those two huge trees that people did not want felled. And this new one appears not only larger but even higher—'

'Mother, can't we move on?' Emily whispers urgently in Kitty's ear and, seeing that the other girls are also restless, Kitty intervenes.

She smiles at the stranger. 'I recall the sparrows that tried to reclaim their home in those trees,' she says. 'Until the Duke of Wellington suggested the employ of a sparrowhawk to discourage them. James dear, the girls and I will walk slowly back, I should like to take a closer look at the grounds.'

She turns to survey what is already a large and well laid out garden of descending terraces with water basins and fountains surrounded by ornamental balustrades and spies a group of workmen at some distance below whence rise the sounds of soft hammering. 'Look girls,' she points. 'Sculptors at work. I have often marvelled at how a lifelike figure can be fashioned from apparently unyielding stone. Let us see how close we may get and watch a while.'

Mary takes her arm to descend a wide flight of steps, while a happier Emily makes pretence of chasing Bertha along a more circuitous path which is edged with evergreen shrubs and small trees. They have just disappeared from sight when there is a sudden scream from Bertha and Kitty and Mary hasten after them in alarm. They find both girls gazing up at a very large stone lizard looming over them out of the bushes with a spike on the end of its nose.

Bertha turns to her mother, her face alight with wonder. 'A dinosaur,' she whispers as if it might be disturbed and pounce.

Emily bends to read from a small sign at the creature's feet. 'It is an "*iguanadonatherfieldensis, so named for the similarity of its teeth to those of an iguana and for Atherfieldon the Isle of Wight where many remains have been found which enabled the first skeleton to be reconstructed. Similar bones were found earlier in a Sussex quarry and others later in Maidstone in Kent.*" Oh Mother, this is more like!' she turns to Kitty. 'We saw many such smaller bones ourselves in a museum on our journey,' she explains to her sisters. 'And fossils. But I was disappointed having imagined I would see just such monsters. I wonder if there are others.'

She walks a little further to where the path joins another at right angles and almost collides with her father who has evidently discovered a faster route down. 'Look what we've found, Papa!' She takes his hand and pulls him back to see the monster.

'An iguananadon,' mispronounces Bertha, still wide-eyed. 'Emily says there may be others.'

'There most certainly will be,' replies James. 'Thirty three to be exact. According to my well-informed new acquaintance. But we shall have to come back next year after it is all finished if we wish to see them. Although I'm not sure if we should.' He affects an air of genuine indecision and begins to walk on which teases Bertha into a frenzy of persuasion.

'Oh we should, Papa, most certainly we should, please Papa, please.' She takes hold of his hand and jumps up and down at his side until she gains his full attention and sees his smile.

'And there is to be an Egyptian pavilion housing recent discoveries from the Pyramids that I should especially like to see,' James continues as the others follow close behind. 'How thrilling it must be to be the first to set foot inside a tomb that has been closed for thousands of years. And to find it full of wondrous treasure.'

Kitty notes his wistful tone and wonders if they have fortune enough to send him on an expedition. But he soon collects himself. 'How lucky we are to live in such an age of invention and discovery. Even you, my doubting daughter,' he addresses Emily, 'should agree that there are marvels unguessed at so few years ago.'

'Oh Papa,' Emily takes his other hand and lifts it to her lips. 'I do love you.' Which, Kitty notes with pleasure, makes James glow with happiness.

They have reached the carriage and are settled inside and moving off when Emily exclaims. 'I have a present for you, Papa, I had quite forgot. From Lyme. I think you will find it interesting.'

'Thanks to a very kind young man who had purchased the last copy but insisted upon giving it to Emily,' Kitty tells him.

'Oh?' James is intrigued.

'Surely an admirer?' Mary gives a knowing smile.

'Emily has an admirer!' Bertha chimes in.

'Stop it, all of you,' Emily retorts crossly. 'He was just being kind.'

'Though by a coincidence of acquaintance we did see him again in Horsham,' adds Kitty. 'He is the friend of a curate at a church near Mrs Bennett's house. His name is Walpole.'

'And,' Emily declares with great finality, 'he is also going to be a parson. Now do please let us make haste. Can you not tell the driver, Papa, that we are in a hurry and to take the shortest way to Hyde Park?'

39

After again crossing the Thames they continue straight along Birdcage Walk with St James' Park to their right. Just before they reach the end they begin to pass a large complex of new buildings and as they reach its gates a small company of mounted green-coated soldiers carrying rifles and in tight formation turns in ahead of them. Emily cries out in excitement.

'Surely they are from James' regiment. Oh do let's slow down and see, perhaps he is with them.'

'It is Wellington Barracks.' James nods. 'And there are only two rifle regiments.'

But the riflemen have dispersed and disappeared into one or other of the barracks buildings.

Emily clicks her tongue crossly. 'If we had been a minute earlier we could have seen if he were there.'

'Look, Bertha,' Kitty points from the opposite carriage window. 'Do you know that building? Do you know who lives there?'

Bertha frowns. 'Have I seen it before? Or only in pictures?' Her face clears as she remembers. 'Is it where the Queen lives?' she says at last. 'Buckingham Palace?' And when Kitty nods she turns in triumph on her sisters. 'You see! I said James is guarding the Queen. Why he lives right next door and was just riding back from the Palace.'

The carriage continues on past the palace with another park to their right and in through the gates of yet another and much larger park.

'At last.' Emily stands to peer eagerly out across Hyde Park from the window next to her mother. 'Look,' she points to some horse riders. 'That's where I went riding with James and his friends. Rotten Row it is called though I don't know why. Oh I do hope we may go again. I am sure James could find you a mount, Mary, if you wanted to come.'

'Thank you, Emily, but it is hardly why I have come to London,' Mary pulls her shawl more closely about her shoulders. 'I must see about my trousseau before all else. But no doubt Papa would like to go.'

'Of course he may,' Emily says with only the smallest hesitation that Kitty hopes James has not perceived. 'Oh but see ahead,' she leans perilously far from the window causing Kitty to seize hold of her skirts. 'Does that not look like a very large party of Hussars, Papa? Do look and see, their uniforms are dark, they could be blue could they not, of the 7th perhaps, your own? Or the 8th, the King's Royal Irish, for theirs are very similar I believe. Only they are allowed to wear their belts over their shoulder as a result of some victory somewhere, for which reason they are called "The Crossbelts" but it is too far for me to see such detail.'

She stands back to let her father take her place but he remains in his seat and exchanges a quizzical glance with Kitty. 'You have quickly become an expert on military regiments and dress, Emily. But you are right, the uniforms of the two regiments are very similar, especially the dress uniforms which are highly ornamented. They cost a small fortune.'

'Lots of gold braid, all across the chest,' Kitty recalls fondly. 'It was very eye-catching, your father looked extremely handsome. And their regiment was called the "Saucy Seventh" for their smartness and reputation in high society.'

James opens his mouth to respond to this ambiguous compliment but at the same moment the carriage jerks to a halt which causes Emily to regard him with consternation. 'Why are we stopping? I thought we should follow them. Where are we going?'

James opens the nearside door, climbs out and hands down in turn his wife and daughters.

'This is where the Crystal Palace was first constructed,' he tells them. 'I asked the driver to bring us here. I wanted to see how it now appears. And for you to gain an impression of its onetime size.' They walk along a path that leads to what appears to be a low stone wall, so low in fact that it is almost level with the surrounding grass. James leads them along its length, Emily trailing reluctantly in the rear.

'These must be the foundations of the original,' he says. 'I wonder if they will be put to another purpose. Over that way,' he points to the south and west, 'There is land set aside for several great museums, one of which I believe is near completion, so I do not think there will be another building here.' He turns to Bertha. 'Do you know how long are these foundations? How long was the side of the great pavilion? It was a very special length, connected with the year in which the Exhibition was held. Don't tell her.' He holds up a finger in warning.

But Bertha has no time to reply before the sound of an approaching carriage and a loud 'Halloo' makes them all turn. It is young James and a companion who jump down from their hansom cab even before it has come to a halt.

'I thought I should find you here!' James laughs. 'From yesterday's conversation. Mother, Father, my older sister Mary and not forgetting my little sister Bertha,' he indicates each in turn, 'I am delighted to present my great friend Uniacke, Norman Fitzgerald Uniacke to be precise. We saw you passing just now and as soon as we were dismissed we jumped straight in a cab. "*Celer et audax*" that's us. Swift and bold. Our regimental motto,' he clarifies.

The good Devon man is little more than a boy, thinks Kitty, and evidently still a ready victim of embarrassment. His rounded almost beardless face flushes as he bows and mumbles a greeting to each of them in turn. He smiles with greater confidence at Emily whom he has of course already met, before returning his gaze to Mary at whom he stares for some moments in very apparent admiration, while Mary's smile and cast down eyes tell Kitty that she is perfectly conscious of the impression she has made.

'Have you eaten, Mother, Father?' asks James. 'We are unexpectedly free of duties for the rest of the day. There is a reasonable hostelry just outside the gates on Knightsbridge where we could lunch. It is near that very good linen store, Harvey Nicholls? I thought Mary might wish to look there when we have eaten. My sister is filling her Bottom Drawer,' he says inconsequentially but with immediate effect. Poor Norman looks crestfallen and Mary appears none too pleased to have her engaged condition made public.

Her cheeks a little flushed, she turns to her brother. 'Oh there is no hurry if you have more interesting suggestions for how we may all spend the afternoon.' She smiles at Norman.

She needs to see Charles again, thinks Kitty, before she forgets why she accepted his proposal, and she resolves to ask James to write to his future son-in-law without delay, to suggest that he join them as soon as he may.

'As a matter of fact shopping might be just what you would find most interesting, indeed of some urgency if I know my sisters,' James junior replies. 'And I shall tell you why I think so when we have ordered our lunch for I am famished.'

***

'A ball!' Mary and Emily's response is immediate and enthusiastic. 'A regimental ball!'

'Requiring new dresses I imagine?' young James is clearly gratified at the reception of his news. 'Of course you must come too,' he addresses his parents. 'But sadly not young Bertha. Sorry, Bertha.'

'I know.' She sighs before addressing Kitty. 'But perhaps I may in any case acquire a new dress of some description? May there not be social occasions to which I am invited?'

'I am sure there will be,' Kitty assures her. 'In fact, cousin Maria was speaking of hosting some reunion of family and friends before we return to Devon.'

'Then may we all go shopping after we have eaten?' asks Emily. 'For much as I grudge giving my brother any compliment, his eye for fashion has always been good while we are sadly out of touch with London styles. I should like to look at different models and fabrics while you are with us, James, and then perhaps make arrangements through cousin Maria's dressmaker. May we? Mother? Father?'

'We have sent the carriage home,' James senior prevaricates, 'thinking we would walk as it is near.' He looks to Kitty for further direction.

'I believe there are cabs to be hired,' his son parries. 'I thought we could drive up and down Regent Street, perhaps stopping to walk in the arcade for one cannot see all the shop windows from the street, and then, if we have time, return via Pall Mall for there is a very good place, I have been told, by the name of Harding and Howell.'

'I am rather too tired to embark on so ambitious an enterprise,' Kitty responds, but, seeing the disappointment on her daughters' faces offers a solution. 'Do you think we may trust the young ones to make this expedition alone?' she enquires of her husband. 'After all, Mary is of age and Bertha may be too young to dance but she will make a fine chaperone, won't you my darling?'

'So long as they only look and do not buy,' James concurs. 'I cannot say I trust any of my children sufficient to give them an open purse!'

The suggestion is acted upon within half an hour when, having waved farewell to their offspring and Norman, Kitty and James walk arm-in-arm the short distance from Knightsbridge to Belgravia.

'I hope we have not been foolhardy.' Kitty wants reassurance.

'You think Mary is going to break that young fellow's heart?'

'He is *very* young. But I hope she will not be cruel and I had thought already to ask you if you would invite Charles to join us as soon as he may.'

James nods thoughtfully. 'They have been too long apart. And Emily?' he adds. 'Do you not think we must keep a close eye on her now? She is of an age to have her head turned, is she not?'

'She is,' Kitty agrees. 'And I do wonder, as I believe you do also, if she has not already met someone through James.' But then she laughs. 'However, as you may tell from her dismissal of poor Walpole—'

'The parson-to-be?'

'Indeed. She most certainly will not be won by the first man to show her attention. In fact,' Kitty laughs again, 'Walpole fared rather better than another would-be swain we encountered in Hampshire.'

'He was so unsuitable?'

'As a matter of fact I think he was. Rich enough and well-connected, as far as I discovered, but I am afraid quite obnoxious, being very much full of his own importance and eligibility. I confess I was not too sorry to see his discomfiture at Emily's treatment of him. She ignored him utterly for half our journey, obliging me to maintain a show of courtesy!'

'I am sure you were kindness itself.' James hugs her closer and they walk onto Maria's house in companionable silence.

***

Kitty feels well rested, James has also had a nap and both are having a glass of Madeira and making desultory conversation with Maria and Sir John when the shopping party returns. They all look up as the carriage stops outside, smile at the sudden burst of young voices and laughter the moment the front door is opened to admit them and are already watching the sitting room door when it bursts open. The three girls are the first to rush in.

'I am so sorry we are late, cousin Maria, everyone,' Mary declares but her flushed face and sparkling eyes speak otherwise.

'The traffic!' Emily rolls her eyes. 'You wouldn't believe what a jam there was at Hyde Park Corner. A wheel came off a carriage or something.'

'But we had such fun!' Bertha chimes in, utterly uncontrite. 'And I know just what sort of dress I want, Mother.' She squeezes in between her parents where they are sharing a small couch and bestows a kiss on each. 'And the material. Look!' She draws out from her pocket a snippet of lilac taffeta. 'Do you like it?' She jumps up and takes it for Maria's approval also.

Maria laughs. 'Very pretty.' She makes room for Bertha to sit beside her. 'I have already asked my dressmaker to attend tomorrow morning and to be sure to have enough assistants to meet the shortest deadline. And in the afternoon we can all go and buy your chosen fabrics. Perhaps excusing Sir John and your father from the expedition. But where is young James?'

'Here, cousin.' He enters much more quietly than his sisters with a deferential Norman and another young man in his wake, clasping their caps to their chests with eyes lowered, awaiting introduction.

'You were so good as to invite me to invite my friends here, Sir John, cousin Maria,' says young James. 'And so I have pleasure in bringing my two very best friends to meet you. Norman Fitzgerald Uniacke - from Devon,' he emphasises the last word. 'And this,' he turns to draw forward his other companion, 'this is Daniel Byrne of the Royal Irish Hussars who has not yet met my parents either.' As James finishes the introductions Daniel steps forward.

He is strikingly handsome. His eyes are as green as the island from which he surely originated if not that of his birth. His hair, straight and jet black, falls like a crow's wing across his cheek as he makes a low bow and he tosses it impatiently back as he straightens, revealing a strong but finely boned face. Involuntarily Kitty glances at Emily who is still standing with Mary in the centre of the room and instantly confirms her suspicion. Emily's face betrays a mixture of eager admiration and anxiety at this meeting. She wants Daniel to make a good impression, she wants her family to like him. Daniel is the young man whose existence she and James have suspected.

'I am honoured to make your acquaintance,' he says in a low voice that carries the merest hint of a brogue.

'We came across each other in Regent Street,' James explains. 'Quite by chance,' he adds, rather too hastily thinks Kitty. 'We all three met first on manoeuvres in the spring. At Chobham?' He glances from his father to Sir John.

'Ah, in Surrey,' nods Sir John. 'I remember reading in the papers. Expect you do too, James eh?'

James senior nods. 'The first manoeuvres on such a large scale since the wars against Boney. Larger than any I ever took part in. But of course there wasn't the need in my day.'

'Blessedly, we were at peace,' Maria says firmly. 'Whereas surely now we soon may not be. Hence these manoeuvres.'

'It was quite a spectacle I heard, eh young fellows?' continues Sir John. 'Visiting dignitaries, Royals even?'

'Oh yes,' James affirms. 'Crowds of them!'

'It was hard sometimes to remember that it was practice for real warfare,' offers Norman.

'But a good deal better than galloping round and round Hyde Park,' Daniel adds. 'Though to be sure the horses prefer that.'

'I liked galloping round Hyde Park,' Emily objects but then turns quickly to address only her brother. 'I should like to do so again.' She fears herself too bold, thinks Kitty. 'And so I believe would Mary.'

'Oh indeed I should.' Mary blushes, perhaps remembering her earlier adamant denial of having time for such diversions.

'We shall, we shall,' her brother assures his two older sisters. 'Eh you two?' He addresses his friends.

'I very much hope so,' stutters Norman, briefly catching Mary's eye.

Daniel bows slightly towards Emily which causes him again to toss back his hair. 'And I only meant it is not such good preparation for war, not that I did not, do not enjoy it.' He turns to James senior. 'And I daresay, sir, we might find a spare horse for a fellow cavalryman should you wish for exercise.'

James seems a little taken aback at this unexpected tribute. 'That would be grand, excellent, I thank you. One does get a little - stale in London after a while.'

He is very pleased and Emily smiles at Daniel, her approval plain to see. He however does not meet her glance and there are several moments of silence after this exchange despite the general air of goodwill. Kitty stands in sudden decision.

'Girls, it is late. You must go and dress for dinner. We are all ready. I will come up and help you.' She turns to young James. 'Goodbye darling, we will see you tomorrow? You are coming to the dinner with Mr Carlyle, I believe?'

'I most certainly am,' he assures her as he replaces his cap and salutes the company in general. 'And we must be off, my friends, or we shan't get any fodder.'

Kitty shepherds the girls from the room as the young men take their leave and Maria protests that they simply must come to supper another day.

40

The family is again gathered before dinner, excepting James junior for whom they are waiting. Sir John is in his preferred position, standing warming his back in front of a large fire in the sitting room and making genial survey of his company. Today this compasses the three girls sitting together on one long sofa engaged with more or less enthusiasm on small pieces of needlework, Maria and Kitty in low chairs on either side of the fireplace and Thomas and James at either end of a fine old leather chesterfield.

'I understand that you visited the so-called Crystal Palace yesterday?' Thomas enquires of James.

He is trying hard to make conversation, thinks Kitty, in uneasy circumstances. It is also very nearly their first meeting for when she has visited Thomas over the years James has usually preferred to find some other occupation.

'Both new and old sites,' James concurs. 'And in both places I was very impressed by man's ingenuity. In my opinion the dismantling and reassembly of the building deserves as much credit as the original construction.'

Thomas nods but seems unable to think of a rejoinder.

'My father is very interested in the latest discoveries and inventions,' offers Emily. 'Whether in the sciences or of ancient civilisations.'

'Oh, only in an amateur fashion.' James adds quickly. 'As are many of my contemporaries. Men of leisure.'

Thomas raises a quizzical eyebrow and again appears lost for words.

'I doubt Thomas has much notion of the meaning of leisure,' observes Kitty, irritated that her husband should so soon have felt obliged to belittle himself. 'Nor time therefore to interest himself very widely beyond his own expertise, great as that may be.'

Thomas looks at her, eyes narrowed, at this provocation which she instantly regrets as being unfair in a situation where he cannot politely retaliate. James also glances at her, his expression a blend of embarrassment and surprise. She is glad when Emily again takes the lead.

'Is it not important, Mr Carlyle,' Emily leans forward in her eagerness, 'to understand such developments in order that we may seek to improve our society?'

Thomas' face clears and he turns to Emily with the trace of a smile on his lips, lips that once were so very sensitive, thinks Kitty, so ready to respond to every new emotion.

'Unfortunately, however, one finds that so often the effects of change are not improvements but are in fact malign,' he says gently. 'As with the destruction of employment by machines, which forces so many people to abandon their country homes and seek a living in cities where they find only squalor and disease.'

'Oh Mr Carlyle, have you read Mr Dickens?' Bertha pipes up in some excitement for she has recently begun to follow such narratives with great interest and impatience for the next episode, particularly where they centre on young persons like herself.

'He is my very good friend,' Thomas tells her. 'And we often discuss such matters of an evening. When I have stopped working.' This last he directs at a somewhat chastened Kitty.

'I am attempting to read your books about the French Revolution,' offers Mary. 'Although I must confess to finding them a little difficult. Whilst certainly painting a most vivid picture of those terrible times which otherwise I might not have been able to imagine.'

Thomas is clearly about to express his appreciation of this compliment when young James makes his entrance. 'Greetings everyone, sorry to have kept you waiting.' He strides across the room to kiss Kitty and Maria and turns to the visitor with a bow. 'I am honoured to meet you at last, sir. Your great fame precedes you and I have found my friends envious of my good fortune.'

'Well spoken, young James,' comments Maria. 'Truly Thomas you have amazed us all with your great achievements over the past years. Little did we expect of the young man who first visited our family. Though I was myself much absent abroad with my husband at that time. I am very glad indeed to now renew our acquaintance.'

Thomas inclines his head and no doubt, thinks Kitty, is ready to again express his gratitude for this opportunity of reconciliation with the family from which he was once so abruptly banished, when they are summoned to dine. On her husband's arm as they follow their host and hostess into dinner, she wonders if the evening is proving as painful an experience for Thomas as she is beginning to find it herself. She is proud at the way that her children have variously acquitted themselves in the face of so renowned and erudite a personage, but highly aware of the contrast with their usual light-hearted banter and preference for less serious topics. None of them, she reflects sadly, are likely to make as significant a contribution to the world as has Thomas.

Thanks to James, she has brought up her family in comfort and safety far from the restless cities, unaffected by the ravages of mines and factories, more or less secluded from the poverty and sickness that has blighted so many lives. But, she wonders, has she thereby also blunted their abilities, limited their consciousness, shackled their freedom to explore their horizons? And what might she herself have become had she – she buries the thought as it arises and squeezes James' arm a little more tightly as he leads her to her place at the table. After all, Thomas has no children at all to whom to pass on his wisdom and superior connections in society. What if she had never been blessed with any children? What married woman did not want them?

'Mary is shortly to live in France, in Paris,' she tells Thomas when all are seated and Mary is his nearest neighbour. 'After her marriage. Her husband-to-be has much business there.'

Thomas turns to Mary with some interest. 'Hence your attempt to acquaint yourself with its history? I fear that you will find little there that you will recognise from my pages for Paris is in a veritable frenzy of reconstruction.'

'I guess it was much destroyed by the Revolution and later turmoils?' young James enquires from his position opposite.

'Ha!' Thomas gives what Kitty recognises as his characteristic loud bark of laughter which rather startles his other listeners. 'I fear the explanation is not so simple. No, the wide boulevards and great squares that are rapidly replacing the narrow twisting streets and close packed houses of old are rather designed to facilitate the advance of any army should such incursion be necessary.'

Young James is nodding his understanding even as Thomas is speaking. 'And greatly impede any efforts of the populace to oppose them! Is that not interesting Papa? Sir John? How military organisation changes in response to different situations? It is why my regiment, the Rifles, was formed,' he tells Thomas. 'In North America where great formations of soldiers whether mounted or not were found to be of little use in fighting the natives who run and hide in often rough and mountainous terrain.'

'I see!' Thomas responds politely but it is not clear that he has understood, nor indeed is interested.

Which, Kitty sees, is what James Senior believes for he hastens to his son's support. 'Well now that is interesting,' he says. 'I had not thought of it. Had you John? Changing times, changing weapons, changing tactics...'

'Hmmph.' Sir John frowns and wipes his mouth with his napkin before he speaks. 'Mustn't get stuck in the past you mean? True, true. Although it's different in the navy I reckon...'

The conversation stumbles onwards with varied contributions on topics of unequal interest to all. Kitty admires Maria's careful brokering of some disagreement concerning the condition of the poor (Emily holding to the belief that more charity is the solution while Thomas argues that the Poor Law only fosters idleness and dependence.)Kitty notes that Thomas is a good deal less well-informed concerning current events in the Crimea than most of the others present (Mary and Bertha say nothing on the matter) and then her attention wanders.

She attempts to picture the evenings at the Carlyles with herself playing Jane's role of hostess and facilitator of good relations. Could she have learnt to 'fashion conversational balls' to toss to Thomas when he or the discussion flagged? Could she have entertained the many illustrious men who came to the house in Cheyne Walk? Mr Dickens, Mr Tennyson, Mr Darwin... She had not heard of any women attending though Thomas had once told her of a rich aristocratic patroness whom he visited and of whom Jane was apparently very jealous. Imagine, she closes her eyes, imagine being present at, even being part of discussions of the important new ideas and discoveries that are shaping the world before they have been made public, before they are even written down. How much more interesting than the thousands of quiet evenings she has spent in distant Devon, particularly in Exmouth, when the children were young and early to bed. She had missed London at first, despite the newly discovered joys of being a wife, later mother, and being mistress of her own household at last.

Of course, Kitty realises, her money could have ensured a larger and more prestigious address and given Thomas a more agreeable study in which to labour. There need never have been the careful economies and rural isolation that dogged Thomas' early years as a writer. How would his career have differently developed had he remained in London with her and never returned to Scotland? Would he still have made his mark, his company sought by the other gifted and celebrated men of his generation? Or would he have been distracted by a life of greater ease, her large circle of mostly less learned relations, not to mention their own family had they had any children? Might he have become dissatisfied at what he came to feel the waste of his talents and blamed her for stunting his ambitions? There was no way of telling.

'Mother?' Emily voice startles her. 'Are you feeling unwell?'

'Sorry, I was daydreaming,' she apologises to the company. 'A little tired perhaps, although one could hardly describe our day as arduous!' Then, reflecting that Thomas is the only one present not to know to what she refers, she explains. 'We have been in the clutches of dressmakers most of the day, desiring, if not indeed requiring, new apparel suited to the season and the circumstances. There is to be a ball,' she clarifies. 'And ladies, particularly young ladies, must be appropriately dressed.'

A flicker of a smile crosses Thomas' face as he looks at her, his gaze momentarily intense. She can tell that he knows she is teasing him, as of old, with this affectation of her preoccupation in trivia, but then he would have risen to the challenge with some sharp retort while now his response is brief and non-committal.

'I see.'

'So what were you all talking about?'

223

'I was asking Mr Carlyle on what he is now working,' Emily informs her. 'And he says he is in the very early stages of writing a life of Frederick the Great of Prussia, believing him to be a strong leader of the sort that is needed for an orderly society. I think that is what you intend, Mr Carlyle? Believing us rather to have lost our way in the current mechanical age such that we are easily swayed by the latest ideas and isms.'

Her face is expressionless whether because she has no feelings on the matter or, more probably thinks Kitty, does not at present wish to reveal them. She wonders how contentious Thomas has been while she has not been attending, how much tolerance her family has felt it courteous to bestow. He is surely long accustomed to holding forth on his opinions but at gatherings of persons who are themselves more used to, more skilled in argumentation. Has the expressed admiration of his present audience begun to be tempered by dislike of his tendency to dominate, in effect to preach? What a contrast Thomas must seem compared to James, who has always encouraged his children to speak out and, like a good gardener, given them space to blossom according to their individual inclinations. Emily having spoken, there is an air of uneasy silence round the dinner table which Maria now breaks.

'And I took Thomas to task concerning his views on prisons with which I simply cannot agree,' she says. 'The wretched inmates cannot wait for true reform in an indefinite future and therefore good-hearted philanthropy is essential.'

'I quaked under her assault,' Thomas claims with a small smile.

'I think we were all a little surprised that Thomas disagrees so strongly with Mr Dickens,' adds James. 'Having thought the latter rather the model of enlightened attitudes on the subject.'

Thomas gives a nod of acknowledgement. 'We agreed to differ,' he says, rather too abruptly thinks Kitty.

'Anyway,' he takes a breath and continues, 'Mr Carlyle also said that at present he is spending most of his days in the reading rooms of the British Museum and he has suggested that we might like to visit the Museum, that indeed we should visit it in its new premises and he could accompany us.'

'That big diamond is there,' Bertha interrupts. 'The one from India that the young prince gave to the Queen, the one you and Mary and Papa saw at the exhibition and Emily and I did not. OH can we go? I should like to very much.'

'There are many other acquisitions which I should like you all to see, including dinosaur fossils and other wonders of natural history that I know will interest you,' replies her father. 'There is a big tablet called the Rosetta stone which has unlocked the secrets of the language of ancient Egypt, and beautiful sculptures which are over two thousand years old from Greece, including a very famous frieze from a big temple which you may still see in the city of Athens. There are relics from the Assyrian civilisation which is even older. Only recently I read of some new sculptures that have been transported from the long destroyed city of Nimrud.' James' face, Kitty is glad to see, is uncommonly lit with enthusiasm as he turns to Thomas. 'It is a capital idea, Mr Carlyle. I think we should.'

41

James and Thomas are leading the way up the short flight of steps beneath the imposing classical facade of the new British Museum with Kitty a few paces after them and the girls following a little further behind.

'What a contrast is this to the last time I visited here,' exclaims James turning his face towards Thomas so that Kitty can see his eager expression. 'For so long it has been one great construction site.'

'The largest in Europe it was said,' agrees Thomas, his gaze remaining fixed on the ground beneath his feet.

'But how fortunate are we to have these great public palaces of display and learning,' muses James. 'And more are being constructed to which some of the contents here will then be transferred.'

'And there are to be more galleries of paintings besides.' Thomas turns to include Kitty in the conversation. 'I am myself involved in a project to create a gallery of portraits, of famous individuals through the centuries. Much can be learnt, in my opinion, from a good portrait. The face being something of a window on the soul. At the least, it aids one's imaginings of different times and places .'

Kitty again recognises the sharp contrast between her life as it is and might have been. Where now she is a visitor, a consumer of others' vision and industry, she could have been a patron and provider of such cultural benefits to society. She steps up to join the two men in front of the museum entrance. 'I did not tell you, Thomas, that only last year I had returned to me a portrait of myself with my brother, a fabulous big painting of us made just before we left India for England. When we had already left our parents in fact. Certainly when looking at it you can very easily imagine our state of mind. In fact, I appear to have but recently stopped weeping.'

'I remember you were both very young.'

'Yes. I was three, William five,' Kitty confirms. 'We were dressed in Indian clothes. Perhaps for the last time. It was quite shocking for me when first I saw it again - to recognise myself in that little girl.'

'Kitty had long awaited its possession,' James explains. 'Having discovered its whereabouts by chance and been promised it on its previous custodian's demise. It now hangs in the hall of our home. You must come and see it one day,' he adds gallantly and rather to Kitty's surprise and not quite unmixed pleasure. 'The advent of the train makes us quite accessible these days.'

Kitty smiles to herself reflecting that the prospect of a long train journey will not increase the appeal of the invitation and wonders what Thomas will say. But he only has time to bow in acknowledgment before the girls' arrival makes further response unnecessary.

***

With James as their guide, they have traversed several galleries of objects from a succession of civilisations in the eastern Mediterranean and beyond. It is the first time, reflects Kitty, that she has managed to place some of these once rich and powerful empires in any kind of order or historical context. Thomas too has listened politely, Kitty is relieved to see, having firmly disclaimed any particular knowledge of such ancient history, though he has occasionally wandered off to inspect something not on James' itinerary.

'And the Assyrians were finally defeated by their neighbours and rivals the Babylonians,' James is concluding. 'Of whom I guess King Nebuchadnezzar is the most famous.'

Bertha nods with a badly suppressed yawn. 'Are we going to see the diamond now?' she enquires, a little plaintively.

James gently ruffles her hair. 'Yes, we must move continents entirely before you fall asleep on your feet. Let us find India.'

Halfway up the splendid internal staircase to the area where Indian artefacts are displayed, they reach a small landing whence tall windows give a view over London to the north of the Museum. Kitty stops to take breath and gazes out .

'How London has grown in this direction also,' she remarks. 'I remember when one could see fields and market gardens between here and the hills of Hampstead and Highgate. Now it is one great metropolis.'

'And it has not stopped its insatiable advance.' Thomas' voice at her shoulder has a note of grim relish. She glances at him and dislikes his look of satisfaction at prejudices confirmed as he adds: 'Who knows what will stop it.'

'Or when,' observes Emily coolly from behind them. 'For if I have understood the lesson of downstairs, it is that no civilisation lasts for ever.'

'Indeed,' Thomas agrees. 'As several writers have imagined, one day London and the civilisation of which it is the heart, will cease to be. Fifty and more years ago Sir Horace Walpole described a traveller from Lima marvelling at the ruins of St Paul's Cathedral. Lima,' he tells Bertha, 'is in a country called Peru in South America. And,' he continues, 'more recently the poet Shelley wrote of a time *"when St Paul's and Westminster Abbey shall stand, shapeless and nameless ruins in the midst of an unpeopled marsh"*.' He stares through the window across the rooftops, chimneys and steeples to the distant, still green hills on the horizon, his face a picture less of sorrow, thinks Kitty, than of an avenging deity.

Bertha sidles up to Kitty and takes her hand. 'Will our house and all Torquay also fall into ruins?' she whispers, her upper lip trembling.

'Perhaps,' Kitty says, pulling her close. 'But not for a long long time. Hundreds of years, maybe more. There is no need for us to worry about it.'

'Come,' James calls. 'Who will be first to find the diamond? Finders keepers!' He hastens ahead up the stairs, closely pursued by Bertha with Mary and Emily hurrying behind, leaving a silent Kitty and frowning Thomas to follow at a slower pace.

'I upset Bertha,' Thomas states with a faint air of surprise. 'I am sorry.'

Kitty laughs. 'I guess you have little practice of talking to children!' she observes. Then, reflecting that she has herself now spoken thoughtlessly, she adds: 'Fortunately or otherwise.' And nor therefore does he have a personal link to the future she thinks. He might feel differently about the possible destruction of our civilisation if his descendants would be amongst those to suffer. And feel more common cause with the rest of humanity.

'Isabella's sons liked me.' Thomas is defensive.

'True.'

'Though that was a long time ago.'

'Very true.'

'But I did not relish tutoring.' Thomas glances at her sideways. 'Except that it brought me into your esteemed family.'

'Mama, Mama!' an excited Bertha is racing back towards them. 'I found it first, the diamond. It is so wonderful, *"The Mountain of Light"* it is called in English. It is so big and it has already been cut down from the size it was when it was found.'

'So you will be the one to keep it?' Thomas enquires with every appearance of seriousness.

Bertha throws him a look of scorn. 'That was a joke, Mr Carlyle. My father's joke. Of course the diamond is worth far too much for anyone other than the Queen to own. We are just over there,' she tells Kitty, pointing to a far corner. 'I'll go and tell Papa I've found you.' And she runs off again.

'Touché.' Thomas gives a rueful smile.

They thread their way to join the others through cabinets of small Indian figurines and pieces of jewellery and other artefacts, more or less sorted and labelled as to their date of origin and place of discovery. There are larger statues also: graceful dancing *apsaras*, smiling Buddhas, gods and goddesses intertwined in amorous play. Kitty stops in front of one especially beautiful figure of a nameless slender-waisted goddess, her eyes closed, full lips slightly parted, hips tilted to one side in what seems an attitude of utter bliss.

'I wish I knew more about India,' she says. 'I wish I could have visited, when I was younger.'

'I have sometimes wished I had pursued my studies of India.' Thomas is beside her, frowning doubtfully at the goddess. 'Particularly that I had written of the coming together of civilisations that has occurred through the British conquest of India, in which I first became interested through my meeting with your family. Later, of course, I became more interested in your particular history.' He looks at her, his expression inscrutable, except that in the depth of his eyes she is sure she sees a flicker of the old fire. 'Why your British family broke off all contact with your Indian family, particularly your mother. But as you know I never found out.' He looks away and they move on.

They have rounded the last case of curios from where Kitty can see her husband and daughters waiting at the far end of the gallery. James raises a hand in greeting. She glances sideways at Thomas. 'I have found out why,' she says. 'A few days ago, from the Indian lady, Nur. Her sister was my mother's dearest friend. She was with my mother when she died.'

'Really?' Thomas stops dead. 'What strange coincidence. And what did she tell you?'

Kitty hesitates before walking on, and Thomas quickens his pace to catch up with her. 'Or should I not ask?'

'I will tell you,' she promises. 'Since once you made such effort to discover it. But not now. It is too long a story and not one to be told in such circumstances. I will tell James I wish to travel with you in a separate carriage on our return journey. He will understand that I do not wish our daughters to overhear what I say.'

The girls, Kitty is amused to discover, have each a different response to the sight of the great diamond.

'I wish I could hold it, Mama,' says Bertha. 'See how it sparkles and shines. I should like to peer deep into it and imagine what fascinating stories it could tell. Of the people and places it has seen as it has changed hands over the centuries.'

'I should like to wear it,' laughs Mary. 'And benefit from the fascinating light it would cast on my person.'

Emily is silent, frowning.

'And you Emily? You have no taste for such a bauble?' her father teases.

Emily smiles at him quickly. 'I should not refuse diamonds were you or another to offer them,' she says. 'But this particular one does not I believe belong here. In fact,' she speaks with increasing passion, 'though I have this morning found the sight of so many varied exhibits interesting and instructive, I find that I cannot forget that in most cases they are the profits of pillage. They have been taken from their homes, stolen from their rightful owners. So I wish I could liberate this gem and send it home.'

Kitty breaks the silence that follows Emily's outburst. 'I have not told you all what Nur told me and Emily also knows,' she begins. 'And Thomas you do not even know what the rest of us learned from a letter from her grandson, that she was married in India to a soldier from Savoy who became a great general. From Nur herself I heard that he formed and commanded the army of an Indian king who was briefly the greatest power in India, on whom the Mughal Emperor depended. And if this king hadn't died he might have continued to rule India rather than the British who within a few years had conquered the lands over which he had ruled. For his son was young and weak, and though he begged General de Boigne to remain in his service, the General was by that time very ill and had decided he must go to England and of course Nur and their children came with him. Had this not happened, the course of history might have run very differently.' *And he might yet have returned to India,* she thinks, *if he had not met another woman and abandoned Nur.* 'No-one seems to know this,' she concludes. 'Certainly I did not. And this diamond would then very likely not have been here for us to admire but still adorning the turban of the young king of the Sikhs.'

'Daniel's regiment fought in India at that time,' is Emily's unexpected response. 'He is a friend of my brother, Mr Carlyle. I told him about Mrs Bennett and General de Boigne. He was very interested to think what a distinguished enemy they might have had and perhaps failed to defeat. Of course this was long before he was even born.'

'And your regiment,' Thomas enquires of James. 'Were they also in India?'

'Never yet,' James informs him. 'The year I signed up was the year they came back from France after three years guarding the peace in Paris. And having a very good time indeed or so my colleagues gave me to understand.' He laughs. 'And then we were stationed around Britain, including in Scotland, but with little action beyond occasional confrontations with aggrieved working people who were trying to resist the introduction of machines. But that's army life for you, you never know what you're signing up for, what war if any is to come. You most certainly aren't the master of your own destiny.'

Kitty watches Thomas nodding through James' unusually expansive explanation of matters which must surely seem to belong to another world to his own. Whilst James can hardly paint himself as any kind of a hero, she is oddly proud of his humility in accounting for his lack of any real soldiering despite his rank. And she is even more gratified by his next statement.

'I was glad to resign, after I'd met Kitty and she'd agreed to be my wife,' he continues. 'Life with Kitty has been worth more than all the glory I might have gained in battle I can assure you.'

'Oh Papa,' the girls applaud their father. 'How very romantic, what a marvellous tribute, Mother.' Their chorus of approval quite distracts Kitty's attention from observing Thomas' response, and by the time she does look at him he is entirely composed. James in contrast is smiling broadly if a little embarrassed at his own admission. She puts her arm through his.

'I think it must be near lunchtime, Maria will be expecting us,' she says and, as the whole party begins their exit, she leads him aside to explain why she wishes to travel back separately.

42

Kitty and Thomas set off together in a hired cab leaving the others waiting on the pavement for the arrival of Maria's brougham. It being sunny and quite warm at this time of day, Kitty has asked that the top be let down. It feels more appropriate to be in less private confinement.

'Your husband is very - compliant,' comments Thomas.

To Kitty's ear, his tone suggests that he intends a slur on James' character but she chooses to take the observation as the compliment that she knows it should be. 'Most certainly he is and I am very fortunate that it is so.'

Thomas flushes and for a moment is silent. 'So, tell me of this Indian lady and what she said to you. It seemed, by the way, that you regret the British victory over the Indian king for whom her husband fought. Are your loyalties yet divided? Do you still not feel entirely at home in England?'

They have reached the long street that leads eventually to Oxford. It is a picture of prosperity, lined by shops full of goods for sale and bustling with customers.

'So you remember,' Kitty acknowledges. 'Despite my family's best efforts to make of me an Englishwoman.' She is suddenly tempted to delve further into their common memory. 'Was it not my foreignness that you found – remarkable? Did you not find me *"peculiar among all dames and damosels"*? Or was that only in your writing, in your work of fiction?'

'My only and much confabulated work of fiction.' Thomas sighs and then gives her a conspiratorial smile in return. 'Which however caused such confusion as to the real identity of my heroine.'

'Better it did,' Kitty agrees with a laugh as they negotiate the hazardous crossroad with Regent Street and continue on towards Marble Arch. 'So, do you also remember that my father died very soon after my brother and I had set sail for England? And that he had left my mother in Hyderabad and made haste alone to Calcutta? He had been summoned there to meet the new Governor General. Well...'and Kitty tells Thomas how after some months her mother had travelled to Calcutta, at first been well received by her in-laws but how her developing relations with Henry Russell had become a public scandal, which had led to his abandoning her rather than compromise his career and had resulted also in her banishment for several years from Hyderabad by both the British and Hyderabadi authorities. She relates it quickly, allowing no comment or interruption, and she does not notice any reaction on Thomas' part. As the carriage turns abruptly left into Hyde Park she concludes: 'Is it not the saddest story you ever heard? Does it not explain why she died of a broken heart?'

Thomas passes a hand over his face as if to aid the taking in of so much new information and arrives at a very different conclusion. 'It certainly explains why your family cut all communication with her,' he says. 'That it was a scandal with which no respectable family would wish to have been associated. From which you and your brother should be protected. Were you not shocked to discover your mother's betrayal of your father, so soon after his death? With his *assistant?*'

'No,' says Kitty promptly. 'But I *am* shocked by your response.' She allows her gaze to take in the glorious blazing colours of autumn in the trees along their route while she tries to understand his reaction and explain. 'My mother was alone, apart from her mother. She needed a man to protect her and Mr Russell was more familiar to her than any other. I doubt she would have allowed another even to see her face. It must have seemed to her the best or even the only solution, providing as near a continuation of her life as possible. And, by the way, it was Mr Russell who had kept possession of our portrait all those years, perhaps in memory of her.'

Thomas continues to frown and say nothing, apparently incredulous, she thinks, that she can so defend her mother. A sudden breeze raises a swirl of leaves around their carriage wheels and causes both of them to hold their hats to their heads.

'She was not yet twenty, Thomas,' she points out.

Still he is silent. They have come to the long curving lake called the Serpentine due to its shape. It too is agitated by the wind, thin ripples racing across the surface of the water.

'And Mr Russell was only a few years older.'

Like us, she thinks suddenly, and instantly wants to remind Thomas of his own reckless youthful behaviour. Here at last is the opportunity to ask the many questions that have returned to trouble her over the years. How could he have continued to write to and encourage Jane whilst meeting with, *courting*, her? How could he have cared for her yet risked bringing scandal to her family and damaging her own reputation, let alone breaking her heart? And why was he in such a hurry to propose to Jane which was the final fatal blow to her hopes? She wants to ask him: what did he think he was doing? Did he not know that actions have consequences, that one cannot simply please oneself? Or did he not care if others were hurt? Whether she or Jane. But as quickly she knows that she will not, cannot in all propriety, so confront him. Neither he nor she is as they were then, it all happened so long ago, it is better to continue to act as if it is past and forgotten. But she *can* attack him on her mother's behalf.

'I think you have no idea of how different life could be in a place and time so far from here and now,' she says. 'Despite all your learning.' Kitty sees how Thomas flinches at this but she does not relent. 'And I think if Isabella had told you all this all those years ago you, with your narrow Presbyterian upbringing, would have been as shocked and unforgiving as you are now.' She takes a breath and then abandons all caution for her final thrust as the carriage rattles briskly over the bridge. 'And probably wanted nothing further to do with our family. Or me.'

She sits erect and looks straight ahead as they drive in silence towards the gate that leads to Knightsbridge and thence into Belgravia. It is only when they reach Maria's house and Thomas gets out to hand her down that she sees how she has hurt him. His face is set, his lips a thin compressed line but his eyes are dark and troubled and she cannot bear to meet their reproach. She watches the cab bear him away, his back stiff and straight and is instantly sorry that she cannot make amends.

235

Did I completely misunderstand him, she thinks. Even if he did in my view unfairly condemn my mother for her precipitate liaison with Mr Russell, in springing to her defence I attacked him unjustifiably. There are several emotions he may have felt, some of which he may have needed more time himself to understand, and no doubt he of all people would have soon recognised that his knowledge of her circumstances is limited. In any case, ending the relationship with my family and myself might not have been an outcome he would ever have considered. And perhaps it is my own unresolved feelings about my mother's behaviour that prompted so extreme a reaction on my part.

Oh Thomas, what if you were only thinking how misguided your questioning of Isabella, how unjustified you were in upsetting her, how unnecessary therefore the consequent rupture with my family and your decision to leave London. And asking Jane to marry you. What if you were, with horrified realisation, comparing your own ill-considered behaviour with that of my mother? And seeing how equally fateful were its consequences on the rest of your life and that of others? '*Sartor Restartus*' showed how deeply those consequences were felt by you and were perhaps meant to tell me too. A belated love letter, if in somewhat dense code.

She has never managed to read the whole novel but she knows that the loss of his love causes Thomas, or at least his philosophical hero, to feel utter disdain for all human activity, showing his rejection of the world in '*The Eternal No*'. Later he changes his mind and embraces instead '*The Eternal Yes*' but, as she has wondered in the past, what can it have been like for Jane to live with him through the years when he was writing the book, through all that heart-searching, in the earliest years of their marriage? Surely Jane of all people must have known Blumine the Rose Goddess's true identity.

And does Thomas still regret losing me? As I sometimes do him? This is what romantic novels do not capture, she thinks. They end with a happy outcome whereas life, with all its ambivalence and ambiguity goes on relentlessly and it must be a very strong or simple person who never questions where it has taken them. *I will write Thomas a note of apology*, she decides, *but I shall not see him again, at least on this visit.*

43

That afternoon Kitty throws herself into the continuing frenzy of preparations for the ball. Maria has produced a great number of boxes and bags of long-hoarded treasure for the girls to fashion themselves head-dresses. There are headbands, combs and coronets many requiring repair or the replacement of missing parts. There are also broken necklaces of pearls, crystal, jet and amber beads, semi-precious stones of lapis lazuli, jade, garnet and amethyst that have fallen from some long-forgotten setting, and a quantity of silver and gilt wire with which to make them as new.

'Should you not keep these for your own daughters?' Mary asks, whilst intently examining a sketch she has made of a striking coronet she saw in a shop window in Regent Street. She has already begun to assemble the necessary jet beads.

But Maria dismisses such scruples. 'Bless you, my dear, but I have waited long enough for my girls to show such an interest. They would rather buy such things ready-made. Whereas,' she holds up a lustrous garnet to the light, 'I was always rather good with my hands, though I say it myself. I suppose it was all those days on board ship, needing something to take my mind off the discomforts.'

'And dangers,' says Kitty with affection. 'I wish I had had some such spur to my artistic talents, for I fear I have little aptitude.'

Emily looks up and smiles quickly. 'Nor I,' she agrees. 'And unlike your mother. But let us try.'

By the end of the afternoon, and with a great deal of help from Maria, the girls and Kitty proudly display their creations to their father and Sir John, who have returned from a visit to the latter's tailor. Mary has abandoned her coronet finding it fragile and liable to collapse. Instead she has replaced the missing stones in a simpler arc of rose and cream opals which will match her new dress and which Kitty prefers.

'It is better suited to a young girl,' she says and Maria agrees.

'But you are too modest,' Mary rejoins. 'Maria wanted to lend her this, Father.' She holds up an elaborate crownset with garnets and pearls. 'But she prefers this insignificant band.' She points at a much smaller but prettily worked gold circlet. Do persuade her.'

'I have no opinion in matters of dress.' James smiles. 'I have no doubt you will all look beautiful whatever you wear.'

'Do you like mine though, Papa?' Bertha puts on a narrow band set with amethyst. 'It will match my new dress. And cousin Maria says I may have that one when I am older.' She indicates another wider headband.

James cups his youngest daughter's face in his hand and frowns as if in serious consideration. 'You look quite grown up already,' he says and then he smiles but not before Kitty notes the slight sadness in his voice. How quickly the years will pass, she thinks, when one by one our children will fly the nest.

'You have not admired mine.' Emily produces her choice: a small crown of what look like fragile near transparent flowers the centres of which are of large blue pearls. 'I hardly had to mend it at all,' she admits. 'Isn't it pretty, although mostly of glass.'

'Very pretty,' James agrees.

'Indeed,' agrees Sir John. 'And if you want one of diamonds you had better find yourself a very rich husband!' He laughs heartily, being perhaps the only one not to notice Emily's sudden change of expression.

Maria speaks up quickly. 'Or a generous one like the Admiral.' She smiles at him. 'For I do have a comb set with diamonds, a few diamonds, which is what I intend to wear.'

***

The days that follow are full of outings. They see several plays, visit London Zoo with its wonderful new Aquarium, which they discover to be the first public one in the world, and they walk and drive in various Parks. They make a return trip to Cremorna Gardens, partly for Bertha's sake for she was left at home on their previous visit. At one point Kitty finds they are near Chelsea Bridge where she walked with Thomas and he had so disparaged these pleasure grounds. She wonders if Jane is home again, whether they are holding one of their frequent soirees with a gathering of distinguished guests discussing the important issues of the day.

Then she looks ahead at her young folk gaily treading the network of pathways that are edged with hundreds of flickering nightlights, watches as they stop to look at some juggler or magician, or to drop pennies in the hat of some musician, and she knows where she had rather be, where she belongs. But she is sorry she was unkind to Thomas and hopes that her note of apology made amends.

As he forecast, young James has plenty of leisure to join them and is often accompanied by Daniel and Norman, the latter of whom contrives to diminish the embarrassment of his hopeless admiration of Mary by paying a great deal of brotherly attention to Bertha. He finds her a pony so that she may sometimes accompany them riding, takes her on carousels and, at the Zoo, pretends that he is an escaped crocodile or tiger which of course makes her squeal with delight. He is in fact, Kitty realises with some surprise, almost as close in age to young Bertha as he is to Mary.

Mary also clearly appreciates his antics if only because they allow him to continue his visits. She is very much more light-hearted than of late, thinks Kitty and wishes she herself could remember more clearly the attractions of Mary's fiancé, Mr Molyneaux-Seel, for then perhaps she might find a way to promote them. For Charles is delayed on business and will not even be able to join them for the ball, let alone some of the household purchases on which Mary had desired his opinion.

'I daresay we should wait a little longer,' Kitty suggests one day when they have spent another indecisive hour or two inspecting furnishings and fingering fabrics. 'For he may advise on and prefer French styles as indeed may you. Especially if you are to live there. Does he yet say?'

Mary shrugs. 'He says we shall discuss it when he is here for he is not much of a letter writer,' she says. 'So I guess you are right.' And then she adds with apparent carelessness: 'And if there is then insufficient time we shall have to trust to the resources of Exeter.'

'If not Paris!' Emily has joined them. 'And I agree with Mother that we should abandon this enterprise, Mary, and devote our time to the many far more diverting occupations on offer.' She links arms with her sister. 'And it will soon be lunchtime and everyone will be waiting for us.'

Kitty follows the girls out of the store. It is good to see them in such harmony for they have not always been the best of friends and Mary had drawn away a little from them all since her engagement. *But I will be watchful,* she thinks, *lest either of my daughters act with impropriety. I will not take the risks that Julia did, with only my best interests at heart.*

Yet over lunch in Piccadilly and afterwards walking in St James' Park, she thinks that nothing she could say or do would persuade Emily that Daniel should not be the object of her love. Their heads continually turn to each other in animated talk, their faces are flushed, their eyes bright. There is no question that he is as equally smitten as she. And Kitty cannot fairly fault their behaviour for they do not distance themselves from the company, but continue to laugh and jest with young James and the others. She squeezes her husband's arm.

'They certainly make a handsome couple,' she says.

'But she will have to be patient,' James responds. 'For he will not be in a position to ask for her hand for some years yet.'

Every few days Kitty writes to Nur, her new-found confidante. She tells her about Daniel and even young Norman, of how she doesn't want her daughters to make the same mistake that she did, even more her mother, yet of how impossible it is to guide another's affections even if one can restrain their conduct.

Emily writes to Georgina and Kitty wonders whether she mentions Daniel or prefers not to risk the confidence being passed to Richard and thence perhaps to Walpole. She receives news, which she does relay to her mother, of Georgina's developing romance with Richard. Once or twice, as Kitty already knows, they have together been invited by Nur, wishing to facilitate their meeting since neither has family to do so, besides arranging the charitable donations for which Richard was hoping.

And meanwhile international relations seem to conspire to maintain the happy holiday mood, for, having crossed the Danube, the Turks are consolidating their position. With a view to the oncoming winter, the Sultan has assembled part of his fleet on the Black Sea in order to maintain supplies to the army. A week or two later he orders a second fleet to join them although the British, his principal paymasters, do not permit him to include his larger vessels.

'The Sultan's doing rather well,' observes James to Sir John one morning when they are all sitting awhile together after breakfast discussing the day's plans. 'We underestimated him.'

'For a young'un,' Sir John agrees. 'Only thirty! Mind you, he's got a good Admiral there in Osman or so I've heard.'

'I read that he appears a great deal older,' James responds. 'In one of your *Illustrated London News* I think it was.' He stands and goes to a side table where a number of journals and papers are neatly arranged. 'Here we are,' he picks up one and returns to his seat. '17th September. *"Sultan Ubd-Ul-Medjid is only thirty but looks at least ten years older... his countenance is marked by an indescribable air of languor and debility arising from his early initiation into the worst features of oriental life."*'

'Which we hope will fatally hamper his attempts to restore his crumbling empire,' exclaims Emily with very evident disgust.

'Why so angry, my dear?' Her father is taken aback. 'I did not know you were a partisan in this dispute.'

'I'm not,' Emily retorts. 'What makes me angry is our, the British, attitude. What do they mean *'the worst features of oriental life?'* What do they mean by *'oriental life'* for that matter? China? India? Mother's family there? Mrs Bennett? It is so generalised, so insulting.'

To everyone's surprise it is Maria who first responds. 'Well done, my dear,' she says. 'It was just such an arrogance that I most disliked when we lived in the colonies, despite myself having a perfectly Caucasian lineage, or so I believe.'

There is a short silence during which Kitty reaches to pat Emily's hand in appreciation, which is broken by Bertha.

'Why do you say Caucasian?' she wants to know. 'I thought the Caucasus is practically in Asia.' She looks around her expectantly, perhaps expecting a scornful reply from her sisters, but no-one has an immediate answer.

44

And then it is the day of the ball. Kitty and James are sitting with Sir John and Maria watching the Grand March of couples around the ballroom. Emily had tried to persuade her parents to join them but Kitty had firmly aligned herself with the older generation.

'Emily is right. You look as beautiful as any of them,' James leans to whisper in her ear which makes her blush and fan herself more energetically. 'No Caucasian woman could wear that colour.' He indicates her dress.

It is of a deep apricot, the glow of which is becomingly reflected from her skin and her golden crown is all the adornment that her lustrous hair requires. Maria has lent her a pair of amber earrings, brought back, she fondly recalls, from one of Sir John's trips to the Baltic. They sway gracefully as Kitty moves her head.

But the girls do look very lovely in their blue and pink satin gowns, their faces lit with the excitement of the great occasion. Kitty has cautioned them against allowing any one young man to fill up their dance cards and there has been no shortage of partners. However, for this opening parade they have been claimed by their would-be suitors, both resplendent in their close-fitting dress uniforms. Daniel's is by far the more striking, being dark blue but with so much closely positioned frogging down the front that it resembles a golden breastplate. Daniel himself is so handsome that a lump forms in Kitty's throat as she thinks how quickly youth passes, and how mercifully little aware of this are the young themselves.

Norman's somewhat longer jacket is also intricately decorated with braid but it is of the same colour as the rest of his clothing, a dark green, which however well suits his red hair and pale complexion. Kitty scans the parade for similarly attired young men and spies her son leading a pretty blonde girl with such careless abandon that she is sure he has not yet lost his heart. He even waves to her as they pass.

The first dance is a quadrille which causes a hurried scramble and much hilarity as new couples find each other and form into sets of eight.

'We used to do this.' James taps his foot and nods his head in time to the music.

'And you were very good at it,' Kitty replies. 'There is too much fancy footwork for me to attempt it today.'

They both look on as the dance ends and the dancer regroup for the next.

'And this cotillion?' James asks.

'I am not sure I even remember how to do it.' Kitty watches as couples change partners by exchanging handkerchiefs, once again with much laughter .'And I do not think these young men would readily seek my hand, however pretty my kerchief!'

'More fool they,' James says gallantly. 'But I am determined to get you up on the dance floor soon.'

The following succession of unfamiliar dances, however, leaves them gaping.

'I remember when the waltz was the latest thing,' he tells Emily who is briefly resting on a seat next to him.

'There you go again, Papa,' she berates him. 'Making yourself out to be so much older than you are.'

'It was daring in our day,' Kitty points out. 'But so wonderful to be swung around and around in your father's arms!'

'And how we laughed at the disapproval on the older people's faces!' rejoins James. 'But now there are so many new variations I am afraid it would be us that would be laughed at.'

Before Emily can respond yet another young man, this time in the uniform of young James 60th Rifle Brigade, claims her attention, takes her hand and leads her onto the dance floor.

'It's a polka,' James exclaims, tapping his foot as the musicians strike up. 'And the last dance before supper. Come on, Kitty, we can do this. Let's show them.'

To Kitty's surprise the steps come to her as easily as if it had been only yesterday that she last danced them, while James leads her faultlessly, one hand firmly behind her back to steer a safe passage between the fast moving couples thronging the floor. She throws her head back and smiles up at him, feeling as carefree as in the long ago days of their engagement and entirely trusting in his skilled guidance. After a while she notices how much more space there is and sees how many have made way for them and are standing back and clapping the progress of the few remaining dancers. At the end of the dance there is enthusiastic applause for them in particular and their walk into supper is interrupted by frequent expressions of congratulation.

But as they take their seats there is a sudden ripple of excited talk around the room. Young James leans back in his chair to catch the conversation at the adjoining table where sit a number of his more senior fellow officers and relays the information to his family.

'The Russian navy has gone on the offensive in the Black Sea and captured some Turkish ships,' he says. 'And the weather having deteriorated, the Turkish fleet has been forced to turn into port for the winter.'

Sir John slaps his thighs. 'Well, well, the Russian admirals will be pleased,' he says. 'They've been treated as second class too long. Now their army sees how they need them.' He chortles loudly which causes a few heads to turn in his direction and Maria to tap him sharply on the knee. 'To keep open supply lines,' he adds in explanation. 'Else they'll starve.'

'Which might be a very good thing,' Maria comments sharply. 'And we shall starve if we don't stop talking. Help yourselves everyone and pass the dishes on.'

'Oh the Turks'll be safe enough in port,' asserts Sir John, whilst doing as he is bid and taking a large slice of rabbit pie. 'It's against the rules of war to attack ships at anchor. Osman's done the right thing. In the circumstances.'

James frowns. 'We certainly don't want the balance tipped too much one way.'

Kitty glances around the room and sees that his concern is shared by many whose expressions, which so recently showed only light-hearted pleasure have become grave. Her heart sinks further, however, as she observes a different reaction amongst the younger military men, many of whom are now on their feet and congregating in animated groups. Young James and his friends remain seated but for the rest of supper time their conversation is frequently distracted by these far-away events.

'Well, I am thankful I am marrying a civilian,' Mary remarks loudly to Emily as they walk side-by-side into the ballroom and the musicians prepare to play.

'Sorry, sisters.' Young James inserts himself between them, linking arms with each. 'Come on fellows,' he calls to Norman and Daniel. 'Let's dance while we may.'

'I'm engaged elsewhere for this one.' Norman excuses himself, his face flushed , his expression suddenly downcast.

'Poor boy,' thinks Kitty as she watches him disappear into the crowd, clearly upset by Mary's thoughtless remark which had surely reminded him that she is promised to another .

'I'm coming too,' young James calls after him and goes in search of his own partner.

Daniel bows to Emily. 'May I see your dance card?' he asks and when she gives it to him tears it across and drops the pieces on the floor. 'For who knows when next we may dance together,' he says softly as he takes her in his arms and swings her away in a five-step waltz.

'Should we have said something?' Kitty asks James as they return to their seats by the dance floor. 'People will notice.'

'Oh I think in the circumstances...' James prevaricates, 'the general excitement...'

Kitty sighs. 'Why do men want to fight?' she asks, not expecting an answer, knowing that James may be envying the younger men's probable call to arms.

He reaches for her hand. 'The sooner there is opportunity to fight, the sooner Daniel may make his fortune and marry our daughter,' he points out. 'Which I daresay they wish will be as soon as may be.'

'Look,' Kitty squeezes James' hand. 'Here they come.'

James looks up in time to see Emily and Daniel whirl past them, evidently heedless of their surroundings, entirely absorbed in each other's company.

'With eyes only for each other,' James comments. 'Just as we used to be.'

45

It is the last but one day of their stay in London and the first of December. James and Sir John have gone out together as has become their custom, to read the papers at the latter's club, while Kitty and the girls are have been struggling all afternoon to pack their many purchases into their trunks. Maria has promised to bring anything that will not fit when she and Sir John follow them down to Torquay the following week.

'I wish I might stay and travel with them.' Emily sighs, clearly without hope of being allowed to do so. It is not the first time she has expressed this wish and her parents remain united in their refusal. She sits down heavily on their bed, the picture of dejection.

Kitty sits beside her and takes her hand. 'You know Maria cannot chaperone you everywhere,' she tells her. 'And as your father says, who knows how free the young men will now be. Or indeed how long they may remain in London. What with the strengthening of the blockade of the Turkish fleet.'

'Sir John said the Turkish admiral is sure they won't attack,' Emily objects. 'He has even let many of his crews go ashore.'

'Stop arguing with Mother,' Mary interrupts sharply. 'You cannot be left here on your own and there's an end to it.' She snaps down the lid of the last trunk. 'Come and be useful. Sit on this while I strap it round.'

'It's all very well for you. You will see *your* fiancé very soon,' Emily snaps back but she stands all the same and goes to help her sister.

Mary opens her mouth to retort but bites her lip as Kitty speaks out. 'You must not imply that you are in a similar situation to Mary,' she says gently. 'Whatever has passed in private between you and Daniel. And besides,' she too stands and surveys the now tidy bedroom with satisfaction. 'Mary has waited very patiently for

Charles to join us and we must ensure that we have a very happy Christmas season together. And,' she adds, 'your father says you may write to Daniel. If you wish.'

It is a concession over which Kitty and James have agonised and Kitty wishes James were there to see the joy it has brought to Emily's face. She jumps up to hug her mother at the very moment that young James bursts into the room.

'Come downstairs this instant,' he urges. 'There is great news.' He goes out again and Kitty and the girls follow him.

'But is it good news or bad?' Kitty wonders aloud.

They find James and Sir John together pacing up and down the living room in a state of great agitation while Maria is reading a newspaper. All three look up as the newcomers enter the room.

'The Russians have yesterday sunk the Turkish fleet. Every single ship. In the harbour of Sinope,' Maria informs them. 'So much for the rules of war.'

'Then I guess we must make war on the Russians?' Kitty looks to Sir John who is shaking his head in disbelief.

'And they used Paixham guns,' he says. 'Fired explosive shells, not just balls and shot like we've always done. It's a new era.'

Kitty turns to James who shrugs.

'Oh, I am sure there will be negotiations,' he replies. 'Nothing will happen immediately.'

Young James is standing in the doorway with his sisters. 'So this was the 'great' news?' Kitty addresses him. She cannot disguise the bitterness in her voice.

He steps forward and takes both her hands in his. 'Oh Mother,' he reproaches her. 'As if I did not know how you would grieve at any news of war. No, it is the immediate consequence that is great.' He pauses before bursting out with a laugh. 'We are all given a month's leave over Christmas!'

'So you will come home!' Kitty exclaims and hugs him, the relief bringing tears to her eyes.

'Hooray!' says Bertha. 'It will be as much fun as London. You will bring your friends, won't you James?

'Er...' James hesitates, clearly discomfited as everyone watches him, waiting to see how he will reply to Bertha's innocent request. 'I don't think Norman can come, Bertha,' he says at last. 'He'll probably want to see his own family.'

'Of course he will,' agrees Kitty. 'His mother will want to have him at home just as I do your brother.'

'Right.' Young James nods. 'But – er – is it alright if I ask Daniel to join us, parents? He – um – gave me the impression that he would be able to.'

Kitty sees the look of surprised gratitude that Emily gives her brother.

'I can go riding on the moors with him, maybe do some shooting, keep my eye in,' James continues as if Daniel's visit is to be for his benefit alone.

His parents exchange glances before his father speaks. 'If his family can spare him even some of the time he will be very welcome, will he not, Kitty?'

'Oh Papa, thank you.' Emily runs to her father's side and kisses him on the cheek. 'I promise I will never call you old-fashioned again.'

Kitty sees how James flushes with pleasure even as he laughs and returns Emily's kiss.

'Then I shall expect you to listen with appreciation to my lectures on the wonders of the Great Western Railway on our journey tomorrow.'

Now everyone laughs, including Sir John and Maria who do not entirely understand the substance of the joke. Kitty looks around the room at the smiling faces of her closest remaining family and thinks how very fortunate she is. She catches James' eye and hopes that he can read in hers the love she feels for him, he who has brought her so much happiness. And that is as far as she cares to think today or indeed for many days to come, it not being possible to predict the future in which so much will happen and surely not all of it good.

Afterword

Although *The Rose Goddess* is based upon real people and events, more or less all of the scenes are invented and they include fictitious characters and relationships. The meeting between Nur, aka Mrs Helena Bennett, and Kitty probably did not happen but there certainly was a close friendship between Nur's sister Faiz Palmer and Kitty's mother, Khair-un-Nissa, as documented in William Dalrymple's lovely book *'White Mughals'*.

Making Kitty meet Nur made it possible for her to discover the truth about her mother, besides enabling me to give comfort at the end of her life to Nur to whom I had become very close in writing *The Black Princess*. She died in Horsham just after Christmas 1853 and is buried in St Mary's Anglican churchyard where her grave, unlike all the others, is aligned in an East-West direction, following Muslim custom. I invented Richard but it seems clear that she had a very good relationship with whichever of the then clergy who agreed to bury her there in that fashion.

When preparing to write about Kitty, I realised how very unreliable was her knowledge of her own history and how dependent she would have been on what other people told her. She is on record as saying that she remembered vividly the actual parting from her mother and it is known that she and her brother had no further contact with her and that Khair appeared to die of a broken heart. But it seems very unlikely that their family told them about Khair's relationship with Henry Russell and the scandal it had caused, certainly not when they were children. Dalrymple was several years into his research before he uncovered these long forgotten secrets which I came to see could explain why the children were never allowed to write to or receive letters from Khair.

Lacking much other evidence, I have also made this part of the explanation of why Kitty's romance with Thomas Carlyle ended. Carlyle himself is a somewhat unreliable witness. His correspondence with Jane during the months when he was seeing Kitty are full of contradictions as to his relationship with either of them, while his extensive *'Reminiscences'* sometimes read less as an account of his actual feelings at the time, towards Jane in particular, and more as he wished they had been. He regrets he had not been kinder and pays her many tributes. His novel *'Sartor Restartus'* is the clearest statement of his love for Kitty and the effect its loss had upon him, but it is nevertheless a work of fiction, besides being told in an extremely indirect and convoluted fashion. But he certainly was fascinated by her and jealous of James whose letters to Kitty (according to Dalrymple, I have not seen them) unequivocally show his love for her.

Not surprisingly, history has been less interested in Kitty's more conventional later life and my reconstruction is based on such slim pickings as the online Kirkpatrick family archives, evocative visits to Torquay and its surroundings, and of course more general sources of information about the times in which she lived. In the years after the book ends, Emily did in fact marry the Reverend Walpole Mohun-Harris 'of Hayne', although disappointingly there is no record of the date nor of whether they had any children and the closest place I could find is Haynes in mid-Bedfordshire. I thought Walpole an unlikely first choice of husband for someone who was said to be so like her headstrong and ill-fated grandmother, so I gave her the handsome Daniel, knowing that he would not survive the infamous Charge of the Light Brigade at Balaklava in October 1854 when many of his regiment perished.

Young James's regiment was in India from 1857-9 helping quell the so-called Mutiny and in the United States during the American Civil War between 1861 and 1865. He survived both and married Charlotte Strachey in 1865 and they had three sons, one of whom followed him into the 60th Rifles.

Bertha married another Devon military man in 1868 at the comparatively late age of 28 and had 3 daughters and one son but she died at the age of 35. (Her daughter, Bertha, however lived until 1953.)I wonder if Bertha delayed marrying and leaving home in order to keep company with her mother, who was by then otherwise alone.

Mary married Charles Molyneaux-Seel; they had a son and a daughter and lived in Bruges and Paris. But he died in Hastings in February 1859, perhaps on a business trip to England, and one month later James died in Paris, very likely having gone there to help Mary.

Her daughter was then only two and she might still have been pregnant with her son who was born at some time that year. She returned to Devon where, a few years later in 1862, she married Captain Norman Fitzgerald Uniacke and had five more children. Norman however died ten years later and, presumably when the children had all grown up,(and were in fact each living in a different part of what was still or had been the British Empire), and perhaps after Kitty had died, she went to live with her third son Lucius in Tulare County, California, southeast of Fresno. Her death is registered in Oakland on 30th March 1909.

So Kitty was to experience a great deal of suffering and tragedy after this book ends. At some point she moved to nearby and smaller Villa Sorrento, Torquay, where she died on 2nd March 1889 at the age of 84. It is now a modern block of flats, but it is still called Sorrento. Stitchill House still stands, though it has been altered somewhat, and it is now converted into flats. Kitty did visit Thomas again, very likely more than once. Carlyle wrote of one particular visit:

'Agnoscoveteris vestigial flammae' (I feel the traces of an ancient flame), a line from Virgil. Soon afterwards, in a letter of October 1869 (quoted by Russell's kinswoman, Lady Russell), he wrote to her:

'Your little visit did me a great deal of good; so interesting, so strange to see her who we used to call "Kitty" emerging on me from the dusk of an evening like a dream become real. It sets me thinking for many hours upon times long gone, and persons and events that can never cease to be important and affecting to me... All round me is the sound as of evening bells, which are not sad only, or ought not to be, but beautiful also and blessed and quiet. No more today, dear lady; my best wishes and affectionate regards will abide with me to the end.'

He died in 1881.

Acknowledgments

As must already be apparent, my first inspiration and source was *White Mughals*, one of William Dalrymple's ground-breaking books of Indian history.

I am very grateful to Professor B. T. Seetha, Principal of the Women's College, Hyderabad, who kindly gave us permission to visit the old British Residence, which helped me imagine the long ago days when Kitty lived there. Also to my knowledgeable guide in Hyderabad, Shashi Mohunkumar, who introduced us and showed such interest in my project.

Thank you so much Rob and Carol Voysey for twice taking me to Torquay and finding the site of Sorrento Villa, and Janet Jones for researching the history of the area and discovering that Kitty's first home was the nearby Stitchill House.

As ever, special thanks to my writing group tutor, Todd Kingsley-Jones, who not only refined my prose but kept me focussed on the main story rather than the fascinating byways that too much research can lead one into.

And to Rich Voysey who has again brought my heroine to life in his beautiful and evocative cover illustration.